Vanished Trails

Maddie Castle

Book 4

L.T. Ryan

with
C.R. Gray

LIQUID MIND MEDIA

For information contact:

contact@ltryan.com

https://LTRyan.com

https://www.instagram.com/ltryanauthor/

https://www.facebook.com/LTRyanAuthor

The Maddie Castle Series

The Handler

Tracking Justice

Hunting Grounds

Vanished Trails

Smoldering Lies (Coming Soon)

Want a free copy of the Maddie Castle prequel novella? Sign up for my newsletter and download a copy today:

https://liquidmind.media/maddie-castle-newsletter-signup-1/

Love Maddie? Noble? Cassie? Hatch? Get your very own L.T. Ryan merchandise today! Click the link below to find coffee mugs, t-shirts, and even signed copies of your favorite thrillers! https://ltryan.ink/EvG_

Chapter 1

Heavy. So damn heavy. She hadn't been this heavy two weeks ago, when he'd hoisted her around his waist and that tight, little skirt.

Although, she'd been alive then. This must've been what they meant when they said *deadweight*.

Dropping her into the trunk, he winced when her head hit the corner of the bumper. That made no sense. She was dead. What did it matter if her head hit the bumper? It didn't. She was dead.

She was dead, because of him.

Lifting his shaking hands to his face, he stared down at her in the trunk of the car.

This wasn't what he'd wanted. This had *never* been what he wanted. The only dead person he'd ever seen was his grandpa in a casket. Never thought he'd watch someone die. At least, not until he was old, maybe his wife's last breath on her deathbed. Something like that. But nothing like this.

It hadn't been long, no more than an hour, and her lips were blue. How were her lips already blue? He didn't understand. Was it the cool breeze? It wasn't *cold* by any means, no less than seventy degrees. Did that simply happen upon death? Did the lips just turn blue?

He didn't know. This wasn't exactly his area of expertise. Neither was disposing of a body, but he'd watched enough movies. He could figure it out. He hoped, at least. God, he hoped.

Clutching his knees with blood-caked hands, panting heavily, he bent double and gasped for air. Still, he stared at the girl in the trunk.

How could this be real? How could it have come to this? What would his father have thought?

How could he ever forgive himself?

Should he have called the police? Was it too late for that?

It was. He'd already loaded her into the trunk of his car. It didn't matter that he hadn't intended to hurt her. He had. He'd *killed* her.

How were people so fragile? How could humans have climbed to the top of the food pyramid when death was one hard bump away? It didn't make sense. None of this made sense.

How long would it take before she would be nothing more than bones? Or dust? Why were her lips blue? Was she cold? Did he need to cover her with something?

Yes. He did. Even if she couldn't feel it, her lips were blue. After this, she at least deserved a blanket.

Stretching past her, he grabbed the one he kept back here for drive-ins. While untangling it, wrapping it around her frame, the warmth of her skin brushed his.

That one small touch brought him to his knees, heaving for breath through gasping cries. Reaching out for her pale, lifeless face only brightened by the bluish glow of the moon and stars, he crumbled beside the trunk.

"I didn't mean to," he whispered. "I never meant to hurt you." Sniffling, he stroked some blond hair behind her ear. "I'm so sorry, Liz."

Chapter 2

THIS IS A GOOD THING, I TOLD MYSELF, BUCKLING TEMPEST'S harness around her frame. *Getting back to work is a good thing.*

Standing from my couch once it was secure, I eased out a deep breath. I tried to, at least. Rather than sweatpants—my usual attire—I'd stepped into some jeans this morning, and they impeded that whole breathing thing.

But I was making an effort now. An effort to do better, feel better. The makeup I'd dusted on didn't do much on that front. The jeans weren't helping either. Maybe finding Daisy Miller—or her body—would. That was the hope.

It'd been almost two months since I'd worked a case. Six weeks since I'd killed The Country Killer.

Six weeks since Ox had died in my arms.

A few potential clients had called since then. One woman requested evidence of her husband having an affair. A district attorney wanted me to find something against one of Simeon's dealers.

Both were meaningless. Then Bentley asked if I could find anything about Daisy, his sister-in-law who'd gone missing last year. A case that *didn't* feel meaningless. That's where I was heading now. To meet with Detective Ashley Harper in Pittsburgh and see what she could find for me.

Grabbing my purse off the table, I gritted my teeth at the pain that ached up my knee. Never failed. Although I was sticking to my exercise routine religiously, my pain was the worst it'd been since I'd killed Eric Oakley. But I muttered a curse and kept moving with Tempest at my side.

I was just about to reach for the door handle when a knock pounded against the other side. Tempest barreled to the edge of her leash, nearly swiping me to my feet. Bark so loud it could shatter glass, I had to yell, "Quiet." Rarely did I have to yell when someone came to the door. Meaning the smell on the other side of it was one Tempy didn't recognize.

When I made it to the door, Tempest finally obeyed when I said, "Sit." Pulling it open confirmed my suspicions. A stranger stood on my doorstep.

An attractive man somewhere between forty-five and fifty-five, just over six feet tall, with a wide frame covered in blue jeans and a red flannel buttoned all the way to the neck. Graying blonde hair fell into his pale blue eyes. He had a friendly, familiar smile, but one I couldn't place. In his arms, he held a small bouquet of carnations wrapped in plastic from the local grocery store and a bottle of wine. *Mad Dog* 20/20, to be specific. Ironically, my favorite flavor. Strawberry kiwi. Too bad I couldn't drink it.

No matter how badly I wanted to.

I knew all my neighbors, everyone in this trailer park, and this man wasn't one of them.

"Can I help you?" I asked.

He opened his mouth, but no words fell out.

After giving him another moment, only for him to stay silent, I repeated, "Look, I have somewhere to be. Do you need something?"

"Uh, yeah. Yeah, maybe. I think." He smiled again, but it was strained. Uncomfortable. "Are you Maddie Castle?"

This was a first. "I am. But if you want to hire me, you can find my number online. I'm not a big fan of people showing at my door. So if you don't mind—"

"Oh, no." Shaking his head, he swallowed hard. "That's not why I'm here. Well, I mean, if you want me to pay for your time, I will, but I was just hoping maybe we could talk. But now that I think about it, this was rude. Showing up here like this. I found your address online, so I could've found your number online, which I should've done. That's *definitely* what I should've done. I'm sorry. I just—It's been so long, and I didn't know if a call was enough. Sorta felt like a shitty way to do this. You deserve better than that, so I thought showing in person would be a good thing, but maybe it wasn't. Your face, that's sorta telling me it wasn't. This might be equally shitty."

The man spoke so fast, I barely registered any of his words. I was glad Bentley was working on the flower bed in front of his trailer. He looked as puzzled as I did, straightening from his bag of mulch to see us better. If I needed to use the gun in my hoodie pocket, at least I had a witness to testify that I'd had no other option.

Tempy didn't seem to think this man was a threat. She sat beside me, panting and wagging her tail. She sat as close to her lead's length as possible, not tugging on it at all. I trusted her judgement, but it didn't make this any more comfortable.

"I'm sorry, do we know each other?" I asked.

The smile vanished. Another hard swallow. "We did. A long time ago." Awkwardly extending a trembling hand, he forced the smile back into place. "My name's Sam." His voice cracked when he said, "Sam Castle."

Blinking hard, my heart sank until it wadded into a knot deep in my gut. Staring into those pale blue eyes, time rippled some two and a half decades in reverse. With one blink, he was a few years shy of middle-aged, and the next, he was barely out of his teens with pin pricked pupils, singing *Smells Like Teen Spirit* in sync with the speakers of a Barbie boombox.

Those blue eyes, that blonde hair, didn't look familiar because I knew this man. They looked familiar because I had seen them every day in the mirror since I was old enough to look in one.

Samuel Castle. My dad.

Instinctively, I stepped backward into my home. My safe place. "What the hell are you doing here?"

Lowering the shaking hand I hadn't accepted to his side, he wet his lips. "I'm sorry. I shouldn't have just shown up—"

"No, you should have. You should've shown up the ten thousand times I was staring out that window waiting for Daddy's car to pull in." I waved at the window of my old bedroom. "Why now? Two and a half decades, not so much as a phone call, so why the hell now? What do you want? I don't have money, and you're not staying here, so if that's why—"

"I did." Voice sheepish, confusion pinched his brows. "Not recently, but until Natalie changed the number, I did call. Every night, I called. I wrote you too, but you never wrote back. That's why I haven't since you've been an adult. I thought you didn't want to hear from me. And I get why. You have every reason to hate me. A million zillion *bajillion* reasons to hate me." Hope filled his eyes when he said that.

One of the vague memories I had of my dad was him tucking me in and saying, "I love you times a million, zillion, bajillion." I'd say it back, and he'd say it again, and we'd laugh, and he'd kiss my forehead before turning out my light.

Hearing that silly phrase in his voice again, my heart warmed. Burning fire followed that comfort. Playing on my childhood memories was manipulative.

"I did a lot of bad things. The worst was leaving you." His eyes glassed over. "And I get why you wouldn't want me around. But I did call, Maddie. I swear I did. Ask your mom. I know she'll remember."

He looked sincere. But every drug addict looked sincere when they lied. It was second nature to us.

Swallowing once more, he said, "You didn't get my letters?"

His voice cracked again. I remembered it doing that when he talked about Mom. Like he was dancing around speaking poorly of her. Whether he hated her didn't matter. He wanted me to know a man was not supposed to speak poorly of the mother of his child.

That was when it clicked.

There was a chance he was lying. I didn't know what the purpose of that would've been, considering he didn't realize she was dead. Unless he was lying about that to make his story sound more believable. But he was trying to tell me that my mother hadn't given me the letters. Just like she hadn't given him our new number.

It took far more effort than it should've to unclench my jaw. "No. Where were you? Why couldn't you have driven here when she changed the number? Did you run off to California? You always said you were gonna run to California. If I remember correctly, the deal was that we were gonna go to California together, and we were gonna see the beach. So's that where you went? Southern or northern? Always pictured you doing well in L.A."

Wetting his lips again, his eyes filled with pain and remorse. One more time, he opened his mouth, but no words came out.

"Alright, stop," I said. "You don't get to look at me like that. Like I should feel bad for you. Like you're a victim. I know you were. You were *a* victim, but you weren't *my* victim. Mom's an evil bitch, and you didn't deserve the way she treated you, but I didn't deserve the shit she did to me, either. And unlike you, I couldn't drive off in the middle of the night. I was a kid. You were a grown man. You were my dad, and you were supposed to be there, and you weren't. You left. So either answer the question or leave. Because you're not getting my pity, let alone my forgiveness, without a damn good reason."

"I was gonna..." Swallowing again, he shook his head. "I'm sorry. You're right. You don't owe me anything, and just the fact that you haven't shut the door in my face is more than I deserve. But I didn't go to California. I was in Ohio." Was that supposed to make me feel better? Because he was in another shitty state instead of at the beach, it was no big deal? "And then I was in Ohio State Penitentiary."

Damn it.

I wished I was ashamed to hear that. But hearing my father had been in prison made my heart flutter. Because if he was telling the truth, then there was no way for him to have made certain that I got his letters or his phone calls.

And for some God damned reason, it wadded up a lump in my throat. Like I was that little girl again waiting at the window for Daddy to come home. Daddy was finally here, and hearing he'd been in prison instead of a beach house made me want to collapse into his arms.

He didn't leave because he wanted to get away from you. Look at him, he still loves you. He wants to be here. It's not his fault the other kids had dads while you didn't. It's that darn Uncle Sam's fault.

Pathetic. Stupid.

I didn't know this man. I knew his face, and I knew those eyes, but I didn't know if he was telling the truth. For all I knew, this was a ploy to get me to give him whatever it was he wanted. And what did it matter if this *was* all true? Did that change anything?

One way or the other, that lump stayed in the back of my throat, I would not allow my eyes to water, and I would collapse off a cliff before I collapsed into his arms.

"You didn't know that?" he asked.

I shook my head.

To find a prisoner, you needed the state they were in. Knowing which prison was helpful, depending on the search engine and the crime. Without a docket number, it was difficult to even find them once you had the prison name. It wasn't as simple as a Google search.

Yet, that was all I'd done. Google searches. Ox had once suggested running a standard background check, but I hadn't wanted to know. Sure, I'd assumed he was in and out of prison, but I didn't care to find out.

Why? Because it'd hurt like a son of a bitch if I ran a check on him, only to learn he'd gotten his act together, remarried, and had a happy little life in the suburbs with a new wife and kids while I was stuck with the devil who birthed me.

I'd just wanted to know if he was dead. That's all I'd cared about.

The sun reflected in those glossy blue eyes, and for a second, I swore I was looking in a mirror. "I'm sorry then. I'm sorry I was there, and that I was the one to tell you this. But mostly, I'm sorry I wasn't *here*. I'm sorry I didn't take you to California." He extended the flowers and the bottle of wine. "My number's on the card in there. I'm not far, just fifteen minutes down the road. So if you need anything, or if you just want to call me, I'll answer anytime, day or night. But it looks like you were about to head out." He nodded to my purse. "So I'll, uh, get out of your way. But please, call anytime."

Those last two sentences sounded so sad. They made that lump in my throat thicker, that urge to fall into his arms stronger.

I hated how much my chest hurt as I watched him turn around.

Once he'd walked down the steps, almost to his truck in the driveway, I called, "Why now?" I hated that my voice cracked, too. "What do you want?"

He looked over his shoulder with tears in his eyes and smiled. "I got out last week. I just wanted to see you, kid. Make up for lost time."

Chapter 3

WHILE SAM BACKED OUT OF THE DRIVEWAY, BENTLEY WALKED closer. Eyes wide, mouth partially open, he said, "Was that who I think it was?"

Still watching him back out, straightening once he was on the road out of the trailer park, I nodded. That was as much as I could manage.

Smiling my way before he shifted into drive, Dad waved.

Dad.

No. He didn't get that title. He hadn't been a *dad* since I was in grade school. Sam. That's who he was, and that's what I'd call him. The most he got from me was his name and a wave. He didn't get a smile, either. Not yet. Maybe not ever.

When his old beat-up truck rumbled down the road and he was out of sight, Bentley carefully plucked the bottle from my arms.

Blinking hard, unsure if this was another nightmare, I finally turned to him. His smile was soft, brown eyes grounding me back in reality. "You don't want this, right?"

Remembering the bottle of wine Sam had given me, realizing I'd almost taken it inside with me, I huffed. "Oh, I want it. But yeah, best if you take it."

Bentley let out a half laugh. Pushing a stray strand of hair behind my ear, his smile dwindled. "Are you okay?"

Translation: *Are you gonna go call Simeon Gunn and buy a bag of heroin?*

"I think I'm in shock."

"Hmm." His fingers trailed to the vein at my neck. "A little high, but nothing crazy." Eyes flicking between mine, he lifted his free hand to my cheek. "Warm, not cool and clammy. How's your urine output? Dark in color?"

I pawed him away. "You know what I mean."

"I do. But I made you smile." His got bigger, but his eyes were still gentle. "Do you wanna talk about it?"

"I have to meet Harper—" Pausing, I ran my fingers through my hair and grabbed a fistful at the back. "Shit, I can't leave. He knows where I live. I don't know if he's using, but if he is, I don't have my security cameras anymore, and—"

"I'm gonna be working out here all day. I was gonna cut your grass anyway." Bentley nodded to my overgrown yard. "I'll keep an eye on things. Just go run your errands. Stop and get a coffee. Blast some music. Since you consider caffeine and blowing out your eardrums relaxing."

How did he do it? Sure, music and coffee did the trick too, but nothing got that crawling-out-of-my-skin sensation to settle like Bentley.

Shaking my head, I caught the hand I'd pushed away. "You don't have to do that. That kid down the street said he'd take twenty bucks to do it."

"Give him the twenty bucks to pull those weeds off your propane tank. Those little shits are stuck on there. Just let me handle things here. You go."

He pulled back to look at me, but I caught him by his shirt and yanked him back down for a kiss. This one, not so soft, and not so slow. Realizing I wasn't done with him, he coiled an arm around my waist and held me as close to him as space allowed.

When I let him go, he stayed close. Breathing hard, he rested his forehead on mine. "What was that for?"

"Thank you."

"For confirming you're not in shock?"

"For everything."

* * *

I KEPT WISHING THIS WOULD GET EASIER. KEPT WISHING AND disappointing myself.

Facing the opposite direction at her L-shaped desk, Harper typed away on her keyboard. As usual, she looked gorgeous. Even from the vague reflection in her screen, I knew that much. Pretty blond hair spun into a classy bun with a fancy clip to adorn it. Red lipstick. Big blue eyes framed in thick black glasses. Tack on the pencil skirt and the low-cut button-up, and she was practically the model for *sexy librarian*, or *sexy CEO*, or whatever other career society sexualized when it was a woman doing the job.

And I hated it.

Hated society for sexualizing everything women did, and hated how pretty Harper was. I hadn't always, and I hated that too. I hated how much I hated everything these days.

So why was I still so angry? Shouldn't I have been past anger in the grieving process?

I had to get past it. Especially with Harper. Because she was the highest ranking official I had in my back pocket at the Pittsburgh P.D., and I needed her help.

So, with a calming breath, I forced a smile and tapped the open-door pane. "Knock-knock."

Spinning to face me, she gave a smile far more genuine than mine. "Oh, hey. You look cute."

With a snort, I tapped my hip for Tempest to continue into the room at my side. I held Harper's usual over her desk. "Liar."

"I'm not." She accepted the coffee and laughed. "Are you going out?"

Sitting in the chair opposite hers, I gave Tempest the command to follow suit. She did. "No, just trying to not look like a bum. But thanks for letting me stop by."

"You know you're always welcome. You said this was about a case? I actually wanted to talk to you about one myself."

I arched a brow. "That right?"

"It's up your alley."

"Pretty sure you said the same thing to that D.A. you gave my number to."

"Actually, I told him that *wasn't* up your alley. You're never gonna rat on one of Simeon's guys."

"If I do, three-oh-two me." I sipped my coffee. "Suicide by mafia boss."

"I'll remember that." She took a gulp of hers too. "But I mean it about this job. Right up your alley."

"I'm rusty. Literally just getting back into the game."

"That's okay. Because you wouldn't be the one working it." She nodded to Tempy. "She would." Harper slid a few documents across the desk. "Missing eighteen-year-old. Six kids walked into the woods, five walked out. Search and rescue hasn't found a damn thing. Local P.D. requested our help. I was friends with the girl's uncle back in college, so I guess he pushed for it. But they want more muscle. Me, because he knows me, and you, because of her." Another nod at Tempest. "You're the only P.I. with a K-9 they can find. They want the trail tracked again."

"Search and rescue found *nothing*?" I asked. "No trail at all?"

"No, they got a trail, but it leads to the parking lot. Suggesting Liz got in a car with someone." Biting her lip, she nodded to the papers before me. "But Phil doesn't trust it. Says that she's gotta be in those woods somewhere. I explained that search dogs are next to never wrong, but he's insistent. He wants a private team—or investigator—to run the trail."

"I don't think I'll find anything they didn't."

"Neither do I. But it's easy money. I'm handling most of the investigation too though, and it'd be nice to bounce ideas off you. You're good at what you do, Mads."

Usually, but as established, I was rusty. Also wasn't crazy about working with Harper. But cash was running low.

"Alright," I said. "I'm in. Just make me a deal?"

"What's that?"

"Don't ask me how I'm holding up."

Her eyes softened. I knew exactly what she was thinking. *But, Maddie, I'm one of the only people who knows the truth. I'm one of the only ones you can talk to. You know I'm here for you.*

True, true, and true. But I didn't want to talk to her. Not about Ox. I didn't want to talk to anyone about him, especially not her.

Eventually, she nodded. "Deal."

"Thanks."

"Let me return the favor. Daisy..."

"Right." The reason I was here. Brain fog must've been getting to me. It'd done that a lot lately. Sliding a photo from my purse across the desk, I cleared my throat. "Daisy Miller. Disappeared in September last year."

Harper squinted at the photo, then scoffed. "What prick would use a mug shot for a missing person?"

"One who feels some kinda way about people like Daisy, I'm assuming."

"What kind of person was Daisy, exactly?"

"Foster kid who wound up on crank and dating a meth cooker before she hit adulthood," I said, voice blunt. Harper flinched but didn't wrinkle her nose or roll her eyes. That was why she and I had become friends. Harper hadn't let this job jade her. She had compassion for people like Daisy. People like me. "She has prostitution charges too, but family says they were at gun point. She started running for the boyfriend, racked up a hell of a debt, and the boyfriend pimped her out to pay it off."

"How old is she?"

"In the photo, nineteen. If she's alive, twenty."

Harper cupped a hand over her chest and let out a shaking breath. "Poor kid."

I nodded.

Grabbing the pen and notepad from the edge of her desk, Harper jotted down her name. "You got any theories?"

"Not a one. I can't find shit." Propping my elbows on my knees, I leaned in. "Her family thinks it was one of her johns, a deal gone wrong, or *maybe* the boyfriend. Big maybe though, because he showed up at the family house looking for her and tore the place apart. Really seemed to think she was there. He's got the locals in his pocket. No reason to fake something like that. Just drew more attention to himself."

"Tragic trifecta in cases like this," Harper said, still jotting in her pad. "You ruled out the family though?"

"All she's got is a preteen niece and a brother-in-law who's got the city of Columbus as his alibi," I said. Harper looked up, cocking her head to the side. "He's a paramedic. He was at work the night she disappeared. I confirmed with his supervisor and the partner he was driving with that night. And he's the one who asked me to look into it."

"He *asked* you? He didn't hire you?"

"We're friends."

Tilting her head, leaning back, Harper grinned. "Friends, huh? Same friend you're having dinner with in that?"

"Shut up." Feeling my cheeks warm, I tugged up my top. "It's not any sluttier than what you're wearing."

"It's not *slutty* at all. It's just been a long time since I've seen you in anything other than a baggy hoodie. *And* since I've seen you look so happy."

I snorted.

"Why's that funny?"

"Eh. Guess I'm glad I don't look as messy as I feel."

Her smile didn't vanish. It just got a little sad. Enough for me to know I didn't need to explain. "So who is he? Anyone I know?"

"He is, actually. Bentley Roycroft." Confusion pinched her fore-head. "His daughter was kidnapped by Eric Oakley. He was there." I was amazed I kept my tone level, but I still cleared my throat. "When everything happened."

Jaw falling, she lifted a hand over her heart. "Right. Yeah, Alex has mentioned him a few times." She turned back to her notes, and I didn't miss the way she blinked rapidly and inhaled deeply. "And how's Bentley related to Daisy?"

"Sister-in-law."

"He's *married*?"

"Who do you think I am? You?" I did my best to make sure that sounded like a joke and not an insult. It must've resonated as such, because she snorted a laugh. "He's a widower. And Daisy was like his daughter. She was a little kid when he started dating Bella, and he'd tried to take care of Daisy after Bella died, but she got in with the wrong crowd. We all know that story."

The crude humor in the room dissipated. Harper gave a nod of understanding. "I gotcha. Anything you want me to look for?"

"For now, just anything you can get on the missing person's case. I can access almost everything else. That case is open, though, so there's a lot more red tape."

"I'll try and cut through it for you."

"I appreciate it. If you want anything for helping me out, just let me know. I've got some money in savings."

"I'm good on money. But there sorta is something." She pressed her lips together. "Are you and Teresa in contact?"

"We are. Why?"

"Martinez just moved into Ox's office. I got stuck with all his shit. Apparently, I was the closest friend he had here." Harper nodded to the corner behind me. "So it's all in that closet."

I snorted. "That asshole got his detective shield?"

Rolling her eyes, she gulped her coffee. "But I've called Teresa about getting his things, and she hasn't picked up. I just don't know what to do with it all. Do you maybe wanna go through it? Or take it to her the next time you see her?"

Maybe. Probably not. I didn't know. I really wasn't ready to go through his things.

But Harper was helping me. Wouldn't kill me to load a few boxes into my car to return the favor. "Sure. I'm meeting with her for lunch the day after tomorrow. I'll give it to her then."

"You're a godsend."

Chapter 4

A<small>FTER MY HOUR RIDE HOME FROM</small> P<small>ITTSBURGH WITH</small> O<small>X'S SHIT</small> in my trunk, a wave of guilt moved through me when I limped to my door without the boxes. Like I was somehow leaving Ox in the trunk. Which was stupid. He was dead. They were just boxes of his clutter. Not him.

Plus, I couldn't haul them inside on my own. Why bring them in at all? No, I'd give them to Teresa. She'd get a sad, nostalgic kick out of looking through them. I could just pretend they weren't there.

Much like I pretended he wasn't dead. Just not here. We were in an argument, he was in the city, I was home, and we just weren't talking right now. That was all.

Probably not a healthy coping mechanism. But I moved onto a somewhat healthier one in its place. After Tempy did her business in the yard, I video-called Karen and Phil Turner. The parents of the missing girl that Harper had given my number to.

Although I wasn't sure it was fair to call this meeting "healthy."

"Harper said it was a pre-college camping trip?" I asked. "A pretty large group of kids went out with Liz, right?"

"Six counting Liz," Karen said. Despite the dark circles beneath her glassy eyes, she was a pretty woman. The video was blurry, surely disguising a few blemishes, but her full cheeks had a lovely natural blush to them. A dainty nose complemented her thin red lips. "It was supposed to be their last hurrah before they all went away. Liz is the only one staying in PA for school."

"Do you have their names? All the kids who went with her?"

"Mia Davis, Charlotte Wilson, Danny King, Mike Green, and Caleb Adams," Phil said. He spoke quickly, like he was tired of repeating this to all the law enforcement officials who had yet to find his daughter. "They're bad news. Every one of them. I told her not to go, but she's eighteen. Insisted everything would be fine. I knew it was a bad idea. Any time those kids are together, it's a bad idea."

Phil wasn't a bad looking guy either. Boring though. Thick black glasses framed his dark eyes. A well maintained beard lined his jaw and thick lips. What stood out about him was his demeanor. Sharp, blunt. To the point. I could appreciate that.

I was still writing down all their names when I asked, "What makes you say they're bad news? Drugs? Drinking?"

Karen frowned at him, then turned back to the camera. "They all drink. If they do drugs, it's not excessive. I've smelled weed on Liz a few times, but they're not into anything hard from what we can tell."

"*From what we can tell,*" Phil repeated, glaring at Karen. "Look into Caleb. Do all the digging on him you can. I never trusted that kid. The moment she brought him home, I didn't like him."

"You've never liked any of her boyfriends," Karen said. "Our other daughter, Miranda, she says that they weren't doing well. Something about how Liz was planning on breaking up with him before she started college. Maybe she tried to? That happens, right? Sometimes a boyfriend finds out that his girlfriend is leaving him and he—"

Phil shot her the filthiest look. "What the hell's the matter with you? She isn't dead. Those little shits left her out there, but she isn't dead."

Lip swelling, eyes filling with tears, Karen turned away.

A normal reaction. When it came to missing persons, especially teenagers, everyone knew the statistics. It was almost forty-eight hours now.

"What have they all said?" I asked. "Her friends, I mean. When was the last time they claim to have seen her?"

"The second day of their trip, so two days ago," Phil replied. "They told the cops it was sunset, they were having a fire, drinking"—that word seemed to taste sour on his tongue—"and Charlotte got into an argument with Liz. Something about a boy. Charlotte said that Liz was messing around with one of her friends' boyfriends, and I guess Liz claimed she wasn't, and it turned into a screaming match. Then Liz said she was leaving and stomped off. But I don't believe a damn word of it. Maybe the fight was true, but what does that sound like to you? Because they're all telling the exact same story. Including the boyfriend. Says it was just an argument. She walked off. But Liz wasn't stupid. She wouldn't have hiked seven miles by herself when the sun was going down."

From that bit of information, it sounded like a story that *could* have been true. Teenagers were dumb. If I had slept with my friend's boyfriend, and my boyfriend was sitting at the same fire when the story came out, I might have taken my chances in the wilderness. Especially if I were drunk. Everybody thinks they're invincible when they're drunk.

But Phil's theory wasn't a stretch of my imagination, either. The emotions of teenagers were grotesque. Any of the kids who cared about the girl who was cheated on may have thrown a punch at Liz, but I also understood why Phil was most concerned about the boyfriend. Kids like that—just about to hit the real world with real world responsibilities, possibly with scholarships to great colleges, who witnessed a murder or played some part in it—very well may stay quiet for whoever did the killing.

I, however, couldn't help but notice that while Phil had all but shouted at his wife for mentioning the possibility that Liz was dead, he feared the same.

"When the police found their camp, I'm assuming they did a search with a K-9, correct?" I asked. "A whole search and rescue team?"

"They did. Liz's trail brought them back to the main road," Karen said. "Like she had walked back and gotten in someone's car. But she hadn't driven, and she didn't take any of her friends' cars home, so we have no idea where she went." Karen's lip quivered. "But I just don't understand. Couldn't that trail have been her trail *into* the forest? Maybe the dog got confused? Maybe she's still out there somewhere? Is that possible?"

"It's hard to throw off a well-trained dog's scent," I said.

"But Harper said you have a canine," Phil said. "Can't you go out and do the trail again? Just check? See if maybe the dog did get confused?"

"I can, but it's really not her expertise. Tempest's specialty is in narcotics. Plus the hike you're talking about is pretty long, and I do charge hourly. If I were you, I would trust the search and rescue—"

"We don't care about the money." Phil's tone was rougher than a rusted blade. "And you're the only PI in the area who has a dog. We checked. So we want you out there. Hike the trail, look for our daughter. See if they missed something. Cops make mistakes all the time. That's why people hire you, isn't it?"

Damn. Wouldn't wanna come across Phill in a dark alley. "I just like to be transparent with my clients. There's a very small chance that I'll find anything the search and rescue team haven't."

"Will you do it or not?" Phil snapped. "Because if you won't, just—"

"Oh my God, Phil," Karen said, shaking her head at him in disbelief. "She just wants us to have realistic expectations. She said she can. Right, Maddie?"

This was what it must've felt like to be a divorce lawyer. "Yes, ma'am."

Phil's tone was still sharp as he said, "Alright then. Send me the invoice. Call us when you have something."

It looked like he was reaching to click the end call button on the screen, so I quickly blurted, "I need a little more information."

"Of course," Karen said. "I'm sorry. *We're* sorry. This is just a lot of stress, as I'm sure you can imagine."

I gave a tightlipped smile. "It's no problem. The biggest help would be Liz's login for her cloud? Anything that will grant access to her text messages, social media, direct messages, things like that. It might help me figure out who picked her up, if someone did, and see who potentially has the most motive."

Phil clenched his jaw. "I'll send it."

And the call ended.

Expelling an exasperated breath, I turned to Tempest who sat on the sofa beside me. "Well, got my mind to shut off for a few minutes. That's something, huh?"

Tempest sat up, panted at me, and looked at her crate by the door. Where her silver dog bowl sat.

I scratched her ears. "It's not time yet. You know we wait for Bentley."

"A-woo-wooo." Getting onto all fours, she wagged her tail.

"Don't you howl at me. It's not time yet."

She hopped off the couch and stood in front of the cage. "*A-woo-wooh!*"

"Tempest." I hardened my tone. "No."

Wagging her tail, she ducked her head to the old, beige carpet, kept her butt up in the air, and whined.

It took everything I had to keep my chuckle inside. "No whining either."

Her tail wagged faster. She pawed at her face and whined again.

"You adorable, manipulative little shit."

Again, she pawed at her face. Nothing was wrong with her. I was convinced she just knew how cute she looked when she did that. And she used it to con me into giving her what she wanted.

Every day, all week, we'd gone through this routine. Tempest got her kibble at five p.m. She ate in her crate while I ate with Bentley and

Grace. But Grace left a few days ago for summer camp, so Bentley and I had been eating closer to six or seven. Meaning Tempest was eating closer to six or seven.

Absolutely absurd, in Tempy's opinion. How dare we? She was skin and bones. Famished.

That's how she acted, at least. I didn't want to break the routine of feeding her in her crate while we ate our dinner because of resource guarding when I'd gotten her. So every day, we had this darling little tussle. I told her it wasn't time yet, she whimpered and whined, and I felt like the worst dog mom in the universe.

To cope, I ignored her. The email from Karen and Phil Turner had just dinged on my laptop anyway.

So I picked it up and got to work.

Just as I logged into Liz's cloud, an email from Harper popped up in the corner of my screen.

Hey, it's not much, but here's everything I've got on the Liz Turner case. Looks like the cops are doing everything they can, but the suspect list's a mile long. Good luck combing through it. I'll do some digging on the Daisy Miller case when I get home tonight.

I sent back, *Great, thanks. Do Phil and Karen always hate each other? Or is it the stress of Liz's disappearance?*

Just barely into the file, still waiting for it to load, Harper messaged back, *Ugh, some people shouldn't have gotten married. Let's leave it at that.*

At least a giant chunk of this case would have me alone in the woods. I never loved the social aspect of an investigation, but it was a hell of a lot harder with a hostile client. Maybe I'd try to gear my communications toward Karen.

Once the file loaded, I started leafing through it.

The testimonies from all five kids were similar, but not eerily similar, as Phil had made it sound. Crafted statements often used nearly identical verbiage. That wasn't the case here.

Charlotte referred to Mia and Liz's argument as, "stupid and petty." Danny said, "those bitches are always fighting." Mike made it out to be, "dumb girl shit." Mia cried in her statement, saying, "I didn't think she'd run off alone!" Caleb said it was a "shit show, but no one told Liz to leave. She just freaked out like she always does."

Sort of a suspicious way to talk about your missing girlfriend, but could I blame the guy? No one was exactly chipper after hearing their partner had cheated on them.

I wasn't ruling anyone out until I talked to them in person, but I didn't read reports for witness testimonies anyway. Liz's phone would tell me more than a report ever could. The report was so I could know what the cops knew.

So what did they find at the scene? Not much. Some blood and bloodied tissues, which DNA hadn't come back on yet, but the blood itself didn't match Liz's type. The kids claimed it was Charlotte's. That she'd cut herself accidentally when she was opening a bag of marshmallows for s'mores. I called bullshit. The corner of one of the tissues was rolled up. Like Mia had put it up her nose.

My guess? It was more than an argument. Liz punched Charlotte in the face, and Charlotte got a nosebleed. Or they'd been doing more than drinking. Side effect of snorting anything was a nosebleed.

The search and rescue team hadn't found anything else of Liz's, aside from her sleeping bag and a bag of her clothes at the camp. Which gave me some faith in the kids. If they wanted us to believe Liz left because they'd done something to her, a bunch of teens would've gone overboard and gotten rid of her belongings. The fact that most of her things were still at the camp made me think their story was probable. A fight ensued, and Liz stormed off.

But it was odd. How the hell had a drunk kid hiked seven miles in the dark? Had she brought a gun? Taser? Bear spray? You couldn't have paid me to hike after dark.

Although, as a teen, I would've done it for a free joint. There were few things I wouldn't have done for a free joint.

Which brought me to the big question. Who was Liz Turner? The kinda girl who'd hike seven miles in the forest for a free joint? The kind who was terrified of the wilderness?

Nine times out of ten, knowing the victim told me whether to believe a witness and the evidence. So onto Liz's Facebook I went. Just as I opened her messages though, a *knock-knock* sounded at the door.

"A-woo-wooh!" Tempy howled, pointing to her bowl with her nose.

Otherwise telling me who was on the other side.

Chuckling, I used the arm of the sofa to stand. My knee throbbed as I waddled to the door. Didn't even need to bend to pull Tempest back. She was still at her crate, waiting not-so-patiently for her kibble.

Bentley stood on the other side with a warm smile and a pizza box. He'd just showered, judging by his damp hair and clean shirt. "Waiting for her dinner?"

"I swear she can tell time." Smiling back, I leaned against the doorframe. "Here or your place?"

"Here's good." Brushing past me, he set the pizza down. He caught my cheek and kissed me softly. "You learn anything?"

"About Daisy?" I shut the door behind him and carried the box of pizza to the kitchen. "Not yet. But I'm about to dive into a missing teenager's Facebook. You want popcorn?"

Bentley kneeled to greet Tempest, who only whined at her bowl. He arched a brow at me. "You got a job?"

Reaching into the cabinet for some plates, I smiled wider. "I did."

He scooped Tempest some of her kibble from the container beside her crate. "That's awesome. It's gonna pay better than I do, huh? It gets priority?"

"I'm not letting you pay me for looking into Daisy." Opening the pizza box, I smirked. "Wanna help me snoop?"

"Ah, yes. Let's live vicariously through the missing kid."

Chapter 5

So who was Liz Turner? A bitch.

"Don't talk like that," Bentley said when I verbalized that thought.

I covered my mouth to keep my pizza inside. "Since when do you not like cussing?"

"It's not cussing I have an issue with," he said. "The girl's missing. She could be dead. It wouldn't kill you to have some sympathy."

I leaned forward to read Liz's texts clearer. "But being a bitch is probably what killed *her*."

He frowned at me. "She's just a kid."

"Is being young any excuse to talk to strangers like this?" I angled the laptop toward him. The screen showed a private message from Liz to a random girl on her friend's list. They'd never talked on Messenger before, and Liz had hit her with, *Hey, girly! I'm working with Eternal-Vibe Health Elixirs. They have such amazing products! I've lost 10 pounds with this electrolyte balancer. I know you've put on some weight lately. Since you're getting married next year, now would be the perfect time to get in shape! Use my discount code for 20% off!* "Because Grace is how much younger than her, and she'd never be this mean."

After squinting for a moment, Bentley's nose wrinkled. "Okay, she's kinda rude. But we can try to have a little compassion."

I tried. But from what I could tell, Liz Turner had none of her own.

In her texts and private messages, I found more enemies than I knew what to do with. It started with her boyfriend, Caleb. Seemed like a sweet kid. Each morning, he texted her, *Good morning beautiful :).* Regularly asked her what she wanted to eat for lunch, then brought it to her at the ice cream shop where she worked. Whenever she asked him to buy her some miscellaneous item or another, he'd respond with a screenshot of the order and its estimated arrival date.

She'd ask him to bring her coffee to school, and he'd send her a picture of a cup once he had it in hand. At one point, she'd responded to the photo with, *Wait, does that say whole milk? And regular vanilla?*

Caleb responded with, *Oh, shit. I told them Almond and sugar free vanilla. I'm sorry, baby.*

Liz texted, *Can you go back?*

He texted, *I would, but I'm running late. If I'm late to practice again, coach's gonna kick my ass.*

K.

Not *Okay.* Just *K.* Which was rude enough. The kid stopped and got her what she wanted, without even being asked that morning, and her response was to get short with him over the fact that she had whole milk instead of almond? It wasn't a matter of lactose intolerance either. A scroll through her social media showed how much she enjoyed ice cream. The girl worked at an ice cream shop and sampled the goods daily.

Throughout that day, Caleb apologized a thousand times for the coffee mishap. Liz left him on read. All the while conversing casually with a dozen other guys in her private messages and texts.

Clicking over to the next text conversation Liz had that day with Darren, a friend from her work, Bentley said, "Alright. Maybe I see where you're coming from."

I almost made a smug, playful remark, something like, "I told you so," but Bentley glanced at the screen and flung his head in the opposite direction. "Geez, tell me before you go full screen with that shit."

Turning back to the screen, I was greeted by *way* more of Liz

Turner than I needed to see. I quickly clicked back to her messages with Caleb. "Also something I needed to know, though."

"You needed to see a teenager's entire naked body?" Bentley's head was still turned away, eyes pinched tightly shut. "Because I did not."

"It's put away. You can look."

"I don't know if I believe you."

"Why would I want you to look at a naked teenager?"

"I don't know. Why did you click on it?"

"How was I supposed to know that 'multimedia message' meant nude photo?"

Turning back to the screen, he squinted at the name. "Wait, Darren. We saw him on her Instagram, right? They work together?"

"Yup." Clicking around on the screen, I traveled back to Liz's social media.

When I found the photo of Liz and Darren side-by-side, I turned the laptop back to Bentley. They were both behind the counter, smiling at the camera. Should've found it suspicious that his arm was around her waist, but it wasn't until that photo that it clicked. It almost looked innocent.

Liz was pretty in a cute way. Long blonde hair, big blue eyes, little ski slope nose. Like a porcelain doll, painted to perfection. She couldn't have been more than a hundred-twenty pounds, with all her weight in just the right places. That much, I knew, because even in the photos where she was clothed, she had all her assets on display. There was something bizarre to me about a girl with a face that round, so youthful and innocent appearing, to be wearing fishnets and booty shorts in the next image.

Zooming in, I pointed to the ring on a certain finger of Darren's left hand. "Look at that."

Bentley scrunched up his nose at the image. "Ew. He's married?"

"That's my guess." Liz had tagged him, so I clicked on his profile. His Instagram was private, but there was a link in his bio to his Facebook. And, sure enough, his profile picture there was one of him, his wife, and their infant son. "Graduated in 2018."

"Ugh," Bentley said. "So he's in his twenties, and Liz is eighteen."

"Yep."

"And she sent him a nude last week."

"Sure did."

"Doesn't she have a boyfriend?"

"Yep." I clicked over to Caleb's profile. Fellow eighteen-year-old. The kind of person who didn't gross me out for being interested in Liz. "Think I should add Darren to the suspect list?"

Another, "Ugh," followed by, "Yeah, I'd go talk to his ass."

"Might wanna talk to his wife too." Clicking on to her profile, I scanned for information about where they lived. "Part of me wants to send her the screenshots."

"That'd be cruel, wouldn't it? She didn't do anything wrong."

"How is telling the woman her husband is cheating on her cruel?"

Bentley took over the laptop. "I don't know. Look at what she posted earlier today. 'Leo is teething so bad. I haven't slept in four days. Any moms out there have any advice?'" He shrugged. "Maybe now just isn't the right time."

"There's never a right time to find out your partner's cheating on you."

"Well, sure." Still hadn't so much as looked my way, leafing through Angela's *About* page in search of a rough estimate of where she might live. "But while your baby's teething is an especially shitty time to find that out."

Crossing my arms against my chest, I stared at him for a few moments. He absentmindedly chewed on a piece of pizza. Squinted a bit. Clicked a few times. Tilted his head from one side to the other.

I had been staring at him for quite a while when he finally looked over. Apparently not reading my silence, he smirked. "What?"

"You wouldn't wanna know?"

"Not while Grace was teething." He wiped some pizza from his lip. "She was adorable, but I swear she was possessed."

"So you would—what? Wait for the right time if you were me?

Stalk her on Facebook until then? Wait until she's having a good day to ruin it?"

Smile dwindling, Bentley's brows slowly fell into his gaze. "You're mad."

"I'm not mad. I'm curious. What would you prefer? When would you rather find out something like that?"

"I think this might be a trick question." His voice came out softer, almost sheepish. There was a playful edge to it, like he was trying to figure out if I would return it. Usually, I did. This, however, was a sensitive subject. "Okay, definitely a trick question."

"If there was no right answer, it would be a trick question." Leaning away, I studied him. "This is an opinion. There can't be a right or wrong answer to an opinion."

"It might be the wrong answer if you don't agree with it." His smile was just as timid as his voice. When he realized I wasn't backing down, he cleared his throat. "I'm just saying. If I were where she is right now, I wouldn't want that dumped on me via Facebook. Especially not while my baby is teething, and I haven't slept in four days."

"How *would* you want it dumped on you?"

He opened his mouth, then snapped it shut again. When I only arched a brow, he said, "I'm sorry, I didn't mean to piss you off. If you want to message her, message her."

"If I want to, I will," I said. "But you didn't answer the question."

"Maddie." Another laugh just as uncomfortable as the last one. "What's this about? You don't really care about what I think, do you? Because I know you're gonna do whatever you want—"

"Of course I am. But we have kissed each other hello and goodbye for the last six weeks, so yeah, I do care what you think about cheating and infidelity. If your solution is to avoid it, and wait 'til there's a good time, yeah. I think that is something I deserve to know—"

"Whoa. Whoa, whoa, whoa. That wasn't what I meant. I wasn't saying what the guy did was okay, and I agree she has the right to know."

"Nice backtrack."

"We weren't talking about me, or you, or us." He gave me that inno-cent puppy look of his. "I just meant, if I was going to hear that from a stranger, it would suck already. To hear it from a stranger on a bad day would suck a lot worse."

I didn't disagree with that. What I disagreed with was the fact that he called it cruel. "Alright. But what would you do?"

Bentley cocked his head to the side. "What would I do about what? If I found out that my wife was cheating on me?"

"If you were him. Would you wait for some stranger to send your wife the screenshot? Or would you just wait around for a day that wasn't so shitty? When the baby wasn't teething?"

Still, he looked confused. "I wouldn't be him."

"Nobody thinks they're going to cheat on their spouse."

"I don't." He let out a dry laugh. One that I assumed was intended to lighten the mood. It didn't. "Sorry, Mads, but I don't agree with you. People who cheat think about cheating before they do it. Some people are just cheaters. That whole, 'it just happened,' shit isn't real. It's something people spew when they're ashamed. Unless you're assaulted, you make the conscious choice to do that. I had opportunities when I was with Bella, but I never acted on them because I was married."

My brow was still arched, but my tone was playful. "You had opportunities?"

"That's your response?"

"Tell me about these opportunities."

"Really?"

"You've piqued my interest."

With a huff, he scratched his hairline. "When I still massaged, one of my clients tried to kiss me when I was done with her session. I pushed her away. Gave her a friend's number because I was no longer comfortable massaging her. The other time, it was a coworker. Just a few months before Bella died. Didn't act on it when she died, either." Bentley narrowed his eyes at me. "Did I pass your test?"

"Hmm." I made him wait for a moment longer. "Did you tell Bella?"

"Both times. Immediately after it happened. And she cried, by the way. Because Grace was teething." I laughed, and so did he. "Okay, she wasn't teething. But she did get her shots that day. And I told Bella anyway because it was going to come out, and I didn't want it to look like I'd done anything wrong when I hadn't. So what about now? Did I pass?"

"A minus."

"What did I lose points for?"

"Not understanding where my head went when you insisted on not telling the woman."

"I'm supposed to read your mind?"

"Yep."

Shaking his head, he still smiled. "What about you? What would you do?"

"I wouldn't. We agree on that much. It's very much a choice."

"And? What if the opportunity presents itself?" Dramatically imitating me, I imagined, he propped his chin in his hand. "How would you go about telling your imaginary husband you turned someone down?"

"Depends."

"On what?"

"The guy. Imaginary husband in question," I said. "If he's the jealous type, then I might not tell him. If he's not, I would do exactly what you did."

For a guy who claimed he couldn't read my mind, I was fairly certain he did there. The narrowed eyes softened, and rather than a blank face, sympathy filled his expression. "Did you go through that with Ox? Some guy hit on you, and you turned him down?"

"Something like that." Wishing I hadn't started this conversation, I turned back to the laptop. "Anyway. Looks like my suspect list is ten people long so far, and I've only made it through about two weeks of Liz's phone. The parents want me to go to that forest tomorrow, walk that trail with Tempy, but with a list like this, I don't know where to begin. It's gonna take me a day just to interview half of them."

I still felt his gaze on me for a few heartbeats. While neither of us were mind readers, I was certain I read his. *You're going to throw that at me, and then stay quiet when I ask you the same question? You're not even going to tell me the story with Ox?*

If pressed, I would. But I didn't want to talk about my ex with my... whatever Bentley was. We'd yet to establish the title.

He didn't, though. He didn't press. Instead, he broke the silence with, "That's a long hike, isn't it?"

"About seven miles, yeah."

Fingers trailing from my hand to my neck, massaging there, he said, "Do you think you're okay to do that? Go out into the woods?"

"Yeah. Why wouldn't I be?" I had to glance at him to understand. Those concerned brown eyes said it all. "The woods aren't a trigger for me. I'll be okay."

"Alright. But hey, I'm off work anyway. Grace won't be back from camp until Sunday. You want company?" Smile growing, he thumbed my chin. "I can be your pack mule."

I returned the smile. "I would love for you to be my pack mule."

Chapter 6

PILES—MORE LIKE VERY DISORGANIZED MOUNDS—OF PAPERWORK littered my coffee table. Bentley rubbed a hand down his jaw as his eyes flicked over the sheets. "Is this normal?"

I lifted the corner of a stack with my thumb and shivered at the breeze of the papers fanning back to the tabletop. Rarely did I print out all the details of a case, but I couldn't have kept track of all the conversations, photos, status updates, tweets, snaps, texts, and direct messages without doing so now. Liz Turner lived ninety percent of her life online, and if the internet was good for anything, it was controversy.

"No," I replied. "Almost everyone has someone who would benefit from their death, but it's usually only two or three people."

"And Liz has got, what? Sixteen?"

"Seventeen. And that's just what I could narrow down from the last three months. God only knows how long it'll take me if none of them pan out. I've met drug dealers with fewer enemies."

"Putting it mildly," Bentley murmured. "How long you think it'll take you to interview them?"

Flapping my lips together in a trill, I turned to my notes. "Six of them are on vacation, according to their social medias. I'll have to cross reference that with Harper, but that still leaves eleven. Not counting the five who were with her the night she disappeared."

"Feels kinda stupid to go up in the woods and search for her, doesn't it?" Bentley leaned in and pointed to the makeshift file I had constructed. "I mean, she was screwing this girl's boyfriend." Flipping through my stack of papers, he landed on Zoe Taylor. "This lady lost her job because Liz threw a drink at her when she made her order wrong, and she called Liz a bitch." With a huff, he shook his head in disbelief. "I just can't picture this girl being missing for two days with no rhyme or reason. Somebody killed her."

Hated to make assumptions, but I was thinking the same.

It stood to reason, given the findings of the search and rescue team. Liz had gone to the woods—publicly announced it on every social media, down to the precise campsite—then left those woods willingly after a heated argument with her closest friend group. Truth was, I couldn't blame them for letting her go.

Liz Turner was mean for sport. She thrived on bullying and drama. After learning that she had ruined the relationship of one friend, not to mention her own, I wouldn't have gone running after her either. Probably would've said the same thing they did. *Good luck out there.*

Which brought me back to nothing.

Given the information I had, there was an equal probability that any of these people could've killed her. One of Liz's many enemies may have taken the opportunity to get their vengeance when she'd called them from the woods, drunk and disoriented, desperate for a ride home. It was also just as likely that someone in the friend group had followed her when the others went to sleep, offered her a ride home, killed her in the car, then dumped her body elsewhere.

"If she's out there, dead or alive, the search and rescue team would have found her by now. But this is the one I want to talk to first." I sifted through the pile and handed Bentley what I had gathered so far on Danny King. "He seems the most suspicious."

Bentley squinted at the printed screenshots, then cocked his head to the side. "Which one is he again?"

It would've been cruel to laugh, so I swallowed it back down. There were just so many, it was hard to follow.

"Mia Davis's boyfriend." Going back into the stack, I found the makeshift timeline I had created for Liz's life. I tilted the photo from her dance recital in the first grade toward him. "Mia and Liz have been best friends since grade school. But this private message here"—I scanned through my laptop for the Instagram DM—"is from Danny. It says, *If you ever tell her, I'll ruin you. I've got all the screenshots, Liz. Don't screw with me.*"

Liz had responded with some choice words.

Bentley let out a low whistle and asked, "He's the one who proposed already, right?"

"Yep." I turned the picture of Mia and Danny's low quality engagement photos to Bentley. "Which is already weird. What dumbass gets married at eighteen?"

He gave me a tightlipped, narrow-eyed smile. "Ouch."

Shit.

My whole face heated instantly. "I didn't mean *you're* a dumbass. It made sense for you. And, I mean, it's not always stupid. Things for you two could've turned out—" I pressed my lips together, realizing how much deeper I was digging myself in this hole. "I'm just gonna shut up now."

Bentley laughed. "It's alright. Me and Bella were the exception, but I'm aware of the rule. When it does happen, there's usually a reason. My reason is named Grace."

"That's not the only reason." I did my best to soften my voice. "You were crazy about Bella."

"I was. And I did want to marry her. But she only married me because she was having my baby. She loved me too, but she had plans for her life. Grace and I weren't a part of them. I'm pretty sure the only reason she went through with the pregnancy at all was because I was willing to do anything to help. With the pregnancy, and Bella's career, and then with Grace when she was born. It's not like I was her dream man." Pointing at the image of Danny and Mia, Bentley raised a shoulder. "You think he's hers?"

Hm. A good point, and one I hadn't thought of.

Mia was stunning. *Model* pretty. Her brown hair reached the middle of her back, layered just right to accentuate her round face and high cheekbones. The warm sepia of her skin practically glowed in every photo. In most of the images, she wore very little makeup, but her reddish-brown eyes sparkled like glass. She was somewhere around my height—five foot six—with long legs, a perfect hourglass figure, and just the right poise in her poses and clothes that made me visualize her in a pencil skirt and blazer at the head of a long table as a CEO. The early acceptance letter to Columbia in her profile picture helped to draw that conclusion.

Danny, however? He was cute. His dirty blonde hair, pale blue eyes, and big, playful smile were the most attractive things about him. Although he looked strong enough to carry a body, being on the heavier side, he didn't seem to play sports. Nor did he excel in academics, judging by the photos of him doing keg stands and smoking joints.

To put it mildly, Mia was way out of Danny's league.

"You think she's pregnant?" I asked.

"Not to be an ass, but I don't know why else she'd marry him. If it weren't for the fact that he was screwing her best friend, I might think it was because of his stellar personality, but great guys don't sleep with their girlfriend's friends."

"Another detail to add to the list. And another suspect." Underlining Mia, I made a mental note to interview her privately. "She's going to Columbia next year, so I doubt she'd throw her life away and murder her best friend. But we can't rule it out."

"Don't underestimate pregnancy hormones," he said. "But if she's not, I have no idea why they'd get married. And you know what? I'm not even gonna tell you to wait. You should tell her. Tell her asap. Don't let her throw her life away on this little shit."

"I will when I get back from the hike. Don't wanna drop a bomb like that if I won't be around to deal with the fallout. If Danny *did* do this, he might lash out when Mia confronts him." Swiveling to face him, I shook my head. "But you're wrong."

"About?"

"Bella. You were her dream man."

He chuckled. "You know that?"

"I do."

"You a ghost whisperer now? Or did you guys meet up for coffee or something on your random trips to Ohio?"

"Never been to Ohio, actually." Leaning back on the arm of the sofa, I stretched my legs out over his lap. "And no, no ghost whispering. But I have cyber stalked you. Plus, I've been in your house. In the pictures of you guys, even the ones you're just holding the camera for her, it's obvious. Her eyes when she was looking at you say it all. You were everything to her."

Exhaling deeply, he rested his hand on my knee and massaged it gently. "I don't know. She loved me, and she loved Grace, but where we ended up wasn't what she wanted. My all-time fantasy was what we had. Hers was bigger. Living in the city, traveling the world, surviving off ramen noodles and becoming the next Picasso." Another sigh, and a forced smile. "Did you ever feel that way with Ox? Like you had what you wanted out of the relationship, but you knew he didn't?"

No. Ox was the one who got everything he wanted. I was always the one to concede. But saying so would mean discussing him. Our relationship, maybe his death, and I didn't want to do that right now.

"I don't know," I said. "But I do know that you're wrong. Bella may have had dreams, but they weren't bigger than you."

He opened his mouth, but nothing came out at first. I imagined it was another question about Ox, or maybe another protest to me stroking his ego, but I was grateful when he changed the topic with a throat clear. "Speaking of Ohio, didn't you say that was where your dad was? When he was in prison, I mean. I thought you mentioned Ohio."

Ah, yes. I had.

"Thanks for reminding me." Craning awkwardly to the table for my laptop, I clutched Bentley's forearm to keep from falling. He offered to grab it for me, but I was already waving him off and settling into the pillows. "I don't know why he didn't come up when I searched for him before. If he was in prison for this long, it had to have been for a serious offense, which there should've been news coverage of."

Bentley pressed his thumb into just the right stiff spot on my knee. I had to swallow to keep from groaning my misery. "Is there a way to look that up?"

"Definitely." I typed away on the keyboard. "Especially now that I know where he was, and that he has a record."

"How do you do it?"

"Start with the state correctional records, since I know he was in prison," I said, clicking onto the same site I'd used to find information on Daisy. "Once I get that report, it'll give me an address that'll tell me which county he was in when the crime occurred."

"Then you can search county and police records for the date and find out exactly what happened, right?"

"Has the student become the teacher?"

"No desire to become the teacher. It's just cool. Knowing how you find out all this shit about people." Bentley softened his touch on my knee. "Am I hurting you? You seem tense."

"No." But my heating cheeks must have given me away.

He tugged his hand away. "I'm not gonna be offended if you tell me to stop, Maddie."

"Who says I wanted you to stop?" The file on *Samuel Castle* was loading from the Ohio Correctional website, so I leaned in and put Bentley's hand back where it'd been. "Because I don't."

"What was that face for then?"

"Honestly?"

"Usually preferable to dishonesty."

"It's sore, and that felt amazing, but I'm resisting the urge to groan with relief."

Massaging my knee again, he gave a half smile. "Groan, huh?"

"A throaty, wrinkly old-man-trying-to-get-out-of-his-recliner groan."

Bentley wrinkled his nose. "Hot."

"Ya think?"

"Oh, yeah. Lifetime fantasy."

Laughing as the PDF finally finished downloading, I opened the file. Only to be greeted with another spinning circle. I clicked all over the document. Sometimes that made it load. That's what I told myself, anyway. It probably just kept me occupied while I waited.

"Duly noted. Librarian, or nurse, or cop's more common, but Bentley prefers balding, thick glasses, flannels, loafers, and groaning. You ever take me on a real date, I know what I'm surprising you with when we get home."

I expected a laugh for that. It was a good joke.

But when I looked at him, he was frowning.

"Geesh. Point taken. Old man role play isn't your thing."

"No, I—That's not why I'm looking at you like this."

"Scowling?"

"This isn't scowling."

"Glaring?"

Apparently sensing my sarcasm, he narrowed his eyes. "You're avoiding the bomb you just dropped."

"I didn't drop a bomb."

"You did, and don't think the conversation's ending there." Still, he massaged my knee, but his touch was softer now. Like he was afraid he'd break me. "After everything that happened, the way you've—"

"Ooh, it loaded." I tilted the screen to face him. "Let's see. What'd Dad do? That's so weird. Calling him Dad, I mean. Calling him Samuel feels weird too though. What would you call him?"

His hand stopped moving around my knee. The look he was giving me practically burned a hole in my cheek.

"Maddie."

"Bentley."

"We were having a serious—"

"Holy shit." Stomach suddenly full of knots at the offense typed out on the screen, I tried my best to keep that groan inside. "Shit, I was really hoping it wasn't something like this."

Bentley stayed silent. When I looked up, he was still frowning. His eyes said *Nice deflection.* Verbally, however, he said, "What is it?"

Again, I spun the screen to face him. "Voluntary manslaughter."

Chapter 7

"Shit," Bentley said. "Can you see the details?"

"Not here, no. Remember January 9th, 1998 for me." I minimized the tab and returned to Google to search for police department, Cuyahoga County, Ohio. When I landed on the page, I asked Bentley for the date, entered the other required information, and clicked submit. While it loaded, I harrumphed. "That was, what? Three months after he left? He vanished, started over in a new state, and then killed someone. No wonder Mom never gave me his letters."

Although Bentley's eyes were sympathetic, he tightened his lips to a line. Which he often did when he wanted to say something but wasn't sure how I would react to it. "That's really shitty."

"But?"

"No but."

"I've known you all your life. There's a but."

"Not really a *but*." Bentley shrugged, frowning. "I don't want to impact the decision that you're trying to come to right now. I'm just here to listen."

"Just say it."

"Maddie—"

"We both know that when I'm upset, my instinct is to be aggressive.

Your instinct is to be compassionate. So if you have a compassionate viewpoint, tell me."

"You want to give him your compassion?"

Such a simple question, but answering it felt like tearing my rib cage open for the world to see. "I don't know."

"I think you do." Bentley lifted a hand in defeat. "But if you don't want to talk about it, that's okay. I'm not gonna push."

One of the many things I appreciated about Bentley. Everybody craved a connection with someone who had an ounce of emotional maturity, and I had yet to meet another person who had as much as Bentley. Yours truly included.

I was working on it, though. Wasn't getting very far, but I was working on it. As much as I loved to avoid pain, this was something I would appreciate my best friend's input on.

After a quiet moment, I said, "I remember him, you know? Not everything. I was too young to remember everything. But I remember who he was as a person. He was my favorite parent. Guess that isn't saying much when you consider who my other parent was, but I remember when he cooked dinner, and when he'd pick me up from the bus stop, and the little birthday parties he threw me. I loved him more than I loved anything.

"And then he left. But when I think about him, I think about all those good times. Then I get angry that he wasn't here, but I under-stand it, too. I know who my mom was and how hard it must've been to be her husband. It isn't fair to blame him for wanting to get away. I do blame him for leaving, but I just—Ugh." With a grunt, I ran my fingers through my hair. "I want to hate him, but I also want to forgive him. There was no forgiving my mom. It wasn't just that she did awful things. She was an awful person. But he wasn't. He was an addict, and he was always high, but he was a good person."

Bentley said nothing, only nodded and continued massaging my knee.

Like I knew it would, admitting that felt more vulnerable than streaking through a busy street. There were more feelings bubbling that

I wanted to let out. But I couldn't keep dumping on him. Either this had to be a conversation, or it had to end here. "Do you remember that? What he was like? Or did I romanticize him because of how bad my mom was?"

His voice was soft, along with the pressure he put on my knee. "Maybe you romanticized him a little. But I remember Sam the way you do. He was always messed up on something, but he was never mean." He laughed. "Actually, I take that back. Remember the time he beat the shit out of my dad?"

The most I managed was a somber, breathy chuckle. "I remember when the cops came, but I was asleep when it happened. I don't think I ever got the story."

"He came home drunk. My dad, I mean. And he was just pissed. I don't member what about. The dishes, maybe? That Mom, Phoebe, and me hadn't washed them? Or something like that." Bentley's eyes glassed over, but no tears escaped. "Anyway. He just went off. Like he always did. I remember hearing something bang, and then something shatter, and then mom yelled something like, 'They're sleeping! Just leave them alone!' But he didn't. He opened my door, then Phoebe's, turned on our lights, and screamed at us to get out of bed. To come clean whatever it was. Mom kept telling him that we had school in the morning, to just let us sleep, and he hit her."

Bentley nibbled his lower lip. "Me and Phoebe got up. We were gonna go do it, but I was crying. Like a five-year-old does when his dad hits his mom. He did that whole, 'I'll give you something to cry about' routine. I guess I screamed pretty loud? Your dad heard me. Next thing I know, he's charging in, pulling him off me, and beating the living shit out of him." He managed a smile. "So, I don't know. I might kind of romanticize your dad too."

Damn it. Damn the tears budding in my eyes.

"It makes sense. Forgiving him, letting him back in, that makes sense. But so does keeping your guard up." Gesturing to my laptop, Bentley resumed his rhythm on my knee. "Did that load yet?"

Grateful he gave me a chance to look away, I swallowed the salty water that ran down my throat. The police report had loaded. I told him so, then leafed through it for the good stuff. The meaty part? It read,

On January 9, 1998, at 2100 hours, I was dispatched to [redacted] regarding a breaking and entering and consequent assault with a deadly weapon. Upon arrival, Officer Gabriel Reed and myself met with Sophia Russel and Julian Mitchell outside the residence in the front yard.

Penelope Russel is the six-year-old stepdaughter of Benjamin Russel, the victim. She had a cut on her lip and a scraped knee. She was hysterical, would not respond to questioning. When asked if the assailant hurt her, she said [one line of redacted material].

Inside the home, we found Benjamin Russel in [two lines of redacted material]. Forensics will need to confirm, as he was unrecognizable. Blunt force trauma from baseball bat (found at the scene) likely the cause.

Julian Mitchell, victim's in-house maid, gave us the name, description, and vehicle information of assailant, Samuel Castle, who was not present at the scene. Sophia said Samuel lived at Motel 12, twenty minutes from the Russel home.

Upon arrival, Samuel Castle was standing at the front of his vehicle with the hood open. He fled on foot. After a three-block chase, we arrested Samuel and brought him in for questioning. He asked for legal counsel immediately. The subject was placed into handcuffs. They were double-locked and checked for fit prior to placing him into the backseat of my police car.

"That's it?" Bentley asked. I nodded. "What about court transcripts?"

Speaking through the lump in my throat was harder than I thought it'd be. "I can request them, but it'll take a few days at least. There's less red tape with police reports."

"Hmm. Well, those redacted bits are weird, right? Are you thinking coverup?"

I wished. "Redacting's common. Cops do it on records that'll become public to protect the safety of people involved."

Another, "Hmm." After another quiet moment, Bentley said, "Benjamin Russel. Does that sound familiar to you?"

"No. It does to you?"

"I think? Like, maybe something to do with the Nelsons. The guys Daisy was selling for?"

"They dealt meth, didn't they?" After typing *Benjamin Russel* into Google, I arched a brow at Bentley. "Sam's a downers kinda guy."

"Maybe it's not connected to them then. But I definitely recognize the name."

As soon as the search loaded, I scoffed. "That'd explain why." I turned the screen toward him and read the byline aloud. "'Cleveland Mayor Killed in his Home.'"

His jaw hit the floor.

Mine didn't. Breaking and entering suggested attempted burglary. When the guy fought him, Sam killed him.

Too sickened to read it, I passed Bentley the laptop so he could give me the gist.

So badly, I wanted to believe he was a decent man. And maybe he had been. Maybe killing Benjamin was just a mistake. A horrible, awful mistake. Maybe he'd been on too many drugs that night, went too far trying to get his next fix, and spent every moment of his life since regretting it.

But how could it have just been an awful mistake? How could he have bludgeoned this man until he was unrecognizable by accident? Sure, I could see him hitting him once in fury. But to beat him until he was mush? In front of a child?

Even on drugs, I couldn't justify that, especially considering his drug of choice. It was the same as mine. Opioids. Drugs that dulled the senses, softened the mind, and slowed the central nervous system.

I couldn't see it while battling withdrawals either. They were horrendous. Debilitating, if coming off heroin. Swinging a baseball bat into someone's face would make you hurl if you were dope sick.

If he'd done this, I couldn't let him back in. Could I? I believed in rehabilitation, but prison didn't rehabilitate anyone.

Prison sentences were doctorates in crime. An addict went to jail for possession of meth, and they got out with a PhD in how to cook it themselves. Six-month sentence for grand theft auto? Well, they just met their bank robbing partner. Lock up a rapist? Upon release, they'd learned that if you kill her when you're done, no one'll know what you did.

More often than not, people were a hell of a lot worse after they got out. How could it get worse than this? Sam had broken into a stranger's—

"Wait." I furrowed my brows. "The report said Julian identified Sam. She knew him. The maid knew him on a first name basis."

"Huh," Bentley said. "Yeah, I guess it did."

"So he didn't just attempt to rob the mayor's home." My heart skipped. Admittedly, a pathetic thing to feel so excited about, but I'd never been known for perfect mental health. "They knew each other. So there's probably a reason, right? He didn't kill him in cold blood. Beating his head in with a baseball bat, that's overkill. We usually don't see that with strangers. They had beef. He went there for something, they argued, and Sam lashed out. That makes sense, doesn't it?"

He still stared at the screen, forehead scrunched down in focus.

"Bentley." Legs still draped over his lap, I nudged him in the chest with my knee. "Did you hear me?"

"Sorry, what?"

"They knew each other. He may have had a decent reason for doing what he did." God, I hoped he had a decent reason. "Or I'm a pathetic little girl who doesn't want her daddy to be the villain. But I'm too close to this now, and I need your input here. Am I making excuses for him?"

"No, I don't think you are." He turned the laptop my way. "They never mention him. This is the only article I can find about Benjamin's death, and they never mention Sam by name. If I didn't know better, I would think the cops never arrested the suspect. And what journalist do you know who isn't going to do what you just did to find the police report? Why would a journalist omit the murderer? What's the purpose in that?"

This news should not have made my stomach feel as fluttery as it did. "Not once. They never mention Samuel Castle."

"Not here, and not anywhere else. That's weird, isn't it?"

"Really weird." Sitting up, I read the article over his shoulder. And sure enough, not a single mention of my father. It had almost nothing to do with the victim's death at all. It was more of a biography, or an obituary. They propped Benjamin Russel up on a pedestal, but never mentioned the man who killed him. Why? There was nothing people loved more than a villain behind bars. "You know how you asked if I thought there was a cover-up?"

"Changing your tune?"

"To put it mildly," I said. "It doesn't make sense."

"Who were they trying to protect? Sam? Benjamin? Benjamin's family?"

"The latter, I would think. Sam isn't the type of company a mayor should keep." Squinting at the article, I quoted the section that stood out to me. "'Benjamin Russel was killed by an intruder in his home.' That's it. Doesn't mention that they knew each other, nor that the child was a witness, because Ben wasn't as squeaky clean as the rest of this article makes him out to be."

"Looks like it. But how could he and Sam have met anyway?"

"Beats the hell outta me." Studying that image of Benjamin a moment longer, all that hope that had fluttered in my chest twisted and spun until it landed in my gut as an ill, churning sensation. "Does it matter?"

"Does what matter?"

"If it was revenge or cold blood. Does it matter?" I asked. "I make my living finding out bad things people have done. I send them to jail for it, and make sure they go bankrupt in their divorces, and help cops build cases, and... I don't know. Doesn't this make me a hypocrite? Wanting so badly to believe he's decent when I know he killed a man?"

Silence ticked on for a few moments too long. When I looked over, Bentley was pressing his lips together again.

"Just say it."

"I wasn't gonna—"

"I want your input, so just say it."

Bentley kept his voice softer than silk as he said, "If my neighbor and her husband hadn't been there, I would've killed Kevin when I saw what he did to Daisy. I would've gotten voluntary manslaughter." He slid his thumb over the back of mine. "A few weeks ago, the day everything went down." Again, he pressed his lips together. When I stayed quiet, he cleared his throat. "If Ox hadn't told me to put the gun in his hand, if I hadn't fired it, when it got to ballistics, they would've known he wasn't the one who killed Eric. They knew you were there, and—"

Likely afraid I'd be upset, he stopped again. I appreciated that. But not because I was upset.

"I'm a killer too?" I asked. "Is that your point?"

"No." He frowned deeply. "I'm grateful you decided my side of the story in that arrest *did* matter. You let me explain that it wasn't black and white. That there was a lot of gray. That's all."

Ugh. I hated that he was right. And I loved that he was right.

I still wanted to hate my dad. Hating was easier than forgiving. Forgiving meant opening myself up again. Risking abandonment. Betrayal. Loss. Hatred was safe. Hating my mom, keeping her at a distance, was how I moved on from the pain she caused me. How I moved on from the pain she could cause me again.

But I loved that Bentley was right because it made me feel less pathetic. Like I wasn't a sad little girl desperate for her daddy. Like I was a rational, open-minded person, ready to discover the gray, muddled truth.

"I guess I'm just thinking that solving the puzzle," he said, "knowing the real story, that's how you make decisions. Most people just feel things, but you decide how to feel off of the facts." Bentley shrugged. "If you want to forgive him, or if you want to hate him, you're gonna need the facts for that. And it doesn't look like you're gonna find those in public records. You'll have to talk to him."

Closing the laptop, I forced a smile. "I'll think about it. But that's a lot of work for one day. Onto lighter topics."

Bentley returned the smile, but his was more sincere than mine. "Sure. How about a movie and something sweet? I'm in the mood for ice cream."

I was also in the mood for something sweet. Not the type of sweet that Bentley seemed interested in. The kind of sweet that didn't just taste good but dulled the world from existence.

"I think I'll pass on the ice cream." Brushing his cheek, I leaned in and touched our lips together. Against them, I whispered, "But I'm down for the movie," before doing it again.

Slowly, softly, he kissed me back. His hand came to my neck, bringing me closer to him. Each caress was tender, gentle, dragging me farther and farther from the reality that today and the last six weeks had been.

Something about Bentley allowed me to do that. To float away. When it was the two of us talking about my case, or what his day had been like at work, or his plans for a little household project he was working on, just talking to him softened my reality. But when he touched me, when our lips were against one another's, it was like nothing else existed. We were every version of ourselves and the possibility of what came next at once. The childhood best friends, the first crush, the first kiss, the addict and the enabler while also boyfriend and girlfriend, parents and spouses, the healed and stable. His friendship and the community that came with it gave me life again, but his touch gave me hope.

Until he pulled away. He *always* pulled away.

Clearing his throat, he stood. "I think I have some at my place. I'm gonna go grab it. You want to pick the movie?"

My hope had been that the movie would be background noise. Apparently an empty hope.

And I didn't understand it. Whatever was happening between us, I didn't understand. I wanted more than friendship. Admitting it had felt as vulnerable as admitting that I wanted my dad in my life again. But Bentley had said it first. He'd said he wanted the same thing I did.

Since then, we'd kissed hello and goodbye. He tucked an arm around me when we watched movies on the couch. A few times, when my knee was particularly irritable and I needed to lie flat, he'd lain in bed with me. We'd made out like a couple hormonal teenagers, and I'd fallen asleep in his arms.

Any time I attempted to get it past that? He pulled away, just like he did now. When I suggested going out to dinner, he always said sure, then said something about how Grace was just talking about this or that restaurant. How about we go there? With Grace, of course.

Which was fine. I loved Grace. But that suggested something different than where I'd thought we were headed. And again, that was fine. If he wasn't interested in a relationship, that was okay. It'd hurt like a son of a bitch, but I'd live.

Then he'd kiss me or say he liked my jeans with a certain smirk, and I'd scratch my head for hours.

What were we? What was happening here? Did he want what I wanted or not?

But I didn't know how to verbalize that. Asking felt like pushing. And what good would that do? He already pulled away. At least for now, he was pulling away and coming back with ice cream.

"Sure," I replied. "I'll be here."

Chapter 8

Lush foliage whooshed past in a blur, blinding sun making it impossible to discern where I was. Sharp breaths heaved in and out of my lungs. Hands throbbing, knee no different, I looked left and right. Only trees and verdant blooms stared back.

"Where are you?" A hardly audible whisper. "Where'd he take you?"

"Maddie!" she cried. "Maddie, help me!"

"Grace!" I ran as fast as I could toward the sound of her voice. Left? Right? I couldn't tell. Everything echoed in the peaks and valleys of these mountains. "Talk to me, Grace!"

"Help m—" A trembling sob cut her off. "Don't let me die, Maddie. I want to make it to eighth grade. Don't let me die!"

Right. Her voice came from the right.

"Nobody's gonna die." Feet slamming against the soil, I listened for the sound of her voice. "You're gonna be okay. Everything's gonna be—"

Pushing a branch in my path was like opening the door to the cabin. Behind me, bright sun shone, trees swayed in the wind, and birds chirped, but straight ahead, Grace stood with her back against his chest. Eric Oakley. The Country Killer.

Silver glinted at her throat. Hands tied in front of her chest with red ribbon, she sobbed. "I don't want to die. Don't let me die."

"Yeah, Maddie," someone said behind me. "Don't let her die."

I spun around.

Cold, nearly white, blue eyes glared down at me. Bright crimson spewed from the hole in his side, more from his paper white lips. At hyper speed, his pale, colorless skin fell off in chunks, leaving yellowing white bone beneath. Worms and maggots crawled from his nose and eyes.

"Ox," I whispered, backpedaling further into the room.

Hunting rifle appearing in his skeleton fingers, he aimed the barrel at me.

I stumbled backward and landed on my ass with a *thwack*.

"Don't let her die." He turned the gun around and held it to me, barrel facing himself. "Kill me instead."

"You're not supposed to be here." Shaking my head furiously, tears burned my eyes. "I can handle this. Just go. Go before it's too late."

Wicked grin pulling up one side of his face, he squatted before me. He yanked my arm from my side and put the gun in my hand. "This is what you want. Enjoy it, Mads. Shoot me. Shoot me so she can live."

My lips quivered. "That's not true."

"Of course it is." Gradually, the skin mended on his face and regrew over each finger. In a heartbeat, he was the Ox I wanted desperately to remember. Healthy. Safe. Alive. The only thing that'd changed was his smile. Ox never smiled, but now, he wore the most sick, sadistic grin. "You said you hated me chasing you, but we both know that's not true. You wanted me to *die* chasing you. You wanted me to suffer. You wanted me to beg and plead and squirm and watch you fall for him. You wanted me to watch you choose his daughter over me. Then you lured me out there so I'd die. So you could finally get rid of me."

"I didn't." A gasping weep tore through me. "You weren't supposed to follow me—"

"You knew I would!" Only inches before my face, blood splattered from his lips. The iron pulsed on my tongue. "You knew I wouldn't let you run out there alone. You knew I'd follow you. You knew I was behind you. You knew it when you threw that rock."

"No!" Still shaking my head furiously, I sobbed louder, harder. "I didn't know. I swear, I didn't."

"You *did* do that," he snarled. Grabbing the barrel of the gun, he held it to his chin. "Own it, Maddie. Admit it. You wanted me gone."

Trembling fingers releasing the gun, I struggled out, "I loved you. I didn't want to hurt you."

"I *died!*" Wide blue eyes turning white again, blood sprayed from his lips with each word. "I didn't get hurt. I died because of you. *Own it, Maddie.* Shoot me. Kill me. Be your daddy's little girl. Kill me."

"It's okay, Maddie," Grace said behind me. "Kill him so I can live."

Looking at her over my shoulder, gasping, I crab crawled away from both of them.

The blade that had been at her throat was now in her hand. Crimson coated every inch of her. Eric lay on the ground in a puddle of blood.

"Grace," I whispered.

"What?" She shrugged. "You gave it to me. Remember? You told me to do whatever I had to do to get away. I just stabbed him a couple times."

"You killed him." Lips quivering, I cupped a bloody hand over my face. "You're just a kid."

"Yeah." Grace nodded to my right. "And I'm gonna kill him too."

"No." I staggered to my feet. "No, he didn't do anything."

"It's just the way it has to be," Ox said.

"No!" I lunged toward them.

But my arms caught.

Two hands were tight around my wrists, pinning me in place.

In my ear, Bentley said, "It's okay, Maddie. Everything's okay."

"No!" I screamed, fighting with all my strength against his hold. "Don't let her do this! *Don't let her do this!*"

"It's what you wanted anyway," Ox said, handing Grace the rifle. "Why are you crying?"

"Grace, no! Run! Go!"

"Damn it, Maddie." Bentley's hold tightened. "It's okay. Every-thing's okay."

Propping the gun on her shoulder, Grace lined up a shot through the scope.

"Don't do this, Grace," I said. "Don't do it!"

"Alright." Ox snatched the gun from her hands and aimed it at her instead. "She can die then."

"*No!*"

Boom!

A flash of gunfire lit up the room.

Grace fell to the ground with a *thump*.

Ox dropped the gun beside her.

Yanking free from Bentley's grasp, I collapsed to the hardwoods next to her. The most awful, glass shattering squeal poured from my lips when I couldn't find her pulse. Hot blood pooled around us as I lifted her face in my hands, repeatedly screaming her name.

"You sure you don't want to shoot me?" Ox asked.

Without thought, I grabbed the rifle, spun toward him, and pulled the trigger.

"Told you." Falling to his knees, coughing blood, he smiled. "You'd rather kill me than let her die."

* * *

"God damn it, Maddie." Bentley's voice. "It's not real. Wake *up*."

When my eyes popped open, I still tasted iron on my tongue. I was still on the ground, but this one was carpeted, with an old, meandering scent of cigarette smoke. Two hands still pinned my wrists. They were still Bentley's.

The TV glowing in the corner illuminated his face. Winded, panting hard with wide eyes, something dripped from his lip onto my

55

cheek. Only when it pooled into my mouth did I realize that was where the iron taste came from.

I gasped and jolted backward, attempting to free myself from his hold.

It took a grand total of two brain cells to put the events that led us here into a narrative. Bentley and I had lain in my bed to finish the movie because sitting on the couch was killing my knee. We fell asleep somewhere in the middle of it. While he dreamed peacefully, a horror movie played out behind my eyelids.

Awakening from a night terror on my own was only that. Terrifying. Relief followed. Then shame for feeling the relief. Like I didn't have the right to be relieved when someone I cared about was dead, and my biggest problem was a bad dream. After the shame came grief.

All of that was here now. Terror, relief, shame, and grief. This time, the grief was for the same person it always was. Ox. The relief was the same as well. It was over, and I was awake. But the terror and shame? Those were both for Bentley.

Judging by how sore my throat was, all that screaming hadn't stayed inside my mind. Everything I said in that dream, I had likely said aloud. The flailing to escape Bentley's grasp in the dream had been real as well. I had punched him in the face. That's why he was bleeding.

"I'm sorry." Any frustration that had been in his voice vanished. Releasing my hands, expression gentle, he straightened and held his upright at his sides. "I know that came out kind of aggressive. Yelling at you to wake up, I mean. And then holding you down. I wasn't trying to hurt you. I just—"

"I know," I choked out. No matter how hard I tried, I couldn't meet his gaze as I sat up. "Don't be sorry. You didn't do anything wrong. I'm sorry."

Only the hum of the TV sounded for a few beats. I could practically feel his frown on my cheek.

When he rested his hand on the back of mine, it took a lot of willpower to keep from pulling it away. I reeked of sweat, still tasted his blood on my tongue, and felt the ache through all my knuckles and up my arm from the punch I must have awoken him with.

"I don't accept it."

"You don't accept what?"

"Your apology." Bentley's eyes were always kind, but more than ever now. "You didn't do anything wrong, either."

"Yeah? So you're not gonna have a shiner tomorrow?"

"Just a busted lip." With a smirk, he shrugged. "I'll live."

I didn't return it. Intentional or not, I'd punched him out. I owed him the apology.

"Can we go look at this?" He trailed his thumb over the back of my knuckles. "Put some ice on it?"

* * *

Sprained, Bentley suspected. My joints looked normal, aside from some mild swelling. Apparently there hadn't been a skin-crawling *pop* when I socked him in the face. Although there was pain, it wasn't unbearable when he pressed on the bone. He still encouraged me to go to the hospital, and as usual, I said I would be fine.

While he tended to the minor abrasions with peroxide and Neosporin, he tried to lighten the mood. As usual. Despite how kind I found that, I was about to crawl out of my skin.

In the middle of an anecdote about a six-year-old patient he'd cared for with an injury similar to mine last week, I cut him off with, "What did I say?"

"In the dream?" Bentley asked, and I nodded. Carefully taping the Band-Aid over my index knuckle, he shook his head. "I don't know. It was all gibberish."

The lack of eye contact told me it wasn't. "Bullshit."

He let out a half laugh. "Not bullshit."

"I'm not gonna stop thinking about it until you tell me," I said. "What did I say, Bentley?"

At first, he said nothing. Eventually, he seemed to realize that I wouldn't let this go.

With gloved fingers, he rubbed some of the cream onto my next knuckle. "You were calling for Grace. You said 'Ox' a few times. Then a lot of 'no,' and 'run.' A couple, 'let me go's. Nothing bad."

As much as I wanted to find relief in that, I still scoffed. The *dream* was bad. This screwed up subconscious game where I flipped between blaming myself for what happened to Ox, then blaming Grace, and then blaming Bentley. Doubted Bentley would say it was 'nothing bad' if he had seen it all.

I didn't blame Grace. I didn't blame Bentley. I didn't blame myself. Not really. Not consciously. Since that day, I had felt closer to Grace than ever before. She was alive because of me. Ox had died trying to save us both.

If he were alive, if he had been given the choice between Grace or himself, he would've chosen Grace. No matter how much of an ass he had been, he'd put his life on the line every day for innocent people. He had been proud to die a hero.

So what was this thing inside me? Why did I keep having nightmares like this? Grief was a bitch, but this just didn't make sense.

Thumbing my chin, Bentley brought my gaze to his. "What were you worried you said?"

"Nothing." How fast I answered that surely confirmed that it was something. "The whole thing is just embarrassing. I'm sorry you saw that."

"There's no reason to be embarrassed. I'm sure one of these days, you'll wake up to me crying about Bella. Or my dad. Or an awful scene I dealt with at work. Or Daisy. Or Grace." He tucked some hair behind my ear. "I have nightmares about that day too. So does Grace. Any normal person would. There's no shame in being human."

"Maybe." Doing my best to change the subject, I smiled. "But there *is* shame in punching you in the face. I'm really sorry."

"Eh. I've seen you throw a lot of punches over the years. I knew one would land on my face eventually."

"We're just lucky you got me on the floor before I got my gun."

"Yeah, you should probably put that in a safe."

"I did that a couple weeks ago," I said. "Woke up while I was loading it."

All the color drained from his face. "Maybe you should get them out of the house for now. Until, you know. The shock of everything wears off."

Chuckling, I shook my head. "I'm kidding."

"Oh, thank God." The relief flooding him was palpable as his shoulders dropped and he lifted a hand over his heart. "Because I had no idea how I was going to convince you to get rid of your guns."

He wouldn't have needed to. If I got to a point where I genuinely believed I would harm another person, I would check myself into a mental hospital. As a result, I would lose my guns permanently. Pennsylvania gun permit requirement. Anyone who had been hospitalized for mental health concerns could not own a firearm.

Which I didn't *completely* disagree with. Mentally unstable people didn't need access to a gun. But I'd always thought it only stigmatized mental health conditions more. A car was just as dangerous as a gun, and no one took drivers' licenses away from people because they had sought help for a mental health condition. I couldn't help but wonder how many more people, particularly the hillbillies my home state was so well known for, would've gotten the care they needed if not for that law.

"I'm okay." I raised a shoulder. "It took me a while to get back to work, but I really am okay."

"I know." The confidence in his voice shocked me. So did his smile. It wasn't that pitying one he'd given me when I woke up. He held up his thumb and pointer finger, as if to signify, *a little bit.* "I'm only a healthy amount of worried about you."

"You don't need to worry at all."

"I'm always gonna worry about you. Also worried about the fact that we've only eaten pizza for the last two days. Pancakes, eggs, and sausage?"

The sun was rising outside the window. Not like I ever turned my nose up at a meal Bentley made. "I hope you have that at your house, because I do not."

As he stood, he nodded and stretched his arms overhead. The way his shirt lifted and exposed the bottom of his torso did not escape me. "I'm out of coffee though. You want to bring some over after you get dressed?"

"Sure," I said, just as my phone dinged. The text came from an unfamiliar number.

Hey, it's Sam. I found your number online. I'm sorry to bother you so early. I'm sorry to bother you at all. Really, you can tell me to shut the hell up and leave you alone at any point. I'd completely understand. I'd respect it too. But I'm working at a job that isn't far from your place, and Imma stop at Moonbeam Cafe for breakfast. I don't start until nine, but I'm in the habit of waking up early. Anyway, I know you were rushing out yesterday, and I sort of bombarded you, but I'd love to have breakfast. My treat, of course.

Bentley was not so subtly reading over my shoulder.

Time to provide some commentary. "He sure talks a lot, doesn't he?"

"Probably where you get it from," he said. I playfully smacked him in the stomach. He laughed. "He is being respectful. It's a small thing, but he introduced himself as Sam. Didn't just assume you were gonna call him 'Dad.'"

"Respectful of him to reach out, too." A deep breath escaped my nostrils. "Giving me his number put the next move in my hands. Which is nice, in a way."

"But sort of put the pressure into your hands too." Bentley tucked his arms around me from behind. "Breakfast with me? Or breakfast with him?"

Another deep breath. Everything I'd learned last night pulsed through my mind. Specifically, Bentley's remark about needing the full story before deciding whether to let Sam back in.

I craned my head back to meet Bentley's gaze. "You still gonna keep me company in the woods?"

"You'd have to shoot me to keep me away."

Chapter 9

Sam looked like a teenager waiting for his date to the prom.

After pulling into the lot, I sat in the driver's seat for a few minutes and watched him through the window. He kept adjusting his posture. Sat up straighter, then slouched slightly. Fixed his hair, then tousled it. Took his jacket off, then put it back on. When he'd gotten up and moved to the other side of the table for the second time, I decided to head inside.

I didn't know him well, but I knew people. This wasn't the way a man who wanted money or a place to stay behaved. He was nervous. Nervous, and eager to impress. Not in a boastful manner, but a scared one. Like the outcome of this meeting decided the fate of his existence. Or at least his joy. Like whatever I said here, however I behaved, could make him happier than he'd ever been or suffer more than he ever had.

That pressure was like an eighteen-wheeler sitting on my chest.

As I approached the red leather lined booth, sneakers squeaking against the checkered tile, he stood to change seats for the third time. Our eyes met when he spun. Despite the initial shock, apparently realizing that I had seen his dance with himself, he put on a big smile and gestured to the bench. "I, uh, saw you in the reflection of the window. Do you want to sit here?"

"Sure." Commanding Tempest to sit alongside me outside the booth, I did my best to appear kind. Two steaming mugs of coffee already rested on the laminate tabletop. A few scones sat beside them. Ordering those before I arrived, so they'd be there when I sat, was a considerate gesture. Matching it, though, being just as friendly in response, was easier said than done for me. "Thanks."

"No, thank *you*. I didn't even know if you'd be up." He bent beneath the table and held out a hand for Tempest, murmuring, "Hi, puppy," before giving me that awkward smile again. "She's a service dog?"

"These days, yeah. Her specialty is in narcotics though."

I expected a snort for that. Mom had laughed her ass off when I told her I was going to become a cop.

Sam did neither. He just said, "That's cool. I didn't know they could do that. Both, I mean. Be a canine officer and a service dog." He cocked his head to the side. "Wait, are they considered officers? Is that how it works?"

"Not exactly. Hurting a cop's canine is as punishable as hurting a cop, so in a way." The fact that he hadn't asked why I needed a service dog confirmed what I should've already realized. "You googled me, huh?"

Pink tinged his cheeks. "I could lie and say it was just to find your number, but I've been keeping tabs as much as anyone can with the Internet. I had a printout of you in the newspaper in my cell." Another pause. "That's probably not anything to announce with pride, but I did. It was you accepting an award. Something to do with K-9 handling? About ten years ago now, I think."

Damn it. Damn how warm my chest felt.

"The USPCAK9 Founders Award." I nodded. "Yeah, I got that not long after I was certified. I'm surprised you found it."

"Wasn't much else to do on the Internet but look for you." He strained a smile. It fell a heartbeat later. "That came out weird, didn't it? It did. I wasn't, like, stalking you or anything. Just keeping tabs, you know? But if I've crossed a boundary or anything, just let me know. I'll stop googling you. And I'll wait for you to tell me things, if you want to tell me them. You don't owe me your life story or anything. I just— Whew, I'm choking on my words here, aren't I?"

Awkward. He was so awkward. Had he always been like this? Did I fail to notice because I was a child? Or was he where I inherited it from?

I smiled. "You're in therapy?"

"Huh?"

"You keep saying you don't owe me anything. That you're sorry. You're not trying to put pressure on me. That you'll respect my boundaries. You're taking accountability, the way an estranged parent should. That's what a therapist would've told you to do."

Another hard swallow. He nodded. "I have been for a long time. Court mandated, at first, but I really like it now. That's what helped me decide to come here when I got out. Practicing this with my therapist, I mean. We've gone through every reaction you might have had to all this, and I did a lot better then than I'm doing now. Guess I was better prepared for you to slam the door in my face. Not that I wanted that, but I didn't want to get my hopes up, so that's what I was assuming would happen, but then—" Pressing his lips together, he shut his eyes and exhaled slowly. "I swear I'm not always this flustered. Or sweaty, if you can smell me."

I couldn't, but it made me smile. I had no memories of him being so anxious, but that look in his eyes brought me far more comfort than I thought it would've.

Lucky for me, the next question wasn't so comfortable. "Was that mandated drug and alcohol counseling? Anger management? Psychiatric?"

"Never anger management." That, he said with confidence. "But yes to the other two. I have substance abuse disorder, anxiety, and depression. No personality disorders, psychosis, or anything like that."

The substance abuse trifecta. Almost everyone with substance abuse disorder had anxiety and depression. It was reassuring, because if Mom had ever seen a professional, she would've been diagnosed with narcissistic personality disorder.

"Are you clean?" I asked.

Avoiding my gaze, he rubbed a hand down his beard. "I took a couple hits off a joint the night I got out."

Damn it, why did he always look like a puppy? Was that what my eyes looked like? Everyone said I had Dad's, but I wasn't sure I ever looked so innocent and sad in my life.

"That's it, though. And it was legal. Only took me an hour to get a card online. Weirdest shit. You can just get legal weed now." An awkward laugh, which I didn't return. Forcing his smile down, he cleared his throat. "But it *was* legal. I'm not risking going back to prison. And I won't risk ruining my life. If you don't want to be around me if I'm high though, I get it. If you want me to throw my card away, I will. It isn't that important to me. You are."

I didn't care if he smoked weed. Sure, it was a *gateway drug*, but when obtained legally, it didn't gateway into anything. As an opioid addict myself, I could confidently say that using cannabis was nothing like using heroin.

"Not around me," I said. "Do whatever you want on your own time, but I don't want drugs in my life."

"Sure. That's not a problem."

Every time he spoke, each nervous mannerism, made me think that same sentence over and over. *He's like a kid at prom.* In part, yes, because he desperately wanted me to like him. But it went deeper than that.

He'd been seventeen when he'd met my mom, and eighteen when she'd gotten pregnant with me. By that time, he was already on drugs. When someone developed a substance abuse disorder and continued to use said substance, mentally they remained the age they were when the addiction began. Occasional drug use would only hinder the brain's development during that time, but chronic use halted growth all over the brain, especially in young people.

If he got clean at twenty-five, shortly after he left me, he gradually would've caught up with his peers. But he went straight from addiction to prison. In other words, he had the mental development of a teenager when he began serving his sentence. While his brain and body had time to recover from the substance abuse, without having gained the real-world experience of the average middle aged man, he wasn't too far off. Between the addiction and incarceration, he had almost no real world experience.

I knew beyond any doubt that I would be diagnosed with a substance abuse disorder if I were honest with a psychiatrist. I used casually as a teenager, but not in excess the way Sam had. My addiction didn't begin until my late 20s and only lasted a few years. Supposed watching him and Mom taught me the easy way.

Tying all this together made something ache deep in my chest. Putting aside how different I wished things were, he'd practically been a kid when he'd killed Benjamin. He *had* been a kid when he'd had one of his own. Mom was six years older than him, twenty-four when they met. Then she abused the shit out of him. He was bigger, stronger, and there wasn't as much discussion of intimate partner violence then, let alone intimate partner violence initiated by a woman.

It wasn't an excuse. But it was an explanation.

"But enough about me," Sam said. "As long as you don't mind me asking about you. If you don't want to open up to me or anything, then I understand—"

"I don't mind. What do you want to know?"

Breath of relief loosening his shoulders, he smiled. "Was that Bentley? Who walked over when I pulled out yesterday?"

"It was. Does he look that much like he used to?"

"Not really, no. But I saw 'Roycroft' on a little rock in front of his house when I was walking up the driveway. Then I saw him walk over to you, and he looked just like he used to. Always running to the door to see Maddie." I must've smiled at that, because Sam smiled wider. "Just friends?"

"More. But it's early. It hasn't been going on for that long."

"Really? I always thought it would start going on as soon as you two hit puberty." Apparently realizing that I hadn't found that comment appropriate, Sam cleared his throat. "Is he good to you?"

That much, I could smile for. "Can't complain."

"Always figured he would be but had to check." He was still smiling, but it was awkward again. Supposed I wasn't giving him much to go off of. To his credit, he was a good conversationalist. I just wasn't. "So you never stopped loving dogs, huh?"

I reached below the table to pet Tempest. "One of the few things I'm very passionate about."

"You always were," he said. "Golden retriever's still your favorite breed?"

Shaking my head, I laughed. "Definitely not."

He propped his forearms on the table, smile softer. More natural. "Why's that? What's wrong with golden retrievers?"

"Nothing. And that's what's wrong with them. They're the easiest breed. Absolutely adorable, and great for families. Older people, younger people. Training them is a piece of cake, and they're highly affectionate. Eager to please their owners. And it's adorable. But it's boring."

"Yeah, you always did like a challenge. That's where your nickname came from. Mad dog. Do you remember that? Anybody still call you that?"

"Some people I know from high school. Greg. Bentley. I always just thought you gave me that nickname because it sounded like the liquor."

"Really inappropriate, but that did play a part. But no, it was because of a dog. Greg's dog, I think." Cocking his head to the side, his eyes scanned the room, as if trying to focus on a distant memory. "Or maybe somebody else's in the park, I don't know. But you were, like, two years old. Maybe three. I'm up on the porch with a friend, and you're down there playing with your toys in the grass, and this big pit bull comes barreling toward you. I see it, but I don't put two and two together until it's tackling you to the ground.

"You played with this dog all the time. He was always in our yard.

But then he's tackling you, and I start to panic, you know? You screamed, so I thought you were hurt. I go running off the porch, I'm terrified that it's eating your face-off, but then this other dog comes running. The pit bull turns around. It's practically sitting on top of you. And this little shit. It was one of those—Shit, what are they called? The Target dog. You know, the one from those commercials?"

"Bull terrier?" I asked.

With a snap, he wagged his pointer finger. "That's it. Bull terrier. It came lunging at you, and this pit bull wouldn't let it get within an inch of you. He literally guarded you with his life. And these two dogs start going at it. You get out from under the pit bull, and I'm trying to grab you, but you run away. And I chase after you, but you're just gone in a heartbeat.

"But my friend, he comes running off the porch. He starts trying to break the dogs up. I'm still trying to find you. And then I hear you screaming, 'Get off him! Don't hurt him!' So I turned around, and the pit bull has got the terrier by its flank, and he's not letting go. And my friend is hitting him to get him to release. That's what you were yelling about, because he was hitting the dog. And you got the hose in your hand." Sam laughed. "And you tell me, 'Grab that one!'" He laughed again, and so did I. I didn't remember a bit of this, but the excitement in his voice as he told the story was heartwarming.

"So I do what you say. I grabbed the terrier by the choke chain it's wearing. You come over, and you start spraying that hose. Soaked the hell out of all of us. The pit bull released though, and my friend is still holding him back. I had the terrier, but the little shit starts bucking like a bull. I fall down, and it goes running back at the pit bull, but you step between them." His smile was somewhere between proud and awestruck. Like even now, almost thirty years later, this was one of his favorite stories to tell. "You yell at it, 'Go home! You go home!' He starts walking toward you again, and you put that hose to use.

"The little demon dog finally starts to run out of the yard. Then you tell me to get the pit bull in the house. My friend does, and I scoop you up. Next thing I know, we're inside, the terrier is barking outside the door, and you're scolding the pit bull. Just wagging your finger in his face, saying, 'Don't you ever do that again. You let go. When I say let go, you let go.'"

I still didn't see how they got Mad Dog from that, but I had to assume they were high while this was occurring. Or maybe drinking Mad Dog. It was an endearing story either way.

Still chuckling at the memory, Sam shook his head. "Your mom never tell you that story?"

"No, I don't think so." I considered adding, *Mom didn't tell me many stories at all* but decided against it. This meeting wasn't too bad so far. Talking about mom would veer into a territory I wanted to stay far away from.

"Well, she never had the best memory." The light in his eyes dimmed when she came up. "The trailer you're living in, it's hers, isn't it?"

I guessed we were talking about her anyway. "It used to be. It's mine now though."

"Yeah, it looks like it. I was confused when I saw it there. It used to be on the other side of park, right?"

"Yep. There was a water main break under the ground five or six years ago. Messed up a lot of foundations. A lot of the trailers on that side of the park got moved over."

"That makes sense. Is she still in the park? Or did she move somewhere else? I know she always said she wanted to go back to school and get a"—he held up air quotes—"'house that didn't have wheels under it.'"

I didn't know if he would take this as good or bad news. For me, it had been a bit of both. As much as I loved Mom, I'd been grateful she was dead because it eliminated the burden of having to come when she called. As much as I hated her, I'd still cried over all the things we would never do together.

But she had been his wife. That had to have hit different.

"No, she's not in the park anymore."

"Oh. Alright," he murmured. "I was just asking because I was wondering if you talked to her about me. If you let her know I was in town, I mean."

Inhaling deeply, I shook my head.

"Take it you don't know where she is then, huh? She still using?"

Damn it. I had to tell him. If I didn't, somebody else would. Maybe it was best to hear it from me. Treading lightly over people's feelings wasn't my specialty. Saying, *She's rotting in a casket*, was far too abrasive. Blurting, *I know where she is, and it's six feet under*, wasn't much better.

Eventually, I said, "She died using."

His skin paled and he opened his mouth, but no words came out.

"I'm sorry. I'm sure I could have phrased that better. It was a little more than a year ago. Just sort of old news for me."

"No, no. You don't need to apologize. I'm sorry for your loss. And to dredge all this up. Your mom, I mean. I'm sure that isn't easy to talk about."

"Wasn't much of a loss." That, I said under my breath.

"What's that?" he asked.

How glad I was that he had not heard me. "Just thinking out loud. But why were you asking about her? She owe you money or something?"

Sam snorted, giving a half smile. "I would have let her keep it if she did."

I chuckled at that. This much, I remembered. He did everything in his power to not make me hate her. Even though she was awful to him, he respected her. That was the gentlemanly thing to do.

"No, it's nothing like that. I was wondering if you had told her about the letters. Or the calls. I guess you couldn't have, so now I'm just wondering. Do you believe me? When I say that I wrote you letters?" Shaking his head, Sam cleared his throat. "I'm sorry. This is all a big enough mess for you, and the way I said that came out like I was *expecting* you to believe me. And you don't owe me that. You don't owe me anything. I guess, a better way to phrase it, would be asking if you *want* to believe me?" He paused again. "I don't think that's better.

That's still putting too much pressure on you, and I'm not trying to do that. So let me just..." He reached into his jacket pocket and laid an envelope on the table. "That's yours. If you want to know if I'm lying, what's in there will prove I'm not. But if you don't want to, you don't..." Another long pause, followed by a hard swallow. "I'm sorry. I don't know what I'm doing here."

Neither did I. Sam was putting in the most effort he could. I knew that. He didn't want to emotionally manipulate me into forgiving him. The chips were all mine. That much, I was grateful for. But how could he prove that he had written me letters?

How could I ignore a chance to look at said proof and decide for myself?

Chapter 10

I GRABBED THE ENVELOPE AND TORE AT THE SEAM, KEEPING MY voice soft. "I get that you're nervous. And you should be, all things considered. But thank you for being so respectful. I appreciate it."

"You don't need to thank me. For anything." Although relief loosened his shoulders, his voice cracked, and the whites of his eyes turned red. "I owe you the world, kid."

Chills bubbled over every inch of my skin and a wet lump formed in my throat. He was right but damn it. He was what she wasn't. The parent she could have been. The one she'd chosen not to be.

Kind. Loving. Compassionate. Sure, a killer, but still a better person than my mother.

How screwed up was that? I wanted so badly to forgive him, despite it all. Despite him abandoning me. Despite what had landed him in prison for almost all my life. Just because he was kind, I wanted to grant him absolution. I wanted to drop into Daddy's arms, because at least Daddy's were open. Mom's had never been.

I didn't know what else to say, so I turned to the papers in my hands.

. . .

OHIO STATE PENITENTIARY
   Outgoing mail
   1-11-1998, Maddie Castle, 123 Circle Drive.
   1-12-1998, Maddie Castle, 123 Circle Drive.
   1-13-1998, Maddie Castle, 123 Circle Drive.

A FORMAT LIKE THAT SPANNED THE ENTIRE PAGE, FROM JANUARY 11th, 1998, to February 8th, 1998.

Daily. Every day, he sent a letter to my home. A stack of papers lay beneath this one, and when I fanned them out, they stretched on until the following year.

"There were more than that, but I ran out of quarters at the library to have them printed," Sam said, voice sheepish. "They keep track of the letters going in and out. Checking for paraphernalia, mostly, but I guess they want to know who everybody is writing in case something were to come up later? I don't know. But I was there for a long time, so I made friends with the guards. Even the warden. He got me those. You can call him and verify, if you want to. Well, you're a PI. I'm sure you will."

Damn it. Shit. What the hell?

That horrible, cruel bitch.

I could scream a dozen more profanities, because the longer I stared at those dates, the thicker my throat got. My eyes burned, but I couldn't let him see me cry. I couldn't look up, because then he would know how I felt, but I couldn't stop staring at the pages either.

It pissed me off. It pissed me off that this hurt so badly. Mom was dead. She was nothing more than a skeleton now, and I couldn't tell her to go screw herself. I had wanted to forgive her for so long, had tried so hard, kept trying to be a good daughter to her until the day she died.

All my life, I'd done everything imaginable to make her love me. To make her stop treating me like a doormat, or a punching bag, or dog shit on the bottom of her shoe.

And she had done this? She'd told me he never wanted me. She'd let me believe he just walked out, without any care for my well-being.

There was no way for a decent person to comprehend the cruelty that had lived inside Angela Natalie Castle. Nobody with a soul could beat a nine-year-old in places that clothes would cover for failing to take the frozen lasagna out of the freezer before school. Years ago, I had concluded that. As badly as I'd wanted to be loved by my mom, she'd been an awful person, and that would have never changed. But even for her, this was a new brand of evil.

And Sam. How could he?

"Why'd you leave me with her?" Anger replaced that heartache, allowing me to look up. There was nothing but remorse in his eyes. Some part of me wanted to stop. Continuing felt like kicking a sad puppy. But damn it, I had the right to be mad. "How the hell could you have left me with her? You knew who she was. You knew *how* she was. You knew she wouldn't let me see these. I couldn't even read yet. She would've had to read them to me, Sam. You really thought that she would read me the letters that you wrote? Knowing how jealous she was that I loved you more than I loved her, and that you loved me more than you loved her, how the hell could you just leave me with her?"

His mouth fell open, but no words came out. I waited. He was going to answer me, damn it. Either he had a reason, or he didn't deserve my forgiveness. He may not have been the abuser, but he'd left me with one when I was defenseless, and I needed a reason not to hate him too.

"I'm sorry," he choked out.

"I didn't ask for an apology." My voice was pure acid. "I asked for an explanation."

Now he was the one having a hard time holding my gaze. But again, I waited. Just like I had waited for his car to roll into the driveway every day throughout my childhood. And just like then, every second that ticked by caused a deeper and deeper ache in my chest and stomach.

"Why? Why did you leave? What was so important, Sam? What mattered so much more to you than I did?"

Tears bubbled in the corners of his eyes, but he blinked fast to disguise them. "Doesn't make sense if I say nothing did. That's the truth, but it doesn't make sense—"

"*Nothing did?*" I repeated, leaning over the table. "Nothing mattered more than I did? Yeah, you're right. It doesn't make sense. That's bullshit. Something did. Something ranked above me in your priorities, or you wouldn't have left me with that God damned monster." He frowned deeply at that. I half expected him to say, 'Don't talk about your mother that way,' but I continued before he could. "Do you have any clue what my childhood was like? Do you have any idea what I went through? She beat me for sport. Just like she did you—"

"Maddie, I'm so—"

"No, you're not. You're not sorry. Or you weren't sorry then, at least. You didn't care." Pain scrunched up his face, and he shook his head, but I kept going. "You can't sit here and tell me you're sorry when you knew. How many times did you pull her off me?" Tears stung my eyes too, but I didn't let them bead over. "How many times was she going bat shit in the living room, and you locked us up in my bedroom? How many times did we blast music on my Barbie boombox while she tore the house apart because she was pissed about whatever she was pissed about that day?"

For half a second, his lip trembled. He bit down to steady it.

"You knew, Sam. You knew how she treated me. You knew how she treated everyone, especially people who couldn't fight back. You knew what you were damning me to when you left. You knew I was only safe when I was with you." I hated my voice for cracking. "I needed you, and you left, and I need to know *why*."

For second or two, he chewed his lip. "Did you hear us? The night I left, did you hear me and Nat fighting?"

Slowly, I nodded.

"I'm guessing you didn't hear what we were fighting about," he murmured, rubbing a hand down his tense jaw. Expelling a deep breath, he massaged his eyes. "You, Maddie. We were fighting about you."

Damn my heart for fluttering.

"I'd been planning on leaving her for months." Leaning over the table, he lowered his voice. "Had it all perfect. I was even sober. I knew I would have to be, because I knew what Natalie was going to do. I was working that security job. You came with me a couple times? You remember that?"

Shaking my head, I crossed my arms and prayed that I didn't look like a giddy little girl ready to lap up whatever he spit at me.

"That's not the point anyway. I'd saved up money. Not much, just a couple grand. Enough to get started. I'd already put the security deposit down on an apartment. I lied to Nat. Told her I was working that night, and I wasn't. I gave you your bath, I got you into your PJs, and I kissed you good night.

"Then I got in my car, and I drove around for an hour. I loaded up a cooler. Got snacks and drinks, and gas in the car, and then I drove home. It was midnight. I thought she was asleep. But she came onto the porch smoking a cigarette as soon as I pulled in. And I've got all this shit in the backseat. Suitcases, road trip food, blankets, and pillows with your Barbie pillowcases on them. But I'm thinking, *Okay, she can't see the backseat from the porch. She doesn't realize.*

"So I try to hurry up and get out of the car. I tell her I was wrong. I don't have work tonight. I walk up the steps, give her a kiss, trying to seem natural, but she isn't. She's... Calm. Calmer than trees on a windless day. And the moment I saw that look in her eyes, I knew. I still tried to act like everything was normal. Then she steps in front of the door. The bi—" Gritting his teeth, he shut his eyes and forced out a deep breath. "She told me to leave. I told her to go to hell. Then some other colorful language that I'm not proud of."

There was only one reason he would've gone back to the trailer if his things were already in the car. I wanted so badly to believe *I* was that reason. But I had no reason to trust him. I wanted one—*God*, did I want one—but he could have made up every word of this. I didn't want to think he would do that, but how was I supposed to know? Mom wasn't around to ask.

"I don't know how she knew. Maybe she realized I'd packed our things. I think about that every damn day. I shouldn't have packed our things. I should have just started over with nothing. It's too late, but I regret packing our bags every day, Maddie." His eyes, his voice, were so soft. Just like they had been when he'd sung me to sleep. "We start arguing on the porch. She's body blocking the door. I'm just trying to move around her, and she won't let me through. I keep telling her that you're my kid too. She can't just keep me from my kid. I'm on the lease. She can't just not let me into my home."

Shutting his eyes again, he swallowed hard. "And she says a lot of shit. The mother always wins in court. I'm on probation. She's older than me. No judge is gonna take me seriously. I'm never gonna see you again. Not unless I calm down and talk about things." To get him to stay. That's what I was to her. Collateral. "And I pushed her." There was no faking the shame in his voice, his eyes, when he said that. "I shouldn't have. That was wrong, and I'm not proud of it, but I did do it. I was trying to get inside so I could get to you, but then I hear the click of a gun.

"And she starts sobbing. I hadn't pushed her that hard. Yeah, she stumbled, but she didn't fall. And she's sobbing, and she got the phone between her ear and her shoulder. She says, 'My husband just hit me. He's trying to run off with our daughter.' And I screamed that's not true, I didn't hit her. I was just trying to get in the house. But she screams over me and tells the nine-one-one operator that she has a gun. If I charged her, can she shoot me? I yell at her to put the gun down. And she shoots.

"It missed me. Went straight out the door. She hangs up the phone. She's aiming the gun at me again, and she's calm again. She says to get out of her house. And probably best to do it before the cops come. But I don't. We keep screaming, and screaming, and then I hear sirens, and I leave.

"But I just went to the park down the road. I could see the entrance to the trailer park from there on top of the hill. So I figure I'm gonna watch it. She'd done shit like that before. Pretended like she was calling the cops, and she wasn't, just to manipulate me into getting whatever she wanted that day. Sure enough, no cops came. So at this point, I know I don't have any warrants out, right?

"And I'm thinking that this works. I can pick you up from school, and we can go. I was the one who always picked you up from school anyway. That same day, I had picked you up from school. But I get to the school, and I try to pull you out, and they tell me I'm not allowed. Natalie gave them specific instructions that you weren't to leave the premises with anyone but her or the bus driver. With an emergency custody order in hand."

My chest was warm, and my heart fluttered, and tears threatened to drown my irises. So badly, I wanted to believe him. If this were true, if he hadn't made this up, it would mend the wound that hadn't healed in almost three decades.

"Did you file?" I asked. "For custody?"

"I did." He nodded. "I lost the preliminary hearing, didn't even get visitation, but I filed an appeal. And I got everything set up for you at my new apartment, but then everything happened."

If that were true, I could find proof of it. All I had to do was go to the courthouse and file a request for the transcripts of the hearings.

"When you say everything happened, do you mean when you killed Benjamin Russel?"

His already pale face lost all color. Rubbing down the bridge of his nose, he cleared his throat. "Looks like you googled me too."

"I'm a PI. You didn't think I'd meet a convict on my own without knowing what you went to prison for, did you?"

Despite how evident his discomfort was, he nodded again. "Yeah, I figured you would."

"Funny thing is, I couldn't find a damn thing." Crossing my arms, I leaned back in my seat. "You killed an important member of your community, maybe *the* most important member of your community, and you weren't even named in the articles about his death. Why is that?"

Another hard swallow. "You really want to talk about this?"

"I really want to know if you have a forgivable reason for doing what you did."

"Does it matter?" There was sincerity, regret, in his big blue eyes. "A man is still dead because of me. I'm not a judge. It wasn't my place to do what I—"

"Stop. Stop trying to act like a good, rehabilitated prisoner. You want to use the therapy speak when we're talking about why we are where we are, why I don't know you, I appreciate it. But not about this. I want to know why you did what you did. The police report's redacted. The journalists lied and said that Benjamin didn't know his attacker. But the maid knew you by name. Whatever you did, you had a reason for doing. A reason that someone thought would be bad PR for the dead mayor. I want to know what that reason is."

A frown. "It doesn't matter, Maddie. I killed someone, and—"

"And it isn't black and white. There is no black and white in the world. Humanity is a million hues of gray. Because if you just broke into your friend's house to kill him, or to rob him, I don't know if I can forgive that. But if you had a good reason, maybe I can."

"I've regretted it since the moment I did it." His jaw released, telling me that much was true. "But the ins and outs of it all, they don't matter."

Teeth clenching, I searched for the words. There were none.

Was Sam trying to make me believe the prison system had worked on him? He was cured? He saw the error in his ways and vowed to never commit harm again?

Bullshit. Maybe he could convince me that he hadn't wanted to leave, that he regretted how it all had occurred, but I knew the prison system. I knew how hard he was trying to convince me that he was different. That he wasn't just a convict. If he regretted killing Benjamin, it was because the act landed him in jail. It wasn't because the man deserved to live.

Aside from all that, I may not have known Sam Castle personally, but I knew his character. He was the man who wouldn't hit a woman, no matter how many times she hit him. The one who gave his piece of shit wife the better car, so she and his daughter were safe. A man who tore down his neighbor's door when he heard him beating his children.

There was a reason, damn it. And I didn't like being lied to.

"Right." Reaching into my wallet and setting a twenty on the table, I huffed a laugh. "There's never a good reason for violence. Not when they're shooting at you, or when they're beating you, or when they're beating your kid, or hell, your neighbor's kid. Never a good reason, right? You are and always will be a pacifist, huh?"

When he realized I was getting ready to leave, he shook his head. "Sweetheart, our food hasn't even come yet—"

"I'm not your sweetheart anymore." I stood and lifted my purse over my shoulder. "I'm a grown woman. And I have boundaries. One of them is being lied to. So if you want to have a relationship with me, there's gonna have to be transparency here. You're either going to have to tell me the truth, about everything, or I won't believe you about anything. But it doesn't matter now anyway. I'm working a case. I have a long drive. I won't have service for a day or two, so I'm not ignoring you if I don't message back. If you want to meet again, though, be transparent. Or it will be the last time we meet."

Chapter 11

I HATED LONG DRIVES. NOT THE DRIVES THEMSELVES, BUT THE pain that came with them. Sitting in one position for too long was literal torture for someone with chronic pain. Especially when the chronic pain originated from the leg needed to power the gas and hit the brakes.

There was no better relief than getting out of the car and stretching my legs after a two-hour drive. Even better because for those last two hours, I couldn't stop thinking about Sam. Forgive him? Believe him? Let him back in? Drill everyone who lived in the trailer park for their recollection of what'd happened the night Sam left? Track down that little girl who had witnessed her father's murder and ask her why Sam had done it? Add another deadbolt to my front door? Reinstall my security cameras? Trust him? Damn him?

I didn't know, but I was ready to get to work and out of my head.

When I arrived at the little coffee shop Phil had sent me to, however, I was ready to load back in and drive for another two hours with my racing thoughts and aching knee. Because an all-too-familiar black, shiny Audi idled in the parking lot across the street. Ashley Harper's car.

Waving, she smiled at me from the driver's seat. Had to assume I wasn't the only one who had gotten a text from Phil Turner. Wasn't sure why he'd hired me if he was going to have Harper work the case, but I had faced my father today. It couldn't be that much more difficult to interview a couple of teenagers with an old friend.

Once I parked, I secured Tempy's service dog vest, then had her help me out of the driver's seat. On two feet, clenching my jaw at the pain that ached up my thigh, I worked my lips into a smile for Harper. She was out of her car in a quarter of the time it took for me to get out of mine.

"Wow, that's so cool." Harper propped her hands on her hips. "Narc turned medical professional. She helps you walk?"

It never bothered me when people asked about Tempest's skills, but that did. Maybe because it felt like she was saying I couldn't walk. "Sometimes. Helps more with getting up and down than actual walking. But what are you doing here?"

Harper scratched the back of her head. "Phil didn't text you?"

"He did." To ask me to come here. Melody Morsels Cafe. A small-town shop where Liz and her friends spent most of their time. When I was twenty minutes from the Turner home, Phil said he had driven past and saw the group of kids she had gone into the woods with were here. He asked me to interview them before meeting at his and Karen's home. "But he didn't mention you."

Pressing her lips together, Harper cleared her throat. "He just asked me to be nearby. Maybe lend some insight while you interview."

"He wants you looking over my shoulder."

"I don't have to." She held up her hands in surrender, blue eyes soft and sincere. "I can stay out here if you want me to. But we're old friends, and they trust me. It's not that they think you're incompetent. I showed them your astounding record. All the arrests you made when you were a cop, and your dog training accolades, and everything with The Country—" She stopped before finishing that sentence. I appreciated that. "If the roles were reversed, and your friend asked you to help where you could in the investigation of their missing child, you would show up too, wouldn't you?"

Considering I was helping Bentley investigate Daisy's disappearance where other professionals had failed, yes. I didn't like it, but I understood it. "Yeah, yeah." A vague nod toward the coffee shop. "But you're getting the coffees."

A smile stretched across Harper's lips. "Medium mocha latte?"

"Since you're paying, large." Despite all the old resentment, there was no stopping my smile. "And cream cheese Danish."

"Ooh, I was gonna say just like the old days," Harper said, continuing beside me towards the café, "But danishes were my thing. You were always a coffeecake girlie."

Had to admit, I was surprised she didn't see what I was doing here. "I'll take one of those too."

Laughing, Harper pressed the crosswalk button. "One of each, and we split them down the middle?"

"Now *that* is just like the good old days."

She chuckled again, but it was softer than the other had been. Hopeful light shined in her eyes. Like just this bit of banter meant the world.

It did for me too, more than I cared to admit. A big part of me wanted to mend the friendship I'd once had with Harper. Was there any chance of that?

* * *

MAHOGANY BOOKSHELVES LINED EVERY WALL, THE SCENT OF JAVA and pastries filling my nose. Cool, indie guitar music floated from the speakers in the corner. Instead of a boring tile beneath my feet, warm cedar wood lined the floors.

It was a cool spot. I could see why it was a popular destination for kids in this town.

And there they were. Mia Davis, Charlotte Wilson, Danny King, Mike Green, and Caleb Adams. I recognized them from their social medias. They sat at a table in the corner. None of them were laughing or smiling. None of them seemed overrun with guilt, but they didn't look their best.

Neither of the girls wore makeup, their hair was tied up in messy buns, and none of the guys had seemed to do more than shower since they returned from their trip. Mia leaned against the window with her hand in her hair, staring absently into the distance. Red eyes chafed in the corners. Danny had a hand on Mia's back, coasting slowly up and down. Charlotte rested her head on Mike's shoulder. His unblinking eyes were glued to the tabletop.

Caleb slouched low in his seat. With a taut jaw, messy brown hair fluttering into his eyes, he stared at something in the distance.

Passing me my coffee, Harper spoke low. "Do you want to get them as a group? Or talk to each of them individually?"

"As a group first," I said. "You looked over the case, right?"

"Yep. I agree with Phil. My money's on the boyfriend."

Mine wasn't. After reading their texts, I just couldn't see it. Emotions ran high after discovering a partner's infidelity. I had been livid when Ox slept with Harper, but killing him had never been an option, not even on purpose. No matter how much I'd loved him, that hadn't been worth my life, my future. Caleb seemed the same way.

The kid had a scholarship to a great school. There was a good chance he would end up playing for the NFL in a few years. He wasn't the stereotypical jock, either. Not cocky, not mean, not a bully. Liz meant a lot if not *everything* to him.

"Mine's on that one." I nodded to Danny, then explained what I had found. "He had the most to lose. Also big and strong enough to carry an unconscious teenager to his car. If it was any of them, which I'm not convinced it was."

"Neither am I," she said. "The girl has a lot of enemies."

"Lot of people with motive." I took a sip of my coffee. "You take the left, I take the right?"

"Sounds like a plan."

The kids didn't even notice us approaching until we boxed them in at their table. I had already told Harper to keep her badge put away until we made the introductions, but she still reflexively reached for it. Luckily, she let me start the conversation.

After the awkward, "Can I help you?" and, "We already talked to the police," followed by my typical, "I'm not a cop, I'm a PI," spiel, I told them, "I was just hoping you guys could tell me a little more about where you were the last time you saw Liz. How familiar she was with the woods, if there were any trails she wanted to take, things like that."

"Oh," Danny said, nodding slowly. "So you don't think we did something to her, right?"

Letting out a half laugh, I cocked my head to the side. "*Should* I think you did something to her?"

His full cheeks flamed. "No, of course not."

"But since you brought it up," I said, lowering myself to the chair at the end, putting Tempest between us. "Would you guys mind telling me what happened that night? There was blood at the scene, but I don't believe it was a mishap with a hunting knife."

"It was." Charlotte's tone was quick and sharp. Not defensive, but nervous. "What else could it have been? And it wasn't Liz's anyway."

"It was yours, right?" Propping my elbow on the table, I leaned in. "I know we're still waiting on DNA, but you did admit that it was yours."

"Is it a crime to accidentally cut yourself?" She held up her pointer finger, exposing a cut that was much too big for the small amount of blood found on those tissues. "Because I didn't do anything wrong."

"You know, I worked with the FBI briefly," Harper said. "They taught me a few tricks about how to know when someone's lying. Like how they'll avoid direct questions by countering them with other questions. Sort of like you just did there."

"Out of everyone, you are the most likely suspect," I said, even though it was a lie. "You started the altercation. Your blood is at the scene. You're not big enough to carry Liz's body, but all of you together?"

"I thought I was the most likely suspect," Caleb said. "I watch crime shows. It's always the boyfriend, right?"

85

"*Was* it the boyfriend?" Harper asked. "I mean, I'm sure I wouldn't have been too happy to learn my girlfriend was sleeping with half the town."

"I didn't hurt her. I never would." Caleb clenched his jaw. "I sure as shit wasn't *happy* about it. Killing her though? That's what you think I—or we—did? You think we all killed her as a group? Like some horror movie? I'm hurt, and I'm pissed, and not just at Liz. At her too." He pointed to Charlotte. "She knew for weeks and didn't tell me. She wasn't even *going* to tell me. I overheard them arguing. But I'm sitting here having coffee with her. Because it's not that big of a damn deal. I love Liz, but not enough to ruin my life. Everybody gets cheated on at some point, right? Not everybody kills because of it."

Like I thought. He was annoyed, but not incredibly defensive. Caleb was reacting the same way I would. "You overheard them?"

"Yeah. Me and the guys were getting firewood, we heard Liz and Charlotte yelling, then my name came up, and so did Isaac. That's the guy she slept with. We ran to them, heard Charlotte call Liz a slut, said something about how Liz screwed Isaac, and then Liz saw me. She said she was sorry, that she wanted to talk, and I told her we were done. Then I went to my tent, chugged a fifth, and passed out."

"Was that before or after Charlotte nicked herself with a hunting knife?" Harper asked.

Silence.

Caleb broke his and my staring contest. The others all turned away as well.

"Look," I said. "If they find Liz, dead or alive, and she has marks on her knuckles from a punch, or skin cells under her fingernails, even if you guys weren't the ones to kill her, and the cops pair that with the blood found at the scene, you're going to be the one who goes down for this." I nodded to Charlotte, then glanced between the rest of them. "And the rest of you are going to get accessory to murder. She couldn't carry Charlotte's body on her own, but with all of your help, she could have. So somebody better talk now, because eventually, Liz is going to turn up."

"Isn't she?" Harper asked. "Or do you guys know where she is? Did you find a good spot to keep her in? Somewhere the cops wouldn't think to look?" Cocking her head to the side, she narrowed her eyes at Danny. "I think I read that you live on a farm. It doesn't happen to have an incinerator for dead cattle, does it?"

Danny's mouth dropped open, head shaking quickly. "We didn't kill her."

"But you did hurt her." Another point at Charlotte. "And she hurt you. That's why the tissues they found were rolled up like you stuffed them up your nose to stop a nosebleed."

Tears bubbling in her eyes, Charlotte swallowed hard. "I didn't kill her. She walked away."

"But you did hit her," I said.

"No, she didn't." Mia frowned deeply at me. "Liz hit her."

Charlotte shot her a look. The kind that said, *Shut the hell up.*

"She's right," Mia said. "Whenever they find Liz, if she's dead, they're gonna know that she punched you. My skin cells are probably under her fingernails from when I pulled her off you." Mia tugged up her sleeve, exposing a scratch on her bicep. "I told you it was stupid to lie. We didn't do anything wrong. Lying is just going to dig us into a hole."

Didn't surprise me that she was the one to call the others out. She was the smart one. "What happened then?"

"What Caleb said." Mia waved at him in gesture. "It was sunset. We were drinking. The guys left, and the three of us were talking. Charlotte told Liz that she needed to fess up to Emily about sleeping with Isaac. The girl is driving herself crazy trying to figure out what happened at this party a few weeks ago, and Charlotte was just saying that it was wrong. She has the right to know. She and Liz started going back and forth, and Liz stood up. Charlotte stood up too, and they were screaming in each other's face, and Liz punched her. Charlotte pushed her away, but Liz kept on, so I got Liz off Charlotte, and that was when the guys came back. We were all still arguing for a while, and then Liz started crying and saying that she was just going to leave."

"We told her not to," Mike muttered. "She had her own tent. We told her to just go there until the morning and then we'd hike back with her to reception so she could get a ride home."

"But she told us to go screw ourselves," Charlotte said under her breath. "She said a lot of really mean things. About how she and Mike had a fling before he and I got together. Then she fat-shamed Danny, and she called Mia a whore, and told Caleb she wished he would've succeeded when he attempted suicide last year, and a lot of other terrible things. That's who Liz is. She's the best friend you can have whenever she's in a good mood. But when she's mad, or drunk, she's the worst person on earth."

"So we let her go," Caleb said. "She had bear spray and a knife."

"But I still chased after her," Mia said. "I knew she didn't mean it. I didn't want anything to happen to her. But then she sprayed *me* with the bear spray. I couldn't exactly chase her after that."

Ouch. I'd gotten maced by someone I was arresting once. Not a fun time, but I did recover within a day or two.

"And that was it," Charlotte said. "Looking back on it, we shouldn't have let her go. But what were we supposed to do? Tie her up and walk her back to the car in the morning? I don't think that would make us look great either."

"We didn't hurt her though," Caleb said, eyes sincere as he looked between me and Harper. "I swear, we didn't. And if anyone here had, you might be investigating *their* disappearance. She cheated on me, but I care about her. Now, can you go out there and find her?"

The kid made a convincing argument. He seemed the least likely from the get-go, and the girls close behind, but I still wasn't sure about Danny. If she was still in those woods, having somehow evaded the bloodhounds, it had already been too long. I needed to meet with her family, get out into those woods, and search.

Turning to Harper, I raised a brow. She gave the slightest nod, informing me that she agreed. As I stood, I passed a few business cards down the table. "I believe you." Which was true. Most of them, I did believe. The one I wasn't so sure of I would track down for a private interview. "But if you think of anything that might help, give me a call."

"If you need to get a hold of her tonight, you can call me." Harper held up her badge. "Pittsburgh PD. There's an extension for Detective Ashley Harper. It'll connect you to my..."

She was still talking, but a kid walking inside caught my attention. Judging by his round face, he was younger than the group that sat before me—probably fifteen or sixteen—with curly blonde hair, light eyes, and pale skin that turned green when he heard the word *detective*. Our gazes locked for half a second. With a hard swallow, he spun around and hauled ass past the window straight ahead.

Cutting Harper off with an elbow jab, I tapped my hip for Tempest to join me. "We got a runner."

Harper stopped cold, just before the kid rounded the building. "I hate the runners."

I hated that Harper was faster than me, a damn dozen strides ahead, already tearing through the door. Half a damn dozen strides that I was grateful for, though, because I heard Danny say, "Is that Andy McAvoy?"

If we didn't catch the kid, at least we had a name.

Chapter 12

Of course, Harper was ahead of me. No shocker there. Most turtles could beat me in a race.

But who could beat both me and Harper? Not to mention Andy, if that was his name.

"Harper," I called, unsurprised when she didn't turn around. "Stop!"

She did, just as soon as Andy rounded the building.

To Tempest, I said, "Take him down easy."

In the time it took to blink, she was out of sight on Andy's trail. A clunk, clatter, and squeal sounded a few seconds later.

Harper's blue eyes were just as wide as her open mouth. "She isn't a police dog anymore, Maddie. If she just bit him—"

"She didn't." I was 99% sure she didn't, anyway. The worry that she did, however, pulsed enough adrenaline through my body that I could jog past Harper. "And if she did, you didn't see anything. Right?"

I couldn't tell if she snorted, scoffed, or laughed.

When I rounded the bend, a breath of relief eased from my nostrils. Tempy lay atop the teenager. With front paws on each of his shoulders, back paws spread out around him, she put all her weight into her ass on his stomach. As he tried to push her aside, she lifted her lip to expose her canines. The kid froze. She went back to panting.

Finding some treats in my hoodie pocket, I smiled. "Good girl."

She kept panting, but she squared her shoulders with pride.

"She—I didn't do anything." The kid's voice trembled, glancing at me out of the corner of his eye. "Can you tell her to get up?"

"You didn't do anything?" Walking toward his feet, so that Harper could stand near his head, I perched my hands on my hips. "Then why'd you run?"

"I-I didn't." He swallowed hard. "I, um, I just forgot my wallet. I was running back to my car to get it."

"Yeah?" I looked around the deserted alley, a gap big enough for a garbage truck to drive between two rows of brick and stone walls. There were some trash cans, one of which Tempest had knocked over when taking down the kid, a couple flies buzzing about, but no cars.

"Also don't look old enough to have a car." Harper stood a foot or two behind his head. When he tilted back to look at her, I imagined she regretted wearing a skirt today. "How old are you?"

He opened his mouth to speak, but I tapped my hip for Tempest to free him. She used his groin as a launchpad, and he grunted instead.

"Hey, you're lucky I told her to take you down easy." Stretching, I held out a fistful of treats for Tempest. "How old are you? What's your name?"

"Sixteen." Once he struggled forward, I noticed the backpack wrapped around his shoulders. And the intense smell of skunk permeating from it. "And Andy McAvoy."

Waving her hand beneath her nose, Harper took a step back. "Well, that could have been why he ran."

Swallowing hard once more, he looked between us. "Don't one of my parents have to be present for you to question me?"

Harper snorted.

I narrowed my eyes. I couldn't begin to count how many times a teenager had said something almost exactly like that to me, and it irked me every time. Kids saw a few cop shows and thought they knew the law.

For formal questioning, kind of. But Harper did not need a parent present to ask him what his name and age were.

"You have the right to call your parents, an attorney, or to remain silent," I said. "But I'm pretty sure he isn't under arrest, right?"

"Not yet." Harper crossed her arms against her chest. "If he doesn't hand over that bag, though, I just might have to. And we could call his parents while we're at it."

"But don't you need a warrant?" Andy tugged the straps of his backpack in closer. "Or probable cause?"

Harper and I both laughed.

"Tempy," I said. She looked up. "Find narcotics."

She started toward Andy, walked around him to his backpack, then lay flat.

"Smell was already probable cause." I held out my palm. "But there you go, kid. Hand it over."

Breaths quickening, hands trembling, he tugged the bag off his shoulders. Silence stayed as he handed it to me.

While it was stinky, it wasn't as much as I expected. Just an ounce or so. It wasn't split up into smaller baggies, nor were there wads of cash lying about. Given his age, it was a lot for personal use, but I'd been around fifteen when I'd kept an ounce on hand.

Finding her cuffs in the pocket of her blazer, Harper said, "Put your hands behind your back."

Tears streamed down the boy's face as he did.

But I still wasn't sure I bought it. Getting caught with an ounce of weed wasn't a fun time for anyone, but this kid had booked it. All he had seen was Harper's badge and my canine, and he'd taken off. As someone who had partaken in the same extracurricular activities as a teenager, something just didn't click. If I had been in his shoes, I would've acted like nothing was wrong when I'd walked into that coffee shop. Someone may have smelled what I had on me, but everyone knew running from the cops was never a good idea. Unless you were doing something a lot worse than carrying a decriminalized amount of cannabis.

"I'm going to go grab my car," Harper said. "Watch him until I get back?"

"No problem." I had some questions for him anyway. Using the dumpster behind me for stability, I lowered myself to the concrete as Harper disappeared around the bend. "You didn't run because of the weed, did you?"

The tears didn't stop rolling, and he didn't respond.

Sighing, I spread out my palms behind me and leaned back. "She's not sending you to jail. She's just teaching you a lesson."

Andy used his shoulder to wipe the tears from his cheek.

"Is it about Liz?" I asked. Although he still avoided eye contact, he tensed. "Ah. You saw us talking to the group she was with when she disappeared, and *that's* why you ran. Maybe she's gonna arrest you after all. But instead of arresting you for possession, she'll arrest you for murder."

Finally looking up with wide eyes, he shook his head furiously. "I didn't hurt her."

That seemed to be the catchphrase of the day. "Alright. But this has something to do with Liz, doesn't it? Isn't that why you ran?"

"No." He sounded like a puppy whom I had just kicked. "Well, yeah. Kind of. But not really. I know Liz. We work together."

"At the ice cream shop."

He nodded.

"Still not understanding why you ran."

Another hard swallow.

"Look, she's a detective." I gestured the way Harper had vanished. "I can tell her that I suspect you had something to do with her disappearance, or I can tell her whatever the real reason is that you ran."

"Liz sold me the weed," he said.

Interesting. Liz had never looked squeaky clean. From what I could tell, she was a complete bitch. But that was what I found odd. Of all the pot dealers I'd had, none of them were anything like who Liz Turner seemed to be.

"What does her selling you the weed have to do with you running when you see the group of people who last saw her?"

"She said that if I got caught with it, her boyfriend would kick my ass." Andy nodded toward the coffee shop. "Did you see that guy? If he would've seen me get arrested with her weed, I don't know what would've happened."

Also interesting. I didn't know if I believed every word of it. What Andy was relaying, I believed *he* believed to be true. But I also knew that Liz Turner was a compulsive liar. There were no references to drugs in any of her text messages or social media pictures with Caleb. In some of her photos, I caught glimpses of bongs and pipes in the background, nothing too out of the ordinary for an eighteen-year-old, but Caleb was an athlete. I couldn't see him smoking weed, let alone selling it.

Then again, he did say that he would kick the ass of anyone who hurt his girl. Maybe he was aware of Liz's dealing. Maybe he was the muscle behind her business.

"That's all?" I asked.

Andy nodded. "But please don't tell anyone. If they know I ratted on them, I don't know what will happen."

"Is Caleb known for kicking people's asses?"

Eyes turning to the concrete, like he was thinking very hard, Andy was silent for a few heartbeats. Eventually, he shrugged.

Interesting. Odd. I would do more digging here tomorrow. But it was already approaching 10 AM, and I needed to hike seven miles before sundown.

"Where were you the night that Liz disappeared?" I asked.

"Home," he said. "I swear. You can check my location history on my phone. And my parents have security cameras. I don't know what happened to Liz, but I had nothing to do with it."

Like I said. I would do more digging tomorrow.

The crumple of rocks under tires sounded to my left, announcing

Harper's return. Once it was in park, she stepped from the car. "What are your parents' numbers, Andy?"

THE HEAT OF THE SUMMER SUN AGAINST MY ARMS WOULD HAVE been soothing if not for Harper's cigarette smoke wafting into my nose. Years ago, she had quit. I considered asking why she'd started again, but I supposed we had all been under a lot of stress lately.

Standing against the car beside me, she gestured to Andy inside. "Do you believe him?"

I shrugged. "I don't know. It's something though. If Liz was dealing, that changes things."

"Do we know that she was actually dealing? Because offloading an ounce to somebody isn't necessarily the same as dealing."

"True. Pot isn't the most dangerous thing to sell either," I said. "But it's worth looking into after I hike the trail."

"Are you going there next?"

"I'm meeting Karen and Phil first, but I'm hoping it won't take too long. Burning daylight here."

"If you don't want to go alone, I wouldn't mind joining you." A hopeful smile tugged at the corners of her lips. "I can stop by the store and grab my own sleeping bag."

"Oh, can you?" I gave a teasing smirk. "You gonna sleep in a tent?"

"Hey, I prefer glamping to camping, but I can do it. I just don't like the thought of you going out there by yourself. It's pretty deep in the woods. And after what happened last time you were in the woods..."

The concern was genuine. Rational, even, given the fact that I hadn't been at my best lately. But the last thing I wanted was a camping trip with me, Harper, and Bentley. "Bentley's gonna meet me. I won't be alone."

"Oh. That's good then. I'm sure you guys'll have fun." She wiggled her brows, smirk morphing to a smile. "I'm going to Karen and Phil when I leave here too. You just want to ride with me? Have Bentley pick you up from there?"

I didn't particularly want to ride with her. But my knee hurt, and I really didn't feel like driving anymore, so I said, "Sure. Thanks."

"Anytime." With another hit off her cigarette, Harper shook her head slightly. "I want to tell Karen and Phil that we're going to find her, but we're going on seventy-two now. The last time her phone was turned on was at the edge of that forest. It really doesn't seem like those kids did anything to her. But someone did, and figuring out who is like looking for a needle in a haystack."

"And if the dogs didn't find anything, I doubt Tempest and I will," I said. "My time would better be used interviewing people here, or digging through Liz's phone some more, but that's where they want me to go."

Harper sighed. "I'll try and interview some people while you're out there. Who do you think I should start with?"

With a huff, I pulled out my phone and began listing them off by name. The people Liz was sleeping with were the most likely, especially the ones in relationships. I had covered the top ten with the most motive, just as a shiny Toyota turned down the alley.

"Think that's Dad?" Harper asked.

"My best guess." It was confirmed when he stepped out of the vehicle, approached us, and shook both of our hands.

He was an attractive man, not much older than Harper and me. No older than forty. Only a few strands of grey peppered his golden hair. A sharp jaw with a 5 o'clock shadow. Inviting, warm blue eyes like his son. Fit, like he spent a massive amount of his time in the gym.

After the pleasantries, Andy McAvoy Senior said, "Is he gonna have to go to court?"

"No, I just detained him," Harper said. "He isn't being formally arrested. Some pot isn't my top priority. But I am concerned about his connection to Liz Turner. Did you know they know each other?"

"That missing girl?" Blinking hard, he looked between his son inside the back of her car and Harper. "You think he had something to do with it?"

"She sold him the weed," I said. "Were you aware that she was your son's dealer?"

"He mentioned that they work together when her face was on the news, but I didn't know the girl. Didn't know he was smoking weed either." Rubbing a hand over his jaw, Mr. McAvoy's brows furrowed. "He was home the night she disappeared though. The whole night, and early the next day. I had him helping me at my car wash. And I've got the security footage to prove it. I can send you the videos from that night if you want them."

"Please do." I handed him my card while Harper handed him hers. "We just like to cover all our bases."

Chapter 13

On our way to the Turners' home, I did some digging on Andy McAvoy. He and Liz were friends on various social media sites, but they didn't communicate often, if at all. Mainly just Andy liking or heart-reacting to every one of Liz's photos.

Mr. McAvoy sent us that security footage. If not for the evidence, I might've suspected he was involved in her disappearance. Maybe she called him to get her out of the forest, he came to get her, saw an opportunity to make a move on a pretty girl, and he killed her when she denied his advances.

But the video showed he'd been home, and that he'd walked to the family car wash next door the following morning with his father. Either way, I planned to dig deeper into Andy when I returned home and had a better Internet connection. All the lagging on our drive was driving me crazy.

Along the way, I texted Bentley the Turners' home address and asked him to meet me there. He said no problem and that he was only about half an hour away. That was down to fifteen minutes by the time we arrived.

It was a nice, upper-middle-class home. Not in a gated community, but a high-end suburb. I could describe the ornate details of the flowerbeds, or the stonework that comprised the home, but the truth was, it looked like every other house on the block. Brown brick. Winding cement sidewalk. Two stories above a basement garage. A glass storm door before the fancy mahogany one.

Inside was just as cookie-cutter. Plain white tiled foyer. White walls with some stock "Live, Laugh, Love" decor. A couple fake plants. Nothing special.

Karen, Phil, and Miranda—Liz's baby sister by two years—weren't much different. An attractive family, as I had concluded from my video meeting with the parents and from Liz's social media.

After going over the basics, discussing what we had gathered, Phil scoffed and stomped about. "You're out of your mind. Everybody loves Liz."

Karen massaged her eyes between her thumb and forefinger. Miranda stayed quiet, but the audible breath she released was almost a scoff.

"We're just telling you what we know, Phil," Harper said. "We're not trying to tarnish Liz's reputation or—"

He wagged a finger at me. "We're not paying you to dig up dirt on our daughter. We're paying you to go out to those woods and *find her*."

"You're paying me to go out to those woods and *look* for her," I replied. "And I told you, I'm going to do my best. But I read the report. If the dogs tracked her back to the exit of the forest, there's a very limited chance I'll find anything else. Right now, it looks like somebody picked her up—"

"And how would they have done that? Wouldn't there have been a record of her calling somebody? Or you think it was just some stranger in the woods who kidnapped my daughter?"

That was possible. Exceedingly rare, but possible.

When I opened my mouth to speak, Harper said, "I'm thinking that, more than likely, she didn't have enough bars to make a call, but she got an Internet connection. She then used something like Facebook messenger, or Snapchat, to make a call. The police department here has already put in a request for those records, but they take a few days. If it was deleted from Liz's phone, we aren't going to see it in her cloud history."

"Or she got lost out there, and the search and rescue team screwed up." Phil's eyes were red-rimmed and wild as he flailed his arms about, as though trying to conjure his missing daughter right then and there. "I was reading articles about this. If the handler isn't very good, they can miss the dog's cues. Maybe that's what happened. Maybe she's still out there, and those cops didn't know what the hell they were doing, and—"

"Phil." Harper softened her voice, expression no different. "You need to take a few deep breaths. How about we go sit outside? Just settle down a bit?"

There was a bit more arguing and several dirty looks shot my way before he reluctantly agreed. Karen mouthed, "I'm sorry," on her way past.

And then there were three. Me, standing awkwardly in the doorway, Tempest panting casually at my side, and Miranda, who sat on the third to last stair with her shoulders hunched. Miranda was who I wanted to chat with anyway. Sisters knew more about one another's lives than parents.

A pretty girl, like Liz in many ways. The same dainty features, soft blonde hair, and petite stature. Her posture wasn't nearly as strong as Liz's had seemed in her photos, however. Hunching slightly, reserved, she avoided eye contact. Like she had grown in the very large shadow of her sister and had never sat up straight on her own.

Once they were out of sight, I gestured to the step beside Miranda. "Mind if I sit?"

She scooted closer to the wall.

Using the railing for stability, I lowered myself beside her and stretched my legs out straight. "Liz isn't exactly who your dad thinks she is, huh?"

"Daddy's little princess," she said under her breath. "I love Liz, but a lot of people hate her, and she hates a lot of them too."

"Yeah, wasn't hard to figure that out. Doesn't mean I don't wanna find her though."

Miranda managed a smile, then swept away a tear. "I don't know who could've hurt her. I mean, there are at least ten people off the top of my head who would love to see her gone. But they all hate her equally."

"Would you mind compiling a list for me? Just in case there's anyone Harper and I missed?" I asked. She nodded. "Thanks. Do you by chance know how Liz is connected to Andy McAvoy?"

Miranda cocked her head to the side. "They work together, I think. Why? Do you think he did something to her?"

"He has an alibi for when she disappeared, but he ran away when he saw Harper flash her badge. We caught him with a little under an ounce of weed that he claims he got from her."

She harrumphed. "Yeah, that makes more sense."

"So you knew that Liz was dealing?"

"I don't know that I would call her a *dealer*. One of the guys she"— Miranda held up air quotes—"'hangs out' with is. When people can't get a hold of him, they call her."

"Yeah? Do you know who?"

"They call him Trip, I think? I don't know his real name. I've never met him either. I know Liz met him at the coffee shop, but that's it. Do you think it's connected?"

I thought this case was a spiderweb. Liz was somewhere in the center of it, but there were a thousand strings tying it all in place. "I don't know. Nothing about this is textbook. But if you could ask around and try to figure out what Trip's real name is, I would really appreciate it."

"Yeah, of course," Miranda said. "But can I ask you something?"

"Sure."

"I was reading about missing persons last night. They say that if somebody isn't found within forty-eight hours, the chance of finding them is close to nothing." The tears in her eyes thickened. "Do you think that's what is going to happen here? We're never gonna see her again?"

Chest tightening, I searched for the words.

I wanted to find this girl because that was the right thing to do, but I usually got more emotionally invested than I was this time. I didn't know if it was because this was my first case since Ox died, or if it was simply because I didn't like what I had learned of Liz so far. That was awful, and I wasn't proud of it, but the first time I felt anything about this case was when I looked into Miranda's teary eyes.

I didn't have to fake my crackling voice when I said, "We're going to do everything we can."

"That's not really an answer." Miranda wiped some snot from her nose. "What if—"

The front door swinging open cut her off. Phil came through first with a tight jaw. "Your ride's here. And you're losing daylight, so...." He waved toward the door like I was a fly and he was swatting me out. "Probably best you get going."

Forcing a tightlipped smile, I pulled myself up by the railing and tapped my hip for Tempest to join me. As I walked that way, I looked at Miranda over my shoulder. "If you think of anything, feel free to text me day or night."

She nodded.

Karen gave me a warm hug on my way past. In my ear, she said, "He's just worried. You're not doing anything wrong."

After thanking her, I freed myself from her grasp and started outside. But the moment I could see the road, my stomach balled into knots.

Where the yard met the street, Bentley was parked in his pickup truck. The passenger side was closest, but the windows were down on both sides. Harper stood at the driver's side. Smiling ear to ear. Resting her forearms along the sill. Leaning her chest, which she rarely covered with much clothing, practically into his vehicle. Laughing. And Bentley laughed too.

My blood boiled through my veins. My head felt as though it was catching on fire. As if the two of them weren't allowed to laugh. Like they couldn't smile. Like I forbade Bentley from getting so close to a woman.

I shook my head. This was irrational. Silly. Bentley was not Ox, and I doubted Harper would do that again. She was just saying hello. Bentley was friendly and doing the same.

Still, when I got closer, I didn't recognize the voice that left my lips when I said, "Can you help me get my shit out of Harper's car?"

Oblivious to my tone, Bentley shot me a smile and reached for the handle. "Yeah, of course. Is it in the trunk?"

Harper, however, was not so oblivious. Smile vanishing, she stepped away and tucked up her shirt. I appreciated that, but I would've appreciated it more had she'd done so before leaning into his open window.

"It is, yeah." Opening it with her key fob, Harper moved toward her vehicle. "I'll help, too."

"I've got it." On his way past, Bentley kissed my cheek. "Just get Tempy settled in."

Once he was out of sight, Harper asked, "So did you get anything from Miranda?"

Helping Tempest into the backseat, I braced myself on the handle. "Trip. That's where Liz got the weed. If you want to do some digging and figure out who that is, it's another thread we can try to untangle."

Harper forced a smile. "Sure. And Bentley said he borrowed a friend's satellite phone. So if you need anything while you're out, or if you find anything, just give me a call."

"You have the number?"

"I didn't ask for it, but—"

"Wow." I shut the rear door behind Tempest. "I would've thought you had."

Harper frowned. "Maddie."

"Harper."

"We were just talking."

"I know. But I just—" A half laugh left me. "We're trying to work through our shit, right? You want me to let you back in? You want us to be friends?"

Frown deepening, her eyes softened. "Of course I do. I wasn't trying to—"

"You weren't trying to ruin our friendship before when you did either, but you did. So now I've got trust issues, and I wish I didn't feel this way. But I don't want you to be his friend." Discreetly, I nodded to Bentley. "You don't need to be. A 'hello' and 'how are you?' in passing's fine, but please don't give me a reason to be paranoid. Please."

"I understand. I'm sorry." Nothing but remorse. That's all there was in her eyes.

Exhaling slowly, feeling my tight muscles release, I cleared my throat. "Thanks."

A short nod of understanding.

After I swallowed down the emotion choking me, I asked, "Has that name come up in your investigation so far? Trip?"

She shook her head. "No. But I'll find him and pass everything I find your way."

"I'd appreciate it." Using the handle along the truck's doorframe for support, I hoisted myself into the passenger seat. "You gonna interview the kids individually?"

"That's the plan."

"Mind if I look at the footage afterward?"

"'Course not."

The thump of Bentley setting my bag into the bed of the trunk sounded. Harper glanced that way, then at him as he got into the driver's side. Her eyes immediately came back to mine. "I'll send you anything I find. And if I need to interview anyone else, you want in on it?"

"Please." I forced a smile. "Just like the good old days."

Posture relaxing slightly, she returned the smile. "Be safe out there."

"We will," Bentley said. "Nice seeing you again."

Harper only gave a quick nod before backing away so we could pull out.

Once the doors shut, as he turned over the engine, Bentley whispered, "What's the beef?"

Not something I wanted to get into. It was just my stupid caveman brain anyway. "No beef. But it's getting late. I don't want to be stuck halfway through and have to set up camp for the night."

"Alright. But I know a pissed off woman when I see one, so I'm not gonna wave. We are apparently not happy with her." Shifting the car into drive, he did everything in his power to avoid making eye contact in the rearview. "Should I avoid the side mirrors too? Just for good measure? Make sure she knows we're pissed?"

Laughing, I shook my head. "I told you. We're not pissed."

As he slowed for the stop sign, he smiled. "And I know when you're lying. But you don't want to talk about it. So I won't push. Question though."

"Which is?"

"Will it offend you if I offer to give you a piggyback when you're slowing us down?"

His tone was a playful tease, but I leaned back and propped my leg up on the dash. "Whew. You're gonna regret offering. I might make you piggyback me the whole seven miles."

Chapter 14

Hikes were nothing new for me and Bentley. Since he had moved back, we went on regular hikes and walks through the woods. With Grace and Tempest, we explored every trail and state park in our county and neighboring ones.

But this was the first we'd gone on since The Country Killer kidnapped Grace and killed Ox. Not because of me. I didn't want Eric Oakley to ruin one of my favorite things. Breathing in fresh air and exploring the best parts of where we lived.

A few weeks prior, I'd suggested going to Ohio Pyle on a day Bentley was off work. It was a popular summer destination in our area. The beautiful natural waterslide was an absolute blast when I was young. I thought Grace would really enjoy it.

Quicker than I could finish speaking, however, she asked if we could go to a water park instead. That was when I'd realized that, while Eric hadn't ruined the wilderness for me, he'd ruined it for her. I hated him for a thousand things, and that was just one more to add to the list.

The thought left my mind as I realized that I was happier than I had been in a while as Bentley and I trekked this trail. He'd worried my knee would be what slowed us down, but nope. He was.

Every five minutes, he stopped and said, "Oh, look at that!" Then pointed at some rock covered in moss or a tree with a circumference bigger than the two of us combined. He had stopped to pick honeysuckle, then excitedly told me to open my mouth and dropped it onto my tongue. Being the big sap that he was, he grabbed every flower he thought was pretty and gave it to me.

Each time he stopped, Tempest looked back at him with her tongue hanging out of her mouth and cocked her head to the side. When she realized that Bentley was stopping again, she'd chuffed and plopped down. They said dogs couldn't show emotion in their faces, but she glared at him.

By noon, we had covered a little over a mile and a half. By two, we were at the halfway mark. The sun didn't set until almost 9 PM at this time of year, so I knew we would make it to the campsite before dark.

And I was enjoying it.

Over the last six weeks, since it had all gone down, I hadn't enjoyed much of anything. I found some momentary peace in distractions, like watching movies with Bentley and Grace or the little burst of serotonin from eating a dessert. But not joy. When I was alone, the tears would well, and my chest would tighten, and I would cry. Almost every day since, I had cried. Supposed that was grief. There was only one other person I'd had to mourn and mourning her was nothing like mourning Ox.

With Mom, I'd been prepared for her death since I was a small child. She'd been addicted to heroin. She hadn't exercised or eaten healthy. I'd always known I wouldn't have a lot of time with her, and much of the time I'd had, I'd spent waiting to get away.

Ox had been my first love. My partner for almost a third of my life. He'd died trying to save me, and that was a hell of a lot harder to face than my mom's death.

But today, I hadn't cried. My feet patted damp, summer soil. The hot sun shined on my arms, reflecting a glorious golden shimmer. Wind cooled my sweaty cheeks as I swatted at bugs and listened to the birds in the trees. Paired with Bentley's laughter and silly dad jokes, it was practically its own song. Surrounded by luscious greenery, watching butterflies drift by, with the taste of honeysuckle on my tongue, joy returned. Joy and happiness were fleeting emotions, just as every other one was, but at least I knew it would return again.

When we made it to the campsite, dusk was turning the blue sky pink and orange. And when I told Tempest to sniff Liz's shirt again, she began leading me back down the trail. Just as I figured she would.

"We might as well set up camp for the night either way," Bentley said. "Can't exactly follow a trail in the dark."

Tying Tempest's lead to a tree, I agreed and started assembling the tent. Bentley collected some firewood while I arranged the sleeping bags. Half an hour later, just as the sun went down, Bentley got the fire going, and I fed Tempest her dinner.

Of course, when we began assembling our pizza mountain pies, her begging made it clear she would have preferred our dinner to hers. Out of guilt, I gave her a few slices of pepperoni.

I'd just finished eating my first one and started assembling my second when Bentley bumped his elbow into mine. "Looks like I didn't have to carry you after all."

"I think it's all those happy chemicals that release when you're in the sun." A glance at my swollen knee, bent awkwardly from my makeshift seat on the log, reminded me the relief was far from permanent. "Or maybe the exercise."

"Endorphins are the happy chemicals, which go off in the brain when you're in the sun, *and* when you exercise. Also release when you laugh, and I made you do that many times today. So I'm taking partial credit here."

"Oh, are you? Because I'm around you all the time, and I haven't had this great of a pain day in a while."

"Breaking my heart, Mad dog." After tearing open a bag of marshmallows, he searched for a good stick. Finding one, he stabbed it into the marshmallow. "Mindset matters though. You were relaxed today."

I snorted. "Don't."

"Don't what?"

"Give me that bullshit about 'mindsetting' my way out of chronic pain." Another nod at my knee. "I've got a metal knee. I use it too much, or not enough, the tissue swells, it presses on nerves, and it hurts. No amount of positive thinking is gonna cure me."

"Nothing's gonna *cure* you," he said. "But stress makes your muscles tighten, and they compress nerves too. Reducing stress reduces that pressure and lightens the load a little. That's why you feel better. Because you were relaxed today, and you've been stressed."

"I've been fine."

For a few heartbeats, he only looked at me in the dim glow of the fire and the moon. I couldn't place his expression. Disappointed? Frustrated? I was about to ask what that face was for, but he said, "Either way. It was a good day."

"It was." Even though we hadn't found anything that would lead me to Liz Turner. "I know Grace doesn't seem to want to do this stuff anymore, but maybe we could find some parks instead. Like, the kinds that aren't deep in the wilderness. Just walking trails."

"Maybe. I actually wasn't sure if you were all that into this stuff anymore either."

"I am." And that was where we would leave that conversation. Talking about Grace's trauma was one thing. Talking about mine was another. I pointed at the bag of marshmallows and said, "Can you pass me one of those?"

Bentley did me one better and handed me the whole bag. After a throat clear, he said, "So how was breakfast?"

Ah, yes. We hadn't talked about that yet. Although we had had all day to, our hike was more of a break from reality.

Carefully shoving my pie iron into the embers, I raised a shoulder. "Nice? I don't know. I thought it'd be awkward, but it was more awkward for him than for me. He's so different from what I remember. Always thought of him as sort of... I don't know, almost like a superhero." Laughing, I stabbed my stick into the fluffy marshmallow. "That's stupid, I know, but I was seven when he left. Maybe I romanticized him."

"It's not stupid. I pray Grace thinks of me as a hero." I had no doubt she did. "He give you a good explanation?"

"For the manslaughter?" I toasted my marshmallow above the flames and let out a snort. "Nope. Wouldn't tell me anything about it. Swears to hell and back that he came back for me though. That he'd never planned on leaving me. Only planned on leaving my mom."

Chews slowing, Bentley cocked his head to the side. "No shit?"

"No shit."

"That's a big claim."

"Yep."

"You believe him?"

When my marshmallow went up in flames, I brought it to my lips and blew it out. "I don't know. He says he tried to pull me out of school the next day. Right after he left, I mean. Apparently, Mom had filed for emergency custody the day before."

Bentley's eyes were bigger than the full moon. "There'd be a paper trail of that, wouldn't there?"

Eating the burned marshmallow whole, I nodded an answer. Once I swallowed the sugary goo, I said, "After I finish this case, I'm gonna go to the courthouse and file the paperwork. Shouldn't be hard to search for. It'll take a couple weeks to receive them, but if he's telling the truth, there will be proof of it."

"Damn," Bentley murmured, chomping into another marshmallow. "Assuming it is true, how do you feel about that?"

"Sitting on a log doesn't feel right. I should be on a black leather sofa, looking at ink splatters."

"Well, it's a big deal. Shoot me. I'd be jumping out of my skin if I were you."

"No, it's okay." My voice came out quieter than I intended. "I just don't want to get my hopes up. He knows I'm a PI. He knows that I'm going to vet anything he says. And he's smart enough to know that if Mom filed for custody, there'll be a paper trail." I explained the letter roster he had shown me as well. "I still need to vet that, but I just can't see him lying about all of it. I don't know what he has to gain from lying to me either. He got a decent construction job and his own place, which isn't much better or worse than mine. He knows I'm self-employed, so I can't help him out in the job department. By connecting with me, all he has to gain is a relationship. That's what my rational mind says, anyway."

"And your *ir*rational mind?"

"It's all a ploy. That he's using me somehow. But that's what that little voice keeps saying."

"I think that's pretty common when it comes to trauma. And I don't think that's a bad thing. Your mom would've taken you for everything you've got, even if you had nothing. That's why you're having that instinct."

"Probably." A deep sigh billowed from my lips, swaying the smoke from the fire away. "What would you do if you were in my shoes?"

"My dumb ass would let him in with open arms, but as you've said a thousand times, I'm nice to my detriment. You don't have to do what I'd do. Mostly because I don't want to be blamed if something goes wrong."

I shook my head. "I wouldn't blame you."

"You might." He smiled. "But hey, you didn't blame me today. For whatever it is that you were pissed at Harper about."

I rolled my eyes. "I wasn't pissed at Harper."

"Yes, you definitely were." Lifting my mountain pie from the fire, he leaned it up against the log beside him to cool. "And I am dying for the tea, but if you don't want to give it to me, I'll suck it up."

"The tea?"

"Yeah, the tea. You haven't heard Grace say that?" He held up air quotes. "'What's the tea?'"

Using a fork to pry open the pie iron, unable to wait any longer after all those calories I burned today, I shook my head in answer.

"The drama. The gossip. The story to the beef."

"How the hell do you get tea from gossip?"

"Spill the tea. Spill the beans, spill your guts, you know?"

Cocking my head to the side, I could only muster a, "Huh."

"Makes sense, doesn't it?"

"It does, actually."

"But I'm guessing I'll have no tea tonight."

Apparently, he wasn't going to stop. And as much as I did not want to talk about this, I had made him discuss things from his past that he hadn't been ready for. Supposed it was only fair to do the same.

"It was stupid." Rubbing my eyes, I shook my head. "It had nothing to do with you."

"It didn't seem stupid."

"Really, it was dumb."

His face made it very clear he was not following.

Another deep breath. "Harper is pretty. Very pretty. And she has a chest that I do not. And she was leaning into your car, and you were only a few inches away from her, and my stupid caveman brain got angry."

He laughed.

"I'm pathetic." Thank God the fire was a good excuse for my rosy cheeks. "I know that, and I don't need to hear you mock me for it. So you can sleep out here now, and Tempy and I will take the tent, and I hate you."

"I'm sorry." He laughed again, but it was softer. "Fifteen-year-old me just screamed in my ear about how cool it is that Maddie Castle got jealous I was a few inches too close to another woman."

Shooting him a certain hand signal, I carefully plopped my mountain pie onto my plate. Once I had, he thumbed my chin and brought my gaze to his. With a soft kiss, against my lips, he whispered, "I know you. It's deeper than that."

"If you were so sure about that," I said, playfully pushing him away, "you shouldn't have laughed at me."

"I wasn't laughing at you. I was laughing at the part of me that thought this was a dream."

"Cheesy asshole."

"I've been around a lot of your friends. Many of whom are pretty, and many of whom I have stood in close proximity to, and it never both-

ered you. I just wanna know if I'm supposed to hate her." Although his
tone was lighthearted, as was the gesture of holding up his hands in
surrender, his eyes made it clear that he was serious. If I didn't want
him to talk to her, or stand too close to her, he wouldn't. Which was
controlling and insane, and not at all what I wanted. "Knowing the
backstory will just help me know how I'm supposed to handle these
situations. But if you don't want to talk about it—"

"She slept with Ox." Having him understand the context made
me feel less controlling, and it was about time I told him. "That's
what broke off our engagement. It wasn't long after The Country
Killer got away. I was barely walking again, my mom had just died,
Bear had just died, and I found the texts on his iPad. So I got drunk,
took too many pills, and almost killed myself. Unintentionally, to be
clear. Losing Ox and Harper was not worth my life, but it was the
cherry on top of everything else falling apart." I felt his eyes on me,
but I wasn't sure I could finish this if I looked at him. "That was why
I moved back to the trailer park. Which I'm grateful for now. I've
come to terms with a lot of shit I hated about myself back then. But
she and I are trying to mend our friendship. Then I walked outside,
and I saw her, and I saw you, and you were laughing, and the
caveman brain activated." I finally looked into his eyes, staring back at
me with an intensity that made me want to shrivel away. "But really.
It wasn't about you."

His brows were furrowed, lips frowning, but I couldn't tell if he was
sad or angry.

"Sorry for the info dump. But now you know the tea."

He stayed silent for a moment and shook his head. "What a bitch."

I laughed. "After all that, your response is, 'what a bitch?'"

"Well, yeah." He paused. "And sorry. I don't like calling women
bitches. But in this case, I feel like it's warranted. Who would do that?"

"Sleep with her best friend's fiancé?" I shrugged and took a bite out
of my mountain pie. "A bitch."

"Also yeah, but why walk over and say hi to me like we were old
friends with that background? Why put me in that position, and why

put you in that position? I think anybody would have a caveman reaction to that."

That was validating. "Thanks."

"And message received. We don't like her. If you decide to like her again, that's okay, but I will never like her. Friends don't do that. I never would've slept with one of your boyfriends."

Laughing, I grabbed another marshmallow. "I'd hope not."

He joined in, and that's all there was for a few heartbeats. The sound of our laughter, Tempest snoring at my side, and the flickering fire. When the laughter dwindled, his voice was set and determined when he said, "I would never do what Ox did to you either."

That made my stomach flip, and yet I blurted, "Pretty sure you'd have to be in a relationship with me for that, which I don't think you want."

There went his smile. And the teasing tone to a relatively grim conversation. Damn my word vomit.

"I'm sorry." Taking my annoyance out on the marshmallow, stabbing my stick through it, I prayed the heat in my cheeks wasn't as obvious to him as it was to me. "That was meant to come out funny."

"You're full of shit."

"Ah, like I thought." Another playful smile, which he did not return. "You don't want a relationship."

"You're full of shit for thinking I don't want a relationship." Face screwed up in confusion, he shook his head. "Why do you think that I kiss you every day? How many times have we made out now? Isn't it about—I don't know—daily?"

Damn it. And damn me. "This was a really shitty time to bring it up. Ignore me."

"Oh, no." Couldn't tell if he let out a laugh or a huff. "No, we're having this conversation."

Chapter 15

"WHAT HAVE I DONE THAT HAS LED YOU TO BELIEVE THAT I'M NOT interested, Maddie?" Bentley asked, tone somewhere between frustrated and annoyed. "Aside from my daughter, you're the center of my life, so I need to know what the hell I'm doing wrong here."

"You're not doing anything *wrong*," I protested. "But don't act like your signals aren't mixed."

He turned to face me better on the log. Which was a far from ideal place to have this conversation. "How? What isn't clear?"

"Aside from the fact that you stop me every time it seems like we're going to go past kissing? That we don't have a label? That we haven't been on an actual date? The only 'dates' we've had are with Grace. Which is basically just us doing what we normally do. She's been at that camp though, and yeah, we've spent time together, but it's still not clear. I thought maybe it's because the last person you were with was Bella, and you're not ready to jump into something with someone else. Which is also fine. But then you kiss me, and I'm confused. For all I know, you're not interested anymore, but you don't want to lose my friendship, or you're afraid I'll relapse if you cut things off, so you're just kissing me because that feels like the safest way to do things. Which is how you operate in life. The safe way. Avoid the possibility of hurting someone. But I wish you would just tell me if that's the case because—"

"Okay, hold on. That's not fair." I expected him to have the same attitude in his voice that I had in mine, but his was much softer. "The rest of it, okay. I can see why you're confused. But don't try to use my habit of avoiding problems here. That's not what's going on. You're the one avoiding the problems, and that's why we haven't moved past where we are."

My jaw dropped. "Excuse me?"

Exhaling deeply, he rubbed his eyes. "Don't get pissed at me."

"I've made my intentions with you very clear, which wasn't easy for me, and you're saying that I'm the reason we're stuck in relationship limbo? Now I *am* pissed at you."

"That came out wrong. *You* aren't the reason. But your avoidance is."

"What am I avoiding? I've told you what I want. I've been more open with you than I ever have with anyone, and—"

"You don't talk about him." Even though he cut me off, his voice was gentle. "You don't talk about what happened. You can barely say his name, Maddie."

This had felt like our usual bickering until that last sentence. "This is about Ox?" Because he was right. Saying his name aloud made my throat feel like it was closing in. "He's my ex. You're my... whatever you are. Talking about exes is usually a faux pas. You don't think that I have unresolved feelings for him, do you? Because I don't. It doesn't matter now anyway, but I don't."

Easing out another deep breath, Bentley twined his fingers between mine. "I don't think you're in love with him. But you can't tell me there aren't unresolved feelings."

"There aren't. When you moved back, we'd been broken up for eight months. Spring was a year. I'm over him. I've *been* over him."

"I know that." While my tone was defensive, Bentley's was sweet. Compassionate. "But you're not over his death."

I didn't think my throat could constrict any tighter until that last sentence.

"He died in your arms, Mads. You haven't talked about him since. Not *once* have you talked to me about what happened. I don't think you've talked to *anyone* about what happened in that cabin." Trailing his thumb over the back of mine, he searched my eyes. Probably looking for the tears that desperately wanted to form. "You're not dealing with it. You're ignoring it. One of these days, it's gonna come back and bite you in the ass. You're going to feel exactly how you did when you watched him die, and you're not gonna be able to ignore it. You've locked all that shit up behind a dam, and all it's gonna take is one bad storm. Those walls aren't gonna just crack. They're gonna crumble."

That much, fine. Maybe he was right. Eventually, I was gonna need to process what'd happened. I didn't disagree with that. "But what does that have to do with us?"

"Everything." The sparkle of his brown eyes in the light of the fire was just as warm as the flames. "It wasn't the same thing, but someone I thought I'd spend the rest of my life with died in my arms, too. I know what you're feeling because I've felt it. I ignored it too, and I spiraled. Went from happy husband and father to drug-dealer's-doctor. I would've been a lot better off if I'd had someone to help me. Someone to talk to. But you won't let me be here for you."

"That's not true. I haven't pushed you away."

"Yeah? Because I make you dinner? Because we go on walks?" Still, his voice and his touch were tender. "All of that's distracting you. It isn't helping you. Telling me what's going on in those dreams might. Opening up instead of acting like it didn't happen."

"I'm not acting like it didn't happen." The moment I said it, I knew he didn't believe it. Really, neither did I. "And I still don't see what this has to do with us."

"Why do you want to 'move past kissing' so badly?" He smiled, but it was weak. "If you want to define the relationship, we can. But why is *that* so important to you?"

I all but scoffed. "Why don't you? Why *isn't* it important to you? If you're not interested—"

"I have been interested since we were thirteen. It's not because I don't want to. It has nothing to do with Bella either. I love her, and I miss her, but it's been a long time, and I'm ready to move on. In every meaning of the word, I am *ready*." The playful tone of that last word made me chuckle, and he joined in. "But I don't think you are."

Definitely a scoff this time. "And you know what I want more than I do?"

"Wanting something and being ready for it are two very different things." He tucked a stray hair behind my ear. "You want another distraction. You want to feel good. You want to get high, and the closest you can get to that is the excitement of something new. Us. A relationship, I guess. And I'm not saying I don't want that too, but I don't want it to be temporary bliss. I want something real with you. Something that's gonna last."

Bentley wasn't the only one who avoided his problems. That was no secret. Opening up was harder for me than it was for him, but it came down to the same issue.

I was chasing a high. I hadn't gotten one, not since Eric Oakley forced me to take that heroin. But I wanted one. Not drugs. Those would ruin my life. Candy and junk food gave me a rush, but it was short-lived. Exercise helped, but it wasn't enough. I wanted euphoria, in any form I could get it.

"If we jump straight in, I don't think it will last. I think in a few months, you'll realize what I see now. That the excitement of this thing between us is just filling the void of Ox's death. That, and it feels like taking advantage." He held my hand a little tighter. "You pretend like you're okay, but you're not. You're vulnerable. You're not ready for what I'm ready for."

"I was ready before he died." Damn my voice for cracking. "I *am* ready for a relationship. I've been ready for months. You said you wanted to take things slow, and that's okay, but please don't spin this. I'm not the drunk girl at prom. I know what I want, and it's you."

"You've got me. If you want to go on a date, let's do it. But until you start talking and working through what happened, even if it's to a therapist, or Teresa, I don't see how we can go further than where we are."

Face scrunching up in confusion, I shook my head. "I don't get what the hell you mean. We can't be a couple? We're just gonna continue to be friends who hold hands and kiss sometimes? Is that your point? Are we twelve, Bentley?"

"Look, I'm not trying to force you to open up, but—"

"You aren't? Because I think you're giving me an ultimatum. Either I get over Ox's death, or we stay stuck in relationship limbo. And it's not fair. I can't just blink and get over—"

"What happens in the dream, Maddie?" Finding my gaze again, he frowned. "I'm not asking you to 'get over' his death. I'm asking you to work through it. Because last night wasn't the first time I've heard you screaming in your sleep. The first time, right after Ox's funeral, it woke me up. I was in my own trailer, Maddie, and it woke me up. I thought somebody was hurting you, so I used my key to get in, and you were scream-crying in the fetal position in your bed."

The full body cringe of embarrassment that worked up my spine forced me to pull away. To try to release my fingers from his. But he held them tighter, refusing to let go. Which I was about to yell at him for. I was embarrassed, and uncomfortable, and I didn't want to have this conversation, because it would only push us further apart. I'd tell him what happened in that dream, and it would only confirm his theories that I wasn't ready.

But he continued before I could say another word.

"You kept saying, 'I didn't pick them. I love you both, Ox. I didn't want either of you to die. I didn't pick them over you. I didn't pick them.'"

Either I was going to puke or scream. I settled on a bark that had Tempest perking her head up to look at me. "Why the hell did you do that?"

Confusion pinched his brows together. "Why the hell did I do what? Check on you?"

"Why didn't you wake me up?" I snapped. "You listen to me say all this, all these private thoughts, and you thought it was okay to just walk away afterward? Go on for weeks without telling me? You basically read my diary, Bentley, and that's really shitty. That was wrong of you, and you know it."

His frown deepened. "How embarrassed would you have been?"

"That's not the point—"

"It *is* the point. Waking you up, telling you that I heard you saying all that, it would've been forcing you to tell me something you weren't ready to. If that's really what you wanted, I'm sorry I didn't mention it sooner. But don't lash out at me, Maddie. We both know I didn't do anything wrong."

Clenching my teeth, I looked away.

Damn it. Damn my eyes for filling with tears.

No, Bentley hadn't done anything wrong. If I had heard him or Grace screaming, I would've done the same thing. Like any half-decent person would. No matter how embarrassed I was, it was far from ill-intentioned.

A knot the size of Texas bunched itself in my throat, and I was a few breaths from sobbing.

When I tried to look away, Bentley tilted my chin toward him. "I know it was a dream. I know you aren't choosing to think this. But your subconscious is blaming me and Grace for Ox's death, and—"

"I *don't* blame you." Although I had tried to soften my voice, my words came out sharper than the tip of a blade. "I don't blame Grace either. I blame Eric Oakley. That son of a bitch would have taken anyone and everyone I cared about to get to me. I know it was no one's fault but his. And yeah, I feel like shit about the whole thing. That's grief, isn't it? But it isn't fair to tell me I'm not ready for a relationship because I'm going through some shit, Bentley. That isn't fair."

For a few cricket chirps and cicada songs, we just looked at one another. Sympathy filled his eyes. Like he heard me, but he didn't believe me. And damn it, that wasn't fair. What I felt wasn't blame toward him, nor Grace.

Remorse. Shame. Guilt. Those were what I felt.

The remorse made it hard for me to look Grace in the eyes sometimes. My shame came when I thought of Teresa. A woman who would never see her son again, because I just had to stop The Country Killer.

The guilt? I'd chosen to chase after Grace, fully prepared to die if it meant I could save her. Only, I'd made it out alive. So had she. But Ox had been the one who died.

Survivor's guilt, I supposed. But not blame.

In Bentley's shoes, if I had only heard the bits and pieces mumbled —or screamed—out in a dream, I would think the same thing he did. I couldn't in good conscience enter a relationship with someone who silently resented me and my child as deeply as I seemed to.

"Sometimes, it's Josey," I broke the silence. "It's not always you and Grace in the dream. Sometimes it's Rachel. Sometimes it's Amber. Audrey, too. Audrey Kemp. She was his first victim. Just this old lady. We got to the scene, and there was blood everywhere. Except on her. She was so neat and clean. Just a slice across her throat. That was it. But then he painted on the walls with her blood. He must've dipped his fingers into the cut to make the scene look the way it did, and I dream about that sometimes, too. Sometimes it's Grace in Audrey's bed at that scene. Sometimes it's Josey, or Rachel, or Amber. Sometimes it's you."

His skin was a little green, but his eyes were soft when I met them.

"Sometimes, you're the one who was running behind me. Sometimes you're the one who dies, and then I'm so angry. Ox tries to hug me, and I push him away, and I say that it should've been him." The tears running down my throat thickened it, and no amount of swallowing brought relief. "And I mean it. I hate that I mean it, but I do. Because I'm glad it wasn't you. I hate myself for it, Bentley, but I'm happy it was him instead of you. Not because I wanted him to die, but because if I had to choose—"

I heaved in a deep breath and held it there. If I let it out, I would bawl like a baby. So I turned away and shut my eyes.

That was the part I'd kept from him. The part I'd ignored myself.

I'd never wanted to hurt Ox, but I preferred this outcome. Bentley and Grace alive instead of him.

It was awful. *I* was awful. How could I look at it that way? How could I be grateful he was dead? How could I think something like that about a man I had loved for a third of my life?

"Maddie." Bentley's voice was more soothing than the warm evening breeze. "It's okay—"

"It's not okay." Wiping the snot that drained from my nose, I blinked hard at the tears. "I'm horrible. I'm glad I'm alive, and I'm glad Grace is alive, and I'm glad you're alive. Out of everybody who could have died that day, I'm glad it was him. And that's awful. I'm a horrible god damned person."

"You're not." He took my hand again, and I let him. I felt guilty for that too. It was comforting, and why did I deserve to be comforted? What sick, twisted person could look at this situation the way that I had? Feel the way that I did? Why comfort me for thinking, feeling, something so cruel? "You're not, Maddie."

With a huff, I shook my head. The last thing I needed was an ego stroke.

"Have you thought about why? Why you feel that way?"

"Because I love you?" There was no stopping my sharp tone or narrowed eyes. "Because I love Grace?"

"You loved him, too." He swiped a tear from my cheek. "You didn't want anything bad to happen to him. *That's* why you feel like this. Because you love him. And love isn't a competition. You don't love me and Grace more than you love him."

"But it doesn't change that I'm grateful he died instead of you." Voice cracking, I struggled to hold his gaze. "I think that's what the dreams are. Shame for feeling this way. Not because I blame you, and not because I blame Grace. Because I blame *me*. He was the one who chased after me, and he didn't want me to blame myself, but I do, and then when I remind myself that it wasn't my fault, that it *was* Ox's fault, I feel like shit.

"Grace is screwed up because of me, and Ox died because I was trying to help her, and I'm scared that one of these days, she's going to die because of me too. Then you're gonna hate me, or maybe you already do, and—The whole thing's a mess. *I'm* a mess. And not knowing where we stand just makes it worse, because it's like confirmation of those fears. That you blame me, or that you're torn between staying my friend because you're afraid I'll relapse, or because you're obligated to after I saved her, or... I don't know."

Gently, he held my cheek and gazed at me for a while. No words were spoken, only the music of crickets and cicadas and frogs in the distance. Maybe he was waiting for me to say more. But I had said it all. He wanted me to open up, and I had. I didn't know how much more open I could get than I had just been.

Every passing heartbeat was like a hammer in my chest, pounding away at any bit of hope I had left inside me. Waiting for him to do just that. Confirm those fears. Say yes, he was only staying around out of obligation.

He didn't.

Instead, he leaned in and kissed me softly, slowly. Not one of those intense, sensual kisses that begged for more, but one that whispered, *I'm not going anywhere.* But I still didn't know what that meant. He wasn't going anywhere, he was kissing me, because he felt sorry for forcing this out of me? Out of obligation? I didn't know.

Until he said, "I don't blame you either."

Damn how tight my throat got.

"I am worried you'll relapse. That's always gonna be in the back of my head, but that's not why I've been here for you." Tucking my hair behind my ear, he shook his head slightly. "I've tried to be here for you through this because you need me. Because you're my friend. Because I love you. I want you to be more than that. I wanna say you're mine. I'm ready for that, and if you say you are too, then I believe you. I just need you to talk to me more, Maddie. Like this. Tell me what's really going on in your head so I understand, and so you understand. So that we're on the same page. So there isn't this stupid miscommunication about where we stand and how we feel about each other. Because I want you.

I want to be with you, and I don't want you to think otherwise for a second."

That should've made me happy, and it did, but it intensified the sting in my eyes. As though that made any sense. Like crying over something I was happy about was even close to logical. I had never been one of those happy criers, but maybe emotions were higher than usual after that dump of my subconscious.

Blinking enough to dry the tears, I smiled. "Does that mean that we're a couple?"

He smiled too. "I'm down if you're down."

I laughed. "So romantic."

"I think that's as close to romance as we'll get." Snatching another marshmallow from the bag, he shrugged. "But I'm not complaining."

Neither was I.

* * *

ABOUT TWENTY MINUTES LATER, ALL THE WALKING WE'D DONE today caught up to us. Bentley was yawning, and I was dozing off against his shoulder. After tying up our food and snacks in a tree's branches, cleaning up the camp, and making sure Tempest did her business, we retired to the tent. Nothing happened there, and I was sure it'd be a while before anything did, but that was okay. At least I knew what we were now.

As I lay my head on his chest, listening to the crickets outside in tandem with the quiet thump of his heart, our talk played on a loop in my brain. Bentley was right about a lot of things. Primarily that I needed to stop warring with uncomfortable realities. That was the same reason my addiction had developed. I wanted to numb the pain, *forget* the pain, instead of cope with it. Much like my chronic misery that would never go away, Ox would never come back.

I let the tears form when that thought came. Swallowing the lump in my throat that his name brought forced that tension to gather else-where, like worsening the pain in my knee or causing a night terror that woke my next-door neighbor. Bundled beneath the blankets with Tempest in the crook of my legs and Bentley's arm around my shoulders, I let the tears fall.

And this time, when I fell asleep, I didn't have that dream. It was the first time since Ox's death that I didn't have a nightmare pertaining to that day. The sleep was dreamless, and I had never been so grateful for the peace of finite blackness.

Until I awoke to a deep, low growl near my feet.

I patted Tempest's flank and murmured a, "Shh."

The crackle of a branch underfoot sounded outside. A chuff and snort followed.

With a whine, Tempest trembled beside me.

Stomach binding into knots, I peeled open one eyelid. In my peripheral, illuminated by the moon, a shadow three or four times the size of Tempest moved across the tent on my left. The thump of its paws against the ground was like the beat of a drum. It couldn't have been more than ten feet away, drawing closer with every second.

There was only one animal big enough to create that shadow and that much noise with a simple step.

A black bear.

Chapter 16

BLACK BEARS. I KNEW IT WAS A BLACK BEAR BECAUSE WE DIDN'T get grizzlies around here. Black bears were less dangerous than grizzlies by a long shot, but that didn't mean they wouldn't maul you to death.

As that bear stalked closer, dead branches creaking underfoot, every bear safety pamphlet I had ever read rapid-fired through my brain. All bears—especially black bears—hated people. If they happened upon a camp, it was most likely because they smelled food. We had cleaned up, but they had better noses than we did. Maybe that was all it was doing. Just scoping out our camp and hoping to get a snack.

Act like it isn't there, I thought. I remembered that clearly from my teenage camping days. Although I had never encountered one, a friend had. He said that he saw it doing just as this one was—looking around the camp while he slept in his tent. It sniffed around a bit, and it left.

This one stalked closer. When it was within a few feet of the tent, Tempest growled again. The bear stopped.

I hurried toward Tempest's face and clasped my fingers around her snout. Under any other circumstance, I wouldn't dream of doing this. But Tempy had a territorial, protective dog brain. She thought standing her ground would protect me and Bentley.

What she didn't understand was that she stood no chance against a black bear. And that dogs were the number one cause of bear attacks. Dogs provoked the bear, and the bear showed the dog just how stupid it was to mess with them.

Heart slamming against my ribs, I held Tempest's snout tighter, despite the whimper that rumbled in her throat. I hated to do that, but I hated the thought of us all dying more.

The bear still stood a few feet away, staring at our tent. It hadn't moved. Not until Tempest whined again, and it growled in response.

Nope. Nope, nope, *nope*.

Holding Tempest's mouth shut with one hand, I stretched behind me for my rifle. I wasn't a hunter, didn't use the thing often, but I had brought it on this trip for precisely this reason. In case we encountered an animal who ranked higher on the food chain.

No way was I getting out of this tent, and I prayed I wouldn't need to pull the trigger, but I could tell where the beast was. I lined up my shot.

Bears hate people, I reminded myself. If it knew I was here, that it would have to face-off against a human rather than a German Shepherd, maybe it would back off. Normally, they would. Only problem was if *it* was a *she*—and if she had babies nearby.

Bumping my elbow into Bentley—his face, to be exact—I said, "We've got a problem."

He grumbled something indistinguishable.

"There's a bear outside the tent." I spoke sharply, loudly. Making my presence known. Informing the bear that there was, in fact, a human here. "You might want to get up before it eats us."

"What?" Bentley asked, barely opening his eyes.

The bear chuffed, the loudest sound it'd made yet.

Tempest wiggled and squirmed.

"I need you to hold Tempest back in case I need to shoot the damn bear," I said. "And I need you to talk to me. Loudly. Obnoxiously. Make sure this bear knows we're here, and we're a threat. That I will kill it if I have to."

"What?" he repeated, sitting up. I opened my mouth to, again, say there was a bear, but he continued before I had the chance. "You can't just kill it, Maddie. We're in its home. It didn't do anything wrong."

"I have the feeling you'll be begging me to shoot it if it tries to eat you."

"Just stay quiet." His voice was an almost inaudible whisper. "It'll leave us alone."

"Maybe. But it's getting closer." It was no less than three feet from the tent now, huffing every time Tempest made a noise. "I don't want to do it either, but if it's between you, Tempest and me or the bear, I'm picking three of us."

With furrowed brows, he yanked Tempest to his side of the tent. "Shh. You're gonna agitate it."

"Tempest already agitated it. It's not like I want to kill the bear, Bentley."

"Then shut up and let it walk away."

"Don't tell me to shut up."

"Well, don't threaten to kill an innocent animal."

"Would it be innocent if it tried to eat me?"

"Bears don't eat people."

"They'll take a bite out of us if we piss them off."

Glaring, he gestured to the shadow of the bear. "And you don't think that the two of us arguing is gonna piss it off?"

"I think that when I started arguing with you, it stopped moving closer. And I think that if I shut up, Tempest is going to growl at it again, and it's going to charge us."

"It's not going to charge us."

"Oh, it's not? Do you speak bear?"

"No, but it looks like it's walking away."

It wasn't. Its silhouette was still a few steps outside of our tent, standing steady, listening. Watching. The little bastard was close, and I needed to be ready to shoot. On the plus side, it was still. Meaning that so long as the two of us kept bickering, it would likely go on its merry way.

I hoped. God, I hoped. Killing people was one thing. Killing an animal was another.

Carefully, I did my best to angle my gun toward what I hoped was its face. "I don't think it's walking away. And if it gets pissed off, all we've got are some plastic walls to protect us. If it gets close enough to touch our tent, I'm shooting."

"I will never forgive you if you kill this bear." There was sincerity in his voice. "He's just minding his business, Maddie. Don't you dare."

"At the moment, he's minding his business. But if he's a she, and there are babies nearby, that little shit is going to kill us."

"Is it even the season for that? For them to have babies, I mean?"

Hell if I knew. "Do I look like a bear expert, Bentley?"

"It's in January, I think," Bentley said. "That's when they have their cubs. And it's July, so I doubt it has cubs. We should just go out there and try to scare her away—"

"Are you out of your damn mind?" Glancing his way, my eyes widened. "You think the solution to a bear outside the tent is to get out of the tent and try to scare it away. A one-to-two-ton, whole ass bear. That's your brilliant plan."

"It's better than killing it."

"Dying is better than killing the bear?"

He didn't respond, and I had to glance at him again to read his expression. Suddenly, I wished I hadn't. He reminded me all too much of Grace with his face scrunched up that way. I had only seen tears in Grace's eyes a handful of times, and Bentley looked like he was one more mention of bear murder away from sobbing.

"I don't want to do it," I said, softening my voice but maintaining my volume. "You know I love animals. But look at Tempy. She's over there shaking like a leaf. Because she knows that bear isn't out there debating the moral qualms."

"Can't you shoot in the opposite direction? To scare it?"

Bears weren't like people. They didn't comprehend warning shots. "All that will do is piss it off. If I have to shoot, I'm going to shoot to—"

A deep growl sounded outside the tent, drawing my attention.

Bentley must have released Tempest's jaw because she growled in response. And that was all it took.

That massive shadow rushed toward the tent.

I pulled the trigger.

A whine sounded. A thump followed. Then, only silence.

* * *

WHEN WE MADE IT OUT OF THE TENT, A BLOB ABOUT THE SIZE OF Tempest barreled over the hillside. Confirming my theory that Mama Bear was only so upset because she was taking care of baby bear.

Bentley wasn't the only one with tears in his eyes as I bent down to examine her. Luckily, even with limited visibility through the tent, I had gotten her in the head. While I found comfort in that, knowing she hadn't suffered, Bentley said, "Murderer."

Looking over my shoulder, I found his gaze in the dawning sun. "Was I supposed to let her kill us, asshole?"

"We probably deserve it more than she did. Sure, she was going to eat us, but we've done worse, haven't we?"

"Worse than eating a random couple and their dog?" I asked. "Shit, man. What other skeletons do you got in your closet?"

Giving a half laugh, he kneeled toward his backpack. "We gotta report this to the rangers, right?"

"Right," I murmured, trailing a hand over the bear's coarse fur. "I'm sorry, Mama. If you would've just walked away, I wouldn't have had to do this."

Of course, Mama Bear did not respond. Contrary to what Bentley seemed to believe, I wasn't the least bit pleased with this outcome. Killing animals had never been something I was fond of. In fact, this was the first time I *had* killed an animal. Ending a person's life didn't come close to the pit in my stomach I had now.

Against the mossy soil, the black bear lay with her snout in a puddle of blood. Thankfully, the blood came from the other side of her face, tucked against the grass, so I didn't see the extent of the damage.

She was dead, but from this side, it looked like she was just taking a nap. I'd seen bears in movies and at the zoo a few times, but this was the first time I'd seen one up close. She was as cute as Tempest. Like a giant puppy.

Damn it. I had just killed a giant puppy.

While Bentley spoke on the satellite phone with the park rangers, and Tempest explored the campsite on her long lead, I sat with the bear. That pit in my stomach stretched into my chest, hollowing and aching with each second that passed. This was not how I wanted to spend today. It had been a necessary evil, but trailing my fingers through a dead animal's fur was hardly my idea of a good time.

I would much rather have preferred sitting on the boulder a few dozen strides away, looking out at the view from this mountaintop. Pink and orange with hints of purple blanketed the miles and miles of farm-land. Some windmills spun in the distance, cows chomped on the grass of the rolling green hills, and the birds sang the prettiest song in the treetops overhead. Looked like a wonderful place to enjoy a cup of coffee with my dog and my—now confirmed—boyfriend.

But nope. I sat in the dirt beside a dead bear instead.

Trotting back my way with a stick, Tempest grinned ear to ear. As guilty as I felt for killing the bear, she made me smile. I scooted away from the carcass and battled Tempest for the stick. I never understood why she did this. Brought me the stick, then refused to give me said stick. Once I eventually got it off her, I threw it, she chased after it, then brought it back. The cycle repeated a few times.

On the sixth or seventh time, she brought the stick back and dropped it. When I threw it, she didn't run to get it. Otherwise informing me she was done.

"What?" I roughed up her ears. "What do you want, Tempy?"

She jerked her head toward my backpack, still hanging in a tree down the path. The bag that contained her kibble.

"Are you hungry?" I asked.

Wagging her tail, Tempest looked at my bag again.

With a chuckle, I gave her head one more scratch, straightened, and headed that way. "Of course you're hungry. You're always hungry."

Much to my surprise, however, she didn't trail after me. Just like she did at home. She typically waited in her crate for her breakfast, so her patience wasn't a massive shock, but I'd suspected that because we were in a new place, she wouldn't follow her usual routine.

It took a bit of battling to get the backpack out of the tree. Once I had it in hand, I started back to the camp. But I didn't see Tempest.

Heart dropping into my stomach, calling, "Tempest? Tempest!" I jogged as fast as I could, which wasn't very fast at all.

With wide eyes, Bentley stowed the satellite phone in his pocket. He called for her too. Then his face screwed up in disgust. "Eww. No, Tempy." He bent toward the bear. Where Tempest was, apparently.

That dropping sensation in my gut morphed into an unpleasant churn. Could I be surprised? She was a dog, after all. We'd brought her out into the wilderness. Supposed she was going to find her own breakfast.

Jumping back, shaking out his hand, Bentley's jaw dropped. "She snipped at me."

Well, he'd tried to take her delicious snack away. Power-walking closer, I said, "Did she get you?"

"Nah, just snapped in my direction." He shook his hand out at his side. "That's not normal for her."

Now that I could see her, lying on her belly and lapping away at the bear's face, I sighed deeply. It had been a long time since Tempest resource guarded. Really, it'd only been a problem the first month or so I had her. All Tempy had needed was a firm hand and a job, and she was an excellent dog.

But this was different. Fresh meat. The freshest she'd ever seen.

Occasionally, I gave her raw food treats. Common sense told me she thought the bear was another one of those raw food treats. Those, I had always given her from my hand, never in her bowl, for this very reason. She absolutely adored it, and I didn't want to risk her guarding it.

Looked like we were going back to hand feeding for the foreseeable future.

No use in describing exactly what she was chomping on when I made it to her. As adorable as dogs were, we often forgot they were wild animals. This reminded me they were just that.

When I approached, she looked at me out of the corner of her eye. She didn't bare her teeth, but I knew that look. A hint of fear, the stiffness of anger, and a tinge of worry. She knew she wasn't supposed to do this, but she was testing her luck.

Too bad for her. She was still on the lead. It was fifteen feet, so I followed it to the tree I had tied it to. As I walked toward her with it in hand, I told Bentley, "Get back."

Slowly, he walked backwards. "You think she's gonna bite you?"

"She might try." Standing just behind her, I tugged the lead. The leash was standard, but it was clipped to a slip lead collar around her throat. I liked using those when she was tracking so she didn't get too far ahead. When she went farther than I liked, the slip lead would tighten, and it served as an automatic correction. The pressure around her neck told her to stop. "Leave it."

Almost too low to hear it, Tempest growled.

I didn't know who this bitch thought she was.

"Leave it, Tempest." Voice firmer, I yanked the lead again. She whimpered. "Mine. *Leave it.*"

With blood on her lips, she looked up at me. The moment our eyes met, hers fell to the soil. Shame. She'd growled at Mom, and she felt guilty for it. Good. She should have.

"Come," I said, pulling the lead farther from the bear.

This time, she stood. Head hanging between her shoulders, tail between her legs, she let the bear be. Once I walked her back to the tree the lead was tied to, I shortened it so that she couldn't get within five feet of the carcass.

Squatting before her, I wagged a finger. "No bite." Again, Tempest hung her head in shame. "No guard." She plopped onto her belly, unable to even look at me. "You stay."

She rested her bloody chin atop her paws. Still couldn't look at me, which was for the best. It was better she felt guilty rather than combative for disobeying.

"Do you think that's going to hurt her?" Bentley asked.

"Eating the bear?" I asked. He nodded. "Probably not. It hasn't been dead long enough for bacteria to be an issue. Bear snatched a robin mid-flight once. Ate the little shit before I could get across the yard to him, but he was fine after. A few bites of bear shouldn't kill her."

Gagging, he shuddered.

I laughed as I walked back to the bear. Again, no need to specify exactly what Tempest ate for breakfast, but it made me feel worse about the whole situation. Then again, what was there to feel guilty about? This was the cycle of life. Nature at its finest. A sad but an unavoidable thing.

What upset me was the guarding. Tempest could have taken off Bentley's hand if she'd tried hard enough, and *that* was the problem. Normally, I would reward her for having backed away from the resource she was guarding, but not after that. She would not snap at someone and expect a treat for it.

"You're sure she didn't get you?" I asked Bentley, examining the bear a moment longer. Just to check for signs of rabies. There were no obvious telltales, like foam around the mouth.

Kneeling on the other side of the bear, Bentley gave the beast a few gentle taps. "Nah, I'm okay. Doing better than this girl. Park office said they're sending a couple rangers. Guess they're gonna handle the body. It's a hike, though. It'll be a while before they can get out here."

"Do we need to wait for them?"

"Do you have other plans?"

I hadn't. Not until I lifted the bear's head, which exposed its front right paw. That different angle let me see something that I never would have if I hadn't shot this bear, and if Tempest hadn't taken a bite of her.

A small white wrapper with a label that read, *EternalVibe Health Elixir.*

The adhesive label was stuck between Mama Bear's claws. It was identical to the ones I had seen on Liz Turner's Instagram profile. Some weight loss electrolyte power drink mix-in produced by a multilevel marketing company.

That little wrapper wasn't exactly Gatorade. Bentley and I were both moderately involved in the fitness world. We would've heard of EternalVibe Health Elixir before Liz's MLM advertising if it was popular.

Was it hers?

It was dingy, caked with mud and debris. As though it had been stuck between Mama Bear's paws for at least a day or two. Not like she'd stepped on it only when she'd entered our camp an hour ago.

Still holding up mama bear's paw, I nodded toward the tent. "Can you grab me a Ziploc bag, please?"

"Sure." There was the slightest twinge of a question at the end of that sentence as Bentley squinted his eyes at me and headed for the tent. I knew what that question was, but I didn't answer it yet. Calling this idea a Hail Mary was putting it lightly. When he returned, handing me the bag, Bentley asked, "Is that the shit Liz was selling?"

"Yep." Turning the bag inside out, I used it like a pair of gloves to conceal the wrapper. "You want to hear my theory?"

Bentley leaned against a tree and crossed his arms. "Well, now you gotta tell me."

I held up the bag with the wrapper inside. "This isn't a popular sport drink, right?"

"Right."

"But Liz sold it."

"Uh-huh."

"Since this is where Liz went missing, it would stand to reason that she used this drink pack."

He glanced around the campsite. "Which would make sense since this was where she was camping."

"Except, it was really stuck on Mama Bear's paw. And look how dirty it is." Again, I held it up, gesturing to the caked bits of mud. "Plus, this campsite was spotless when we got here. It still is now."

"I don't know if I'm following."

"The search and rescue teams were here. So were the cops." I hooked my thumb toward the rock where Charlotte's blood had been found. "They took the tissues those kids used. The evidence they collected included all their garbage. But they missed this one little packet, and Mama Bear found it? The cops couldn't, but the bear did?"

Bentley scratched his head. "Yeah, I'm not following."

Straightening, I held up the bag. "What if Mama Bear found this somewhere else? What if Mama came to our campsite because she associates humans with food? As if, maybe, she found Liz's camp somewhere. Maybe she went through Liz's bag of snacks tied up in a tree. Hell, maybe she smelled Liz here. Tempy did."

"Okay. You think Mama Bear got that wrapper from Liz's bag."

"I think it's a possibility, yes."

"And this helps us how?"

"Because Liz's trail disappears here. She turned around and went back to the road. But Mama Bear's trail might lead us to where she found this wrapper. Which might lead us to Liz's bag. Or to Liz."

Understanding finally flickered through his eyes. "You want Tempest to follow the bear's trail."

"I don't see how it could hurt."

"Can dogs do that? Follow where someone has come from, rather than where they're going?"

"Tempest isn't smelling the source of the smell in the distance. She's smelling the skin cells and hair that a person or animal leaves behind as they walk."

"So that's a yes?"

"That's a yes."

Stifling a yawn, he stretched his arms overhead. "Alright. I'm down. I'll pack up. You call the rangers and let them know why we won't be here when they get here."

Chapter 17

"Maddie."

"Bentley."

Bending over and holding his knees, he panted hard. "We've been hiking for three hours."

"And it's only eight in the morning." I held up my watch. "You know the saying. Something about a bird and the worm."

"If you want to go on and get the worm, you go ahead." He wiped some sweat from his brow and sat on a log off to the right of the overgrown path. "I'm gonna need to catch my breath before I worry about the worm."

A mocking scoff escaped me. I lifted a hand to my chest, as if to clutch my pearls. "You're just gonna let your girlfriend go off into the wilderness by herself? There're bears out there."

"Good thing you've got a bear eater." He guzzled from his water bottle as he pointed a nod toward Tempest. "And you say that like you need somebody to protect you. If this trail leads you to Mama Bear's babies, or a grizzly, or a polar bear, or—hell—a T. Rex, you'll kill them too."

"You know what? You're right. I shouldn't have killed the bear. I should've let it kill us instead. Should've let that bear orphan your daughter."

"Oh, yeah. Definitely what I would've preferred." He set his water bottle down and grabbed the canteen of coffee he insisted on making before we left camp. "Does *your* daughter still have the scent?"

Tempest's nose was still pressed to the soil, tail pointed high, ears alert. I whistled to get her attention. She looked back at me over her shoulder, as if to say, *But this is fun! Don't make me stop!*

"Come here," I called.

She made a, "Awoo-woo-wooh," sound.

"We're gonna eat," I said. "Then you can track some more."

With a wagging tail, she bolted back to me.

"Take it that's a yes?" Bentley asked.

"That's yes. But I've got that hair in case she loses it." I wasn't sure if the park rangers would approve, but I had chiseled some of the bear's fur off before we left, just in case Tempest needed a scent reminder. "We've already covered a lot of ground."

"Yeah, but I'm not complaining. It's been nice. This whole weekend has. Thanks for letting me come." Despite his sleepy eyes, his smile was the most joyous I had seen it in a long time.

"Thanks for coming. But I'm really hoping we find something soon. I don't have a clue where we are, and I need food. Real food. Granola bars aren't cutting it."

"And a shower." He paused. "Me. Not you. I'm the one who needs a shower."

I didn't need to look at his sweaty pits to agree. The smell was proof enough. "I say we give it another hour, and if we don't find anything, we go back to that street." About an hour ago, we had crossed a country road. Certainly wasn't part of the park. For all I knew, we were on private property now. There was no trail in sight, aside from the little deer prints speckled all through the woods. "And then, we'll call an Uber to take us back to your truck."

Chuckling, Bentley scooped some kibble from the Ziploc bag for Tempest. "Deal."

As he hand-fed her—because I told him that the two of them needed to reacquaint themselves as buddies since she had snipped at him—I chugged some of that coffee. Despite his chuckle, and his comment about enjoying this weekend so much, there was suddenly a certain sadness in his eyes. It was never easy to sit up straight when using a rotting log as a seat, but he hunched more than usual now.

Aside from the dead bear, nothing bad happened. Our walk had been peaceful, and then fun, and then playful when we hopped through a creek and splashed one another until we were soaked. Even now, the sun was high, the sky was blue, the birds were chirping, and there was something spectacular about sitting beneath the canopy of green leaves while breathing in the scent of fresh flowers. I was high on the summer breeze.

But Bentley's smile was suddenly forced, and he was slouching.

"You sure?" I asked.

"Hmm?"

"You sure you're thankful I invited you?" My tone was a soft tease. "Because you're looking kinda down in the dumps."

"Oh." He shook his head. "I am. Grateful you invited me, I mean. This is a nice little break from reality. I was just thinking about what you said last night. About Grace not liking being in the woods anymore. Two months ago, she would've had a blast doing this with us. Now she doesn't even want to walk around the trailer park by herself. The day before she left, she asked if I'd be mad if she stayed home. She was worried she was gonna wake somebody with a nightmare." Bentley shrugged, doing his best to whoosh the stress off his shoulders. The pressure remained, however, because he was still slouching. "I don't know. Her therapist says it's just gonna take time. But I'm a parent. I worry, and then I worry some more."

This was the first time since it all began that I'd seen Bentley like this. Grace, I worried about regularly. The guilt of what had occurred debilitated me at times, but I hadn't thought about how it impacted him. He was too busy taking care of Grace and worrying about me to think about himself. It seemed so until now, at least.

How ridiculous was that? Of course it impacted him. An infamous rapist and murderer kidnapped and nearly killed his daughter. To escape, she had needed to stab him countless times with a tiny razor blade.

Why hadn't I thought about it? Why hadn't I thought about how it was impacting him? Maybe it was because of everything he said last night. I avoided everything that hurt. Including this. Knowing it hurt him hurt me because, by extension, I was responsible. Even if I wasn't, I was.

Finding his hand, I twined our fingers together. "I'm sorry. This has gotta be really hard as a parent, and I'm so sorry you have to deal with it."

"Eh." He shrugged. "I'm accustomed to chaos."

"You shouldn't have to be."

"Neither should you, but here we are."

A frown tugged at my lips instead. "Yeah, but this was my chaos. I never wanted you to have to deal with it."

"That son of a bitch was going to be her teacher. It would've been my chaos either way."

True. It didn't lessen the guilt, but it was true. This wasn't about me, though. This was Bentley opening up to me about something he hadn't been able to until *I* opened up. He let me put my problems on him, and he was giving me his now.

"I just wish *she* didn't have to deal with this. I can handle all the bullshit, but she shouldn't have to. I wish things were better for her. That's all anyone wants for their kid, you know? Better than you had."

"Grace has a lot better than you had."

"True. She doesn't have an abusive, drunk parent. But she has a dead one." Brushing his sweaty hair from his face, he nibbled his lip. "Then there's Daisy. Not to mention the risk of losing the only parent she has left every time Simeon calls."

My stomach churned. "Simeon's called?"

"Once." A soft sigh. "One of his guys got into a fistfight. The other guy was wearing a ring. I just had to give him a couple stitches on his cheek. He gave me two grand for it, though." Another shaking breath. "Just feels like a matter of time until he shows at my door with somebody bleeding out. Wouldn't be the first time Grace saw that. She was too young to really comprehend it then, but she's a few years from adulthood now. These things are gonna stick."

I wasn't a parent. Who was I to give advice? Especially in this situation. I was the one who told him to work for Simeon again. Not because it was what I wanted for him out of life, but because we needed him. Did Simeon ransacking Eric Oakley's house save Grace's life? I didn't know. Supposed I never would. But it was my idea, and Bentley was indentured to Simeon now because of it.

"Do you think it's best to keep it from her?" I asked.

Bentley snorted. "You think I should tell her that I'm working with a drug dealer?"

"No? Yes?" Shrugging, I fiddled with the lid of the canteen. "I don't know. I don't want to tell you what to do or anything. But if you're worried she's gonna find out anyway, maybe it'd be better to go into the situation honestly?"

"It's not like I'm lying to her." He paused. "I guess I did. I told her I had to go sign some papers at work when I did that." Another long pause. When he turned back to me, there was genuine question in his eyes. Like my opinion on the subject truly mattered to him. I didn't like the pressure that came with that. "Maybe you're right. Maybe I should tell her. But do you think I should tell her how I started working for him?"

Nausea twisted my stomach. "I don't think I'd tell her that. Just because, if something were to happen to you while you're with Simeon, she might blame herself for it, you know? But don't do anything just because I told you. Do what you think is best."

Scratching Tempest's ears when she finished her handful of kibble, his chest broadened with a deep breath. "I don't know what's best."

"You've done pretty good so far. Grace is an amazing kid. Whatever you're doing, keep doing it."

"She is pretty great, huh? But sometimes I wish somebody would just tell me what to do. A rule book on the shit to refer to. I know I screwed up with Daisy, and so far, Grace is a lot better off. But I can't even pinpoint what I did wrong with Daisy so I don't do it again with Grace."

Forehead creasing, I shook my head. "You did nothing wrong. You played a big part in raising her, but she wasn't your kid, Bentley. You weren't the one who screwed her up. Her mom did. The mess was just too big for you to clean up on your own."

"I guess." He took a gulp from the water bottle at his feet. "Guess it's not the same, but you really want to know what your dad's keeping from you, don't you? This is kind of similar, isn't it?"

Both were examples of fathers doing something illegal and hiding it from their children. "Kind of."

"And you're more upset that he's keeping it from you than at the action itself, right?"

Again, kind of. I nodded in answer.

Bentley nodded too. "Then I think I'm gonna tell her."

"If she gets upset, and you need somebody to talk to about it, my ears are open."

"Thanks."

Everything stayed quiet for a while, only the sound of a trickling creek nearby and the music of the early morning birds filling the stuffy, humid air. His shoulders were a bit softer, his jaw relaxed, and that made me feel better too. I didn't know if what I said was any real help, and I hoped it didn't come back to bite him in the ass, but at least his stress lightened for the moment.

Leaning back and stretching my arms overhead, a gust of wind blew down the mountain. The breeze was soothing, but a quiet rattle followed.

I squinted over my shoulder. A few dozen yards away, something white tinged with red fluttered like a tumble weed from bush to bush. The same branding on the electrolyte stuck to Mama Bear's paw.

When I stood, Bentley grumbled, "Can you give me a few more minutes?"

Holding a tree branch to keep me steady as I climbed over a log, I winced at the pain spiking through my knee. "I'm not getting back on the hike yet."

"Then what're you doing?"

"Picking up after the litter bug."

"What?"

I waved him off and kept moving. When I made it to the piece of debris, my suspicions were confirmed. EternalVibe Health Elixir. The same electrolyte packs Liz had sold. The same ones that'd been stuck to Mama Bear's paw.

Using a Ziploc from my pocket, I lifted the empty packet up for Bentley to see.

"No shit," Bentley said. "Your theory confirmed?"

"Not yet." I trekked back to where Bentley sat, bent for my bag, found Liz's jacket for Tempest to sniff, and held it out for Tempy. "Track."

She plopped her nose to the ground and started downhill.

Grumbling under his breath, Bentley stood. "Alright. Guess break's over."

If this worked, at least Mama Bear's death wouldn't have been in vain.

Tempest nearly pummeled me to the ground a thousand times on our way down the mountainside. Between the tree branches and Bentley's occasional support, I managed to make it to the creek at the bottom without wiping out. Bentley did once, even though I was the one manning a hundred-pound German Shepherd.

With the foot of the mountain only a few dozen steps away, Tempy suddenly veered to the right. Some thirty feet from the deer trail we'd taken, camouflaged by some fresh brush, protruded another one of those electrolyte packs.

"Uh-oh," Bentley murmured, stepping backward. "You don't think she's, like, under that, do you?"

The leaves disguising the drink pack? There wasn't enough of it to cover a body. "We'd smell her by now if she were."

I handed him Tempest's leash and dug in my hoodie pocket, fished out my phone, and snapped some photos. I tucked a couple more baggies over my hands, crouched low, and shifted the pile of brush aside. Slowly, the remnants below became visible. I didn't move much. If this was a crime scene—and I was certain it was—it was best to leave everything where it'd been.

I couldn't be sure, but if I had to guess?

I was looking at the charred remnants of a backpack.

"Stay right here," I told Bentley.

He nodded, and I repeated the process with Tempest. Held out the sweater, let her sniff, and told her to search.

On the long lead, it only took her heartbeats to get to the muddy creek at the bottom of the hillside. Heart heavy, I followed her there. The water wasn't too deep. Only five or six feet. Not exactly a summer destination, but deep enough to drop a body into.

A few steps down the creek, and there it was. Drag marks, about two feet wide, spanning from the muddy creek side to the brush.

Chapter 18

WITHIN AN HOUR, ALL THE LOCAL AUTHORITIES JOINED US AT THE site of the burned bag and drag marks. They said I could stay for the search, and as much as I would've liked to, this was day one back on the job after six weeks off. I was hungry, exhausted, and I smelled like shit. Plus, Bentley needed to get back by 5 o'clock so he could pick up Grace. So I declined, but I asked if they could call me if they found anything. They agreed.

One of the local patrolmen drove the three of us back to the truck. From there, we did exactly as we'd planned and found a local diner for breakfast. Although there was no body yet, I had the feeling there would be one soon. So while we ate, Bentley and I debated who was most likely responsible.

"I don't like that Danny kid." Seated on the other side of the booth, Bentley wagged his pancake-coated fork. "There's something about him that I just find suspicious."

"It's got something to do with Trip." Shaking my head, I dumped a sugar packet into my mug. "If there are two things I've learned in law enforcement, they are: follow the money and follow the drugs. Liz didn't have money. But she was dealing drugs."

"She was selling pot," he made out between chews. "Pot dealers aren't usually associated with murderers."

"Just about anybody who has crossed Liz's path has a good reason to kill her."

"Yeah, but it's usually people closest to the victim who are responsible, right?" he asked. "So why would it be the drug dealer over the best friend's boyfriend who she was screwing?"

"Because he didn't have the vibe."

"Not every murderer has a *vibe*."

"And how many murderers have you met?" I asked.

Leaning in so nobody else in the quiet café could hear, Bentley whispered, "Simeon doesn't have the vibe, but he's a murderer."

"Simeon totally has the vibe."

"In what way?"

"It's a vibe." With a sip of my coffee, I shrugged. "Either you can feel it, or you can't. And you don't. You see the good in everybody, all the time. That's probably why you don't feel the vibe. I assume the worst in everyone, and that's why I know the vibe. Danny just doesn't have the vibe."

"Didn't you know that crooked cop?" Bentley arched a brow. "The one who was redistributing the drugs that were in evidence? Did he have the vibe?"

"He did, actually," I said. "But he had been involved in a shooting before. So I knew he was a killer. That's different."

"Damn. And you had no idea he was involved in Liam's death."

"Nope. I should've known that he was dealing from the lockup though." I took a bite of my sausage. "I was one of his customers. Which is also probably why I didn't put two and two together. Drugs kind of make you stupid."

Blinking hard, Bentley snorted. "One more reason to stay sober. You definitely should have figured that out."

"Probably, yeah. But you live, you learn. Won't make the same mistake twice. And don't get me wrong, I want to interview Danny alone. I just don't think he did it." I yawned and reached across the wooden tabletop for the pot of coffee.

"Want to bet?"

"What are we betting?"

"Twenty bucks." He stretched his hand over the table. "My money's on Danny. Yours is on Trip."

"My money is on it being *connected* to Trip. I'm not convinced it *was* Trip. Only that he's connected to it somehow."

Bentley frowned and dropped his hand back to the table. "That's too vague. Everything's connected in a murder investigation."

"It is. But my bet is that Danny had nothing to do with it." Hand still held over the table, I wiggled my fingers. "If you're right, and it was Danny, even if it is somehow connected to Trip, you get the money."

He narrowed his eyes, but he accepted the shake. "Fine."

"Fine." I returned his glare. "But those interviews are gonna have to wait till tomorrow anyway. I promised Teresa I would meet her for lunch today."

"That'll be nice." Glancing at his watch, Bentley stifled a yawn of his own. "Am I taking you back to your car when we leave here then? Because I've got to pick up Grace at the high school around four thirty."

"Works for me. I'll probably be getting home around five or six, so—"

The ring of my phone cut me off. Losing my train of thought as I fished for it, Bentley finished my sentence. "Dinner when you get home?"

Harper's name lit up the screen. As I slid across the green bar, I said, "What would I do without you?"

"Starve, probably."

I shot him a certain hand signal, which he laughed at, and answered Harper's call with, "Did they find anything?"

A heavy sigh sounded through the speaker. "Unfortunately, yeah. Her body floated a few miles downstream. We're pretty sure, at least. Phil and Karen are going to ID her now."

"Damn. I'm sorry. Should I hold off calling them?"

"I would. They're both a mess. I know they want you to keep digging though." Someone said something in the background. "Two minutes!" she called. "Check your email if you haven't yet. I sent what I was able to get from the Columbus PD about Daisy Miller. It isn't much, but maybe it'll help you."

"Sure, thanks. But wait, did you see the body?"

"Yeah, but no obvious cause of death. No blood or strangulation marks. Just a cut on her forehead but looks superficial. She was clothed still, so we aren't thinking sexual assault. Had to have been a dump though."

"Nothing else explains the drag marks."

"My thoughts too."

"When's Alex doing the autopsy?"

"Tomorrow morning. I'm meeting Phil and Karen. You want me to see if they'll grant permission for you to be present?"

"I'd appreciate it. Thank you." I sipped my coffee. "And thanks for keeping me posted."

"Thanks for finding what we didn't."

"Thank the bear."

"May she rest in peace."

After a few more pleasantries, we got off, and I did as she said. Opened my email from her. The email subject line read *Miller, Daisy FILE.* The body of the email said, *Bullshit, dude. I'm gonna keep digging, but... Well, there isn't much to go off of here. Call me if you think of anything I can use to find more. Friends you're suspicious of? Boyfriends? Johns? Get me a name and I'll do what I can. This girl deserves some closure.*

With a sigh, I clicked the attachment. While it loaded, the weight of Bentley's stare burned my cheek.

"What're you looking at?"

He snorted. "You're so polite."

Chuckling, he shrugged. "That smile was cute."

"What smile?"

"When you were talking to Harper." Another shrug. "You miss her."

I saw where he was going with this and waved him off.

"I'm just saying. You guys must've been close." He poured some coffee into his mug. "Promise I won't sleep with her, if that's what you're worried about. Won't so much as look at her."

"Piss off." Swiping open the file, I squinted at the screen. "Maybe you're encouraging our friendship just to get close to her."

"Oh, definitely." Picking up on my sarcasm, he responded in the same tone. "Look, I'm just saying. It seems like you want her in your life. I'll keep my distance if it's an insecurity thing—"

"I'm not insecure about shit. But I am trying to find out what happened to Daisy, so shh." I held my pointer finger before my lips. "You made me talk enough about my feelings last night."

"You say that like it's a bad thing," he muttered.

Because it is.

And irrelevant. I had work to do, damn it.

But there was nothing to work with. Now I understood Harper's note. The file was thinner than a frozen lake in the spring.

Bentley must've read my expression because he said, "Bad news?"

I shook my head. "Not *bad.* Just not exactly good."

I extended my phone his way. He skimmed through it for a moment, then looked up with furrowed brows. "You're the detective. I don't know what I'm looking at, Mads."

"Because there's nothing *to* look at," I said. "The only interview they conducted was with Katie, the friend who reported her missing, and the owner of the club. Did they even interview you and Grace?"

"No. I went to them a week or so after she disappeared, but they told me there wasn't anything they could do." Bentley held up air quotes. "'She'll show eventually. Girls like her vanish all the time. They come back home when they're ready.'"

"Implying she was on a bender."

"In fairness, I thought the same at first." Wetting his lips, he raised a shoulder. "But Katie wasn't Daisy's friend. She's Tommy's baby's mom.

She and Daisy weren't exactly enemies, but they weren't fans of each other either."

Uh, and he didn't think to mention that sooner? "Who's Tommy?"

"Kevin's brother." Kevin was Daisy's boyfriend, the one who pimped her out to pay off the debt she owed his family for drugs they'd fronted her. "A better guy than Kevin. But still a sketchy dealer."

"Wait, Kevin's brother's baby mama got Daisy the job at Xstasy, but she and Daisy didn't get along, and she was the one to report Daisy missing?" I paused to make sure I'd said that correctly. Bentley nodded, confirming I had. "And this bitch also spoke to a journalist and basically accused you of being responsible for her disappearance?"

A deep breath. "She and I aren't exactly friends either." Pressing his lips together, Bentley scratched his head. "I'm sorta the reason she and Daisy didn't get along."

Supposed that explained why she'd painted him as the villain in that interview. "Elaborate?"

He shrugged and took a sip of coffee, wincing as the steaming liquid trailed down his throat. "She was there a few times when I was stitching people up. So were her kids. *Little* kids. Like, two and five. And she was using. In front of them. I sorta..." Another head scratch, followed by a shrug. "I'd met the dad a few times. He was a good guy. Also an addict, but he'd been clean for a few years, and he was trying to get custody of the younger one. She kept fighting him in court, and she kept winning, so I sorta called CPS on her. They tested her, she came back dirty, and they gave the dad full custody. She got supervised visitation. She eventually realized I was the one who called. So yeah, she kinda hates me."

Couldn't say I blamed him. I was pretty sure his job made him a mandated reporter. It begged a question, however. "You think she would've done something to Daisy because of it?"

Frowning, he shook his head. "She wouldn't hurt a fly. She might be an addict, and a bitch, but not a murderer. Kevin wouldn't let that happen either. As much as I hate the guy, he loved Daisy. Or maybe love isn't the right word. He viewed her as his property. And nobody messes with Kevin's things."

"Kevin was abusive, right? That makes him the number one suspect."

"I would've thought the same thing, but he thought she was with me. A few days after she disappeared, he showed at my door screaming that he needed to talk to her. He thought she was just ignoring his calls."

"That would be a good cover. Make it out like he had no idea where she was."

"But that family has the local cops in their pocket. They kill people on a regular basis. Nothing ever comes of it. The cops know, just like they know about Simeon here. There was no reason to come to my house, make me let him in at gunpoint, and search for her. If he wanted to kill her, if he had killed her, he would've done it, and then he would've laughed in my face when I questioned him about it. Definitely wouldn't have brought it to my attention. And they wouldn't have let Katie report her missing. That would just tie the family back to Daisy's disappearance. If anything, it would've been me or her boss who reported her missing." Another shake of his head. "It's possible, I guess. I know the statistics. But I just can't see it. I hate the guy, but I know him. I don't think he killed her."

Valid points. But here was the problem with investigating a case that took place a state away. I needed to interview these people. As much as I trusted Bentley's word, he wasn't a cop or an investigator of any kind. He didn't think Simeon had the *murderer vibe*, for God's sake.

"I could be wrong. Those people do know how to make a body disappear." When I stayed silent, Bentley continued. "You're the PI. Maybe you see something here that I don't."

"I see a whole lot of nothing." Running my fingers through my hair, I skimmed further down the reports. "That's not necessarily a bad thing. Lack of information could mean lack of effort in the investigation. Which is probably the case given the type of person Daisy was. So maybe I need to look at this from another angle. Did Daisy have any close friends? People I can interview?"

He chewed on his bottom lip, then shook his head. "Outside of Kevin, no. She got along with pretty much everybody, but the closest people in her life were Kevin, me, and Grace."

Grace had no idea that I was looking into Daisy's disappearance. Bentley asked me to keep it that way. He didn't want to get her hopes up. But I couldn't investigate with this little information. "Do you think I could talk to Grace about her?"

Bentley furrowed his brows. "We both know that we're more likely to find a body than Daisy. Grace has already mourned her. I don't want her to have to do that again, especially with everything else she's going through. What questions do you have? I know everything about the kid."

He thought he did. But he was the dad here. I made sure to soften my voice when I said, "Parents never know their kids as well as they think they do."

Tracing his tongue along his teeth, he crossed his arms. "You think Grace is going to know something about Daisy that I don't."

I could all but guarantee it. "It's possible. But if you don't want me to talk to her, I'll work with what I've got. It's a lot more likely that I'm gonna find something valuable if I get to talk to everybody who was close to her, though."

A long, shaky breath. He avoided my gaze, but I didn't need to look him in the eye to know what he was thinking.

"Alright," he said after a moment. "I'll talk to her about it when I pick her up. Just don't get her hopes up, Maddie."

"You know I won't." I reached across the table for his hand and twined our fingers together. "All I'm gonna do is ask more about her. If anything is off limits, just say the word."

After another deep breath, he nodded. "Thanks." He cleared his throat. "So. What do you want for dinner?"

Chapter 19

Everlasting Cemetery.

Teresa called when I was leaving the diner and asked if I'd meet her here. So an hour and a half of Fort Pitt Tunnel traffic later, there I was. Stinking of sweat, wearing my dirty camping clothes beside Ox's rotting corpse six feet in the ground, looking at his photo smiling from the black headstone.

He would've liked it, though. Teresa and I had picked the spot together. Nestled beneath a big oak tree, only a few plots down from his father in the mausoleum. On the grassy hillside to my right, the cemetery line ended, and a little creek trickled. He always liked water. Used to say he wanted to live somewhere on a river or lakefront. I always said that I wanted to live on a big piece of land surrounded by trees. He protested for a while, then reluctantly agreed, so long as he got a creek.

I guessed he'd be listening to this creek for the rest of forever.

God, I hated this.

Laying some red roses atop the headstone, Teresa wiped a tear away. "It looks nice, doesn't it? The black?"

"It looks like something he would've picked himself." I pointed to the portrait. "That vain son of a bitch would've loved how good his nose looks. Always hated his nose in pictures."

"I may have told the artist to photoshop it a little." Trying to disguise her embarrassment, Teresa scratched her nose. "I knew he'd be mad if it looked big, so..."

I laughed. "Don't tell anyone else. Let history think he had a little Whoville nose."

Teresa chuckled and I joined in, until neither of us were chuckling and we both had tears in our eyes.

Resting her head on my shoulder, Teresa murmured, "It's unnatural. Parents aren't supposed to bury their children. This isn't something I ever should've seen."

"Death is unnatural." With careful breaths to keep those watery eyes from turning into sobs, I tucked an arm around her shoulders. "Since the moment it happened, that's all I keep thinking. Even if it's where we all end up, even if it's how every story ends, it's unnatural. This feeling, knowing he's never—"

Those droplets of salty water wanted desperately to escape in a glass shattering shriek. I stopped them before they could.

Her touch as soft as her voice, Teresa stroked a hand up and down my arm and said, "It feels that way, doesn't it? Every time I lose someone, I think that. Just not how it's supposed to be. It can't be. What's the point? Why be here, why live, and love, and be loved, if this is where it ends?"

Another question that I had pondered since Ox's death. I'd always considered myself an atheist. It was logical. Organic or not, we were just nuts and bolts. Parts of a machine. The lungs that allowed us to breathe, the heart that pumped our blood, the nerves that traveled to every limb. When I had gotten shot and lived thereafter with chronic pain, it'd only solidified that logic. We were just nuts and bolts.

But when I'd held Ox as he died, when I'd watched him take his last breath, when he'd stayed alive long enough for me to sing him a song, I'd seen more than a machine. Energy and life came from consuming food and water, but where did it go when the breath stopped filling our lungs? I had watched that energy—or his life force, or his soul—vanish. In real time, I'd watched him make the choice to let go, to move on, and I didn't know where he'd gone. Because one instant he was there, and the next he wasn't. The moment he'd stopped breathing, he wasn't Ox anymore. *Then*, he looked like only nuts and bolts, but only once that energy inside him had left.

If he were here, he'd call me stupid. He'd say souls weren't real. The life force I was referencing was only that. Energy converted from food and water, and that energy ran out as his blood poured onto the forest floor.

Ox would say I was just hoping he'd left because if he had, that meant I could find him again. He would say, "Don't let this be what makes you one of those people who praises the clouds."

I doubted I would find religion anytime soon. I didn't think I wanted to. But I watched him become only nuts and bolts. He didn't start out that way. And maybe it was only hope, a way to deal with the grief, and that was okay. If when I died, I learned it was only endless blackness, so be it. But right now, I believed we were more than nuts and bolts, and I liked it that way. I liked the thought of Ox sitting with his dad behind some pearly gates or born again with a new family who had a big black German Shepherd named Bear who guarded his cradle each night.

"I don't think it is," I said quietly. "I hope it isn't, at least."

Teresa swept a tear away from her cheek. "I hope if you're right, he doesn't get mad at me for saying this, but"—she met my gaze with a sheepish one of her own— "I'm tired of bringing him these flowers. He was allergic to the damn things. And all this does is make me cry. I can cry at home."

Laughing, I wiped the cloudiness from my vision. "Want to cry at lunch?"

Teresa chuckled. "How about we try not to cry?"

* * *

METRO MUNCH—A LITTLE CAFÉ NOT FAR FROM THE CEMETERY. IT was only about ten minutes from mine and Ox's condo, too. We'd eaten here a few times a week for years. I loved the place.

I used to, at least. Now, when we pulled up to it, I'd taken a glance inside the windows, and a memory floated back. Me and Ox researching on my laptop side by side in the blue leather chairs over the mahogany tabletop. Our cups were full, and he was sipping his black coffee, and I was chugging my fourth latte, and we were so happy. Our waitress seldom walked our way, because we were so encapsulated in our work, in each other, that she didn't want to interrupt.

And it hurt. That memory *hurt*.

So I asked Teresa if she minded sitting outside instead. There were wrought iron tables, green umbrellas that shielded us from the sun, and a sign that said to seat ourselves. Ox and I never sat outside, so no memories there.

Teresa agreed, and we sat. We talked about little nothings until the food came, all the while I looked at her and the cars bustling down the road on the right. Not into those windows, not into those memories.

"God, how do you do it?" Teresa gestured to Tempest napping at my feet on the cement. "How did you train the little beast?"

"You know. The usual stuff." Chomping into a fry, I waved a hand. "Ritual sacrifice, a little naked dance under a full moon."

She reached down to pet Tempy's ear. "I'm serious."

Teresa had always loved dogs, but she hadn't gotten one since Ox had gone off to college because she hadn't wanted to leave them home alone while she'd worked. Now, her hours were shorter, her son wasn't around, and she was lonely. A dog wasn't a bad idea, so she'd gotten one. And he kept her *busy*.

"Rex still giving you a hard time?" I asked.

"He's a demon," she said. "He has to be. The little brat climbed straight out of the pits of hell, Maddie."

"He's a puppy."

"No, he's a demon." She sat back and bit into a chicken tender. "He thinks his purpose in life is biting my ankles and peeing on everything I own."

"His purpose in life *is* biting your ankles. Corgis are herding dogs."

"He doesn't need to herd *me*." Sipping her coffee, she frowned at Tempy. "Why can't he be like you?"

"He can be. You just have to be firm with him." I roughed up Tempy's ears. She looked up and cocked her head from one side to the other, waiting for a command. "You weren't easy at first either, little miss."

"But it's supposed to be easier with a puppy. That's why I got one, so he'd be easier to train."

"And he would be. If you'd listened to me and gotten a golden retriever."

"Maddie." She stretched out the word, almost like a whine. "Just tell me what to do with him."

Sure, I could tell her what to do. It wouldn't matter what I told her if she didn't follow it, though. "Are you walking him every day?"

"Every day, twice a day."

"Using the command list I gave you every day?"

"Yes, every day. Well, not all of them. We're working down the list. He does good with sit, lay down, and place."

"That's a good start. As long as you're working on the other commands, too. Is he sleeping in his crate?"

Her frown deepened, eyes softening. "Sometimes. But then he cries, and—"

"And you better not let him out." Despite the way those words would look in black and white, my tone was playful. "Because if you let him out when he cries, you're rewarding the bad behavior."

"But he just wants cuddles, and then he quiets down."

"I bet he does. And I bet he bites your ankles as soon as you get out of bed too."

"What does the crate have to do with biting my ankles? He's sweet as pie when he's in the bed with me. And it's only if I walk too quickly out of a room that he nips my ankles."

157

"Control. The fact that he thinks he's your boss," I said. "You let him out of the crate when he cries, and he thinks, 'Oh, I did this bad thing, and she didn't stop me. I won. *I'm* the boss. Not her.'"

"You let Tempest in bed with you."

"Only if she understands it's a privilege and not a right. The second she acts like it's her bed, I remind her it's mine and kick her off. And you should be able to walk at whatever speed you want to in your house."

"What am I supposed to do then?"

"Start with the crate. Give him his meals in there. Let him associate the crate with something he likes. Then, when he's done eating, leave him in there for an hour while you're watching TV or cleaning the kitchen. And don't let him out until he's quiet."

Another frown. "Fine."

"And when he's out of the crate, keep the slip lead on him. Every time he bites your ankles, pull on it to correct him."

"He hates it."

"That's the point."

"But I feel so mean when I use that thing. Doesn't it hurt him?"

"Put it on yourself and see," I said. "Only hurts if you ram your head away from its length. A little pressure doesn't hurt."

"He cries so loud when I do it."

"Then he's dramatic. As corgis tend to be," I said, covering my mouth to chew a bite of my chicken tender. "He only hates it because when you have the slip lead on him, he knows you're in control. He's not crying 'cause it hurts. He's crying 'cause he's mad that you're telling him what to do."

Resting her chin in her hand, she blew out a billowing sigh. "He *is* bossy. When we're walking, he just about yanks me down. And I don't even know how. He's twelve pounds."

"Corgis are big dogs with little legs and the personality of a cat," I said. "Use the slip lead on the walk too."

"Somebody's gonna call animal control on me. I'm not kidding, Maddie. He howls like a banshee with that thing."

"Tell them your dog trainer said, 'Let him cry all he wants.'" After another sip of my pop, watching her frown at the thought of her poor puppy, I slouched in the wrought iron patio chair. "Do you want to go back to your place after we eat? I can show you what to do with him."

Her eyes lit up instantly. "Would you?"

"As long as you promise to do what I teach you. Because he's just gonna get more stubborn the bigger he gets. And I know how cute they are, but a corgis' jaws are almost as big as hers." I pointed to Tempest with my French fry. "They bite hard. Be firm and get him under control now. A lot of them end up in shelters because they're oh-so-cute, but they're tough. You've gotta be tougher."

She shook her head quickly. "I'd never put him in a shelter. I just don't want to hurt him."

"I know you wouldn't. But I promise he's not concerned about hurting you when he nips you," I said. "Don't be afraid of hearing him cry. He's fine. Just a bossy, manipulative, adorable little shithead."

"He really is." Chuckling, she swirled her spoon through her coffee. "But enough about me. How are you? Anything new?"

That was how she asked about Bentley. She rarely used his name, if ever, but she seemed to enjoy hearing me talk about him. She liked him altogether. Never said we were good together, or that she preferred him and me together over her son and me, but she knew he'd tried to save Ox. She'd thanked him with a plate of cookies, even brought Rex over so Grace could meet him, then left teary-eyed.

Which was why I hated talking about Bentley with her. She may have seen me as a daughter, and I saw her as a mom, but I knew the vision she'd had in mind for my life. The fact that that fantasy could never become reality had to be a slap in her face.

Instead of getting into any of that, I said, "My dad showed up at my door two days ago."

Teresa's jaw dropped. "What?"

"Apparently just got out of prison." I took another sip of my pop.

She'd yet to pick up her jaw. "He didn't even call?"

I explained what he'd said and my inferences, to which she still frowned, but her eyes were sympathetic. Sympathy for me, I assumed, but for him too. Which made sense. Teresa knew my family history. She'd invited my mom to holidays, so she had a vague understanding of what Sam had gone through.

"Do you think he's telling the truth?" she asked.

"He thought she was alive, so I don't see what point there'd be in lying," I said. "Unless he was lying about that too. But I could see it."

"You really think?" Confusion laced Teresa's voice, as it often did when my mom came up. "Why would she hide his letters from you?"

I picked at the remaining fries on my plate. I'd been starving when we got here, and now, my stomach gurgled. "She was jealous of us. That sounds batshit, right? What parent would be jealous of her partner having a good relationship with their kid? But she hated how much I loved him."

"I can't imagine," Teresa murmured, tucking her sweater closer around her frame. "Richard and I, we both loved Ox more than each other. That's how it's supposed to be. It's biology. It's how all animals survive. Our children come first because if they don't, the species won't survive."

"My mom was more the 'eat her young,' type." Despite my witty tone, Teresa's expression only softened. Ox would've appreciated that dark humor. "It was just who she was, ya know? Bitter. Mean. She got a kick out of hurting everyone around her. And who knows. If he hadn't been around at all when I was little, maybe I would've turned out like her." Although, I credited Bentley and his family for that too. His dad might've been a prick, but his mom and sister were close to normal. More nurturing than my mother ever could have been. "So maybe I owe him a chance."

"No." Teresa's eyes hardened. She looked far too much like Ox when she made that face. "You don't *owe* him anything. If you want to give him a chance because that's what *you* want, then you do that. But don't do it because you feel you owe him."

I knew I didn't owe him my forgiveness. But I did owe him my understanding. Mom abused him just like she'd abused me. He shouldn't have left me with her, but, God, I understood. If I could've run from her, I wouldn't have cared who I left behind either. And if he *had* come back for me, how could I hate him?

"Yeah, I guess." Clearing my throat, I dug around in my purse for my wallet. "You ready to head out? I found a body today. Gotta do some research tonight."

"In just a minute." Teresa did the same as me. Fished around in her purse. She, however, came out of it with an envelope. "First, I, uh, need to give you this. It's the reason I wanted you to meet with me today, actually."

"You're not paying me for helping you with Rex." I slid it back to her side of the table. "I have a hundred percent family discount."

"It's not that. It's not from me at all, actually." She forced a smile. "It's from Ox."

My brows slowly fell. "Huh?"

"His last will and testament. A good one." A breathy laugh escaped her. "He left you a lot."

A knot the size of the sun balled up in my gut. "That must've been from before the breakup."

"It's not. There's a letter in here too. I hope you don't hate me for reading it. He revised his will after that shooting earlier this year. He left me enough to do his funeral, more for me to put in my retirement, a little for a few people at work. But most of it, he left to you."

That knot grew bigger and bigger. "No. No, he wouldn't have. We hated each other most of the time."

"And you loved each other *all* the time. It's yours, Maddie. You have to fill out some paperwork, but it's yours."

"No." The word came out involuntarily. "No, I'm not taking his money—"

"*I* took his money. His savings, his bank accounts. That all went to me. But the life insurance is yours."

"Then you can take the life insurance too. We were broken up. I don't deserve that. I can't take it. I—"

"Maddie." Taking my hand, Teresa's eyes turned that cold, icy blue

Ox's always were when he was angry. Her voice didn't sound it, but it was clear my arguing pissed her off. "You were his world for a third of his life. When you weren't anymore, you were still his best friend. He didn't care about anyone the way he cared about you. Maybe you're still angry at him for what happened between you, so this feels wrong, but it's what he wanted. He didn't have many friends, but he had you. And he was horrible at showing it, but he wanted the best for you. So we're gonna go to my house, and you're gonna fill out the paperwork, and you're gonna take what he left you because *it's what he wanted*, Madison Castle. And you're not gonna argue with me about it. You're gonna take this money, buy yourself some health insurance, and then you can argue with a therapist about it."

Chapter 20

$500,000.

That was how much money Ox left me. $500,000. Apparently, his policy had been for a million. Teresa had overseen managing the other $500,000. She's paid off his condo, which now went to me, his car, which also went to me, as well as all his credit cards and loans. I didn't know how much she had left, but evidently it was so much that she didn't feel the need to argue with me about her taking the $500,000 he left me.

I tried to stay focused while I helped Teresa with Rex, but I couldn't stop thinking about that money. And that letter. As I drove home from Teresa's house on the other side of the city, that letter taunted me in the passenger seat.

When I looked at it, tears bubbled in my eyes, and my throat thickened. I thought his last words to me would be, "Thank you," but I was wrong. His last words to me were in that letter.

I wanted to know what he'd said. If he'd made a joke about how he knew I wouldn't want the money, but now I had no choice but to take it. If he'd mocked me, as he was famous for. I wanted to read that letter, but I didn't want to hear—or read, rather—his last words again.

The whole way home, my lips quivered, and I swallowed the urge to cry. A character flaw of mine, as Bentley had pointed out last night. Ignoring my pain wasn't dealing with it. Now I was feeling it, and, my god, I didn't want to.

Losing him hurt like nothing ever had. No matter how much I pretended everything was fine, that *I* was fine, it wasn't. I wasn't. I had already mourned him, and now I was mourning him all over again. This time was final. This time had no apology or reckoning.

Ten years were gone. They were gone when he'd cheated on me, but not really. Our relationship, the romantic one, had been gone back then. But any hope of having him in my life was truly *gone* now. His friendship. His fleeting laughs. His mean jokes. That rude, inconsiderate, emotionally inept asshole was gone, and I didn't know how to face it.

Teresa mentioned something today. That I was the biggest part of his life for a third of his life. Likewise, he was the biggest part of my life for a third of it. How could I just shut the door on that? I didn't know how to say goodbye to the Maddie Castle I had been when I'd met him. His death not only hurt because I would never see him again, but it also hurt because I couldn't travel back in time and meet him all over again. I didn't belong in the past anymore—I knew that—but if I could have, at least he still would've been a character in my story.

From here, I got to grow into someone new, and he would stay immortalized as that man on the black stone above a rotting corpse. My new chapter was only beginning when his entire book had ended. Or it would, anyway. It hadn't ended yet because I hadn't read that letter. There was still a story there, no matter how small.

Dodging potholes up the big hill into the trailer park, I forced myself together. A few deep breaths, some sniffles to keep my tears from running out of my nose, and some dabbing the corners of my eyes to dry the wetness. Bentley wanted me to open up, and I would. But not at this very moment.

When I made it closer to my house, I was glad I had taken the time to console myself. Because there, at the front of my yard, kneeled Sam. Wearing gardening gloves, a blue cap protecting his face from the bright sun, he tugged at the overgrown weeds in the decrepit mulch bed. Kneeling was a difficult task for me, so I'd tried to spray all those weeds with chemicals. Grace had lectured me about how bad they were for the environment, insisting that she and Bentley would take care of them for me, but they hadn't gotten around to it yet.

It was kind. I couldn't get mad at him for it. But I couldn't tell if it was kindness or manipulation. From what I'd gathered, he didn't seem the manipulative type. But a short conversation over breakfast wasn't enough for me to judge his character.

When I shifted the car into park, he turned around. His smile was sad, awkward, as I stepped out of the driver's side. Tempest hopped out beside me. She glanced at him, and then at me, as if to say, *Do you want me to do something about that? Is he allowed to be here?*

I roughed up her scruff in answer. Because I had no idea.

Straightening, Sam gestured to the weeds. "I hope you don't mind. I, uh, I saw these when I pulled in yesterday. With your knee and all, I figured you couldn't do it. And I got some numbers I wanted to give you. Lawyers I had from back in the day and all that. I gave them permission to answer any questions you had, but I thought maybe I could talk to you when I gave you the paper. It's tucked in your door. But I saw these again when I was leaving, and I figured..." An awkward scratch of his head. "I'm sorry. I should've asked. I did text you, but you said you weren't in town, so I just—"

"I don't," I said, walking towards him. "I don't mind."

His shoulders softened with relief.

"But you really don't have to do that. I appreciate it, but I can handle it. My knee gets in the way, but I can sit on my ass."

Chuckling, he shrugged. "I wanted to. I was thinking about doing some of the weeds around back too, but they're pretty dense. I might need to use a weed wacker. You have one? I thought about asking Greg, but he never liked me. Unless you don't want me to. I can head out if you have plans, or if I'm in the way, or if... I don't know."

I didn't want him to head out. I didn't particularly want him to pull my weeds, but I didn't want him to leave. Admitting I wanted him to stay felt pathetic though.

It was so confusing. I was torn between wanting a relationship with my father and wanting to protect myself. Keeping a wall between us, one made of steel that an awkward smile couldn't break was safer. I was safer if I didn't let him in. If I didn't risk getting hurt if and when he left again.

"Bentley has one," I said. "But you really don't have to."

"No, I'd like to. Really. And then, when I'm done, you wouldn't want to get dinner or something, would you?" Wiping some sweat from his brow, he glanced at the mud on his jeans. "Or I can cook. I'm a half-decent chef. Have you ever had chili mac? It's kinda prison food, but it is surprisingly delicious. Unless you're busy. I completely understand if you're busy."

I was just about to say I wasn't when the rumble of Bentley's truck sounded down the road. When I glanced that way, Sam said, "Don't worry about it. That was presumptuous of me. Of course you're busy. I shouldn't have just invited myself. Both to your house, and to dinner. That was rude. I'm rude. I don't try to be, but I tend to be, and I'm sorry. Maybe we can have dinner another time. Today, I'm just gonna finish cleaning up these weeds and get outta your hair."

By the time he had finished choking out that mouthful, Bentley and Grace were getting out of the truck. I wanted to tell Sam he wasn't rude. Pushy, but not rude. That I appreciated how invested he was in becoming part of my life.

But just when I opened my mouth to speak, Grace yelled out, "Maddie!" and all but pummeled me in a bear hug. "I missed you!"

"I missed you too." Laughing, I hugged her back. Behind her, Sam smiled his usual awkward one. Like he wanted to say hi, but he didn't know if he should. He already felt like he was overstepping. What gave him the right to interrupt my boyfriend's daughter's homecoming? "Sam, this is Grace. She's Bentley's daughter."

Grace pulled away and offered a friendly wave. Bentley, lugging Grace's ten thousand bags from the truck, gave a nod in greeting.

"I'm sure you know that's Bentley." I gestured that way. "But Bentley, Grace, this is Sam. He's, um—He's my dad."

After dropping Grace's belongings on the sidewalk, Bentley politely shook his hand. Sam returned the shake, but the discomfort, the lack of confidence, in his expression made him look so much younger than Bentley. "Nice to see you again."

"You remember me, huh?"

"Hard man to forget." Bentley's smile was still sincere. Polite.

Yet Sam grimaced. As if he wasn't sure if that was a jab or a compliment. In fairness, neither was I.

"Like, *the* dad?" Grace asked, voice low, but not low enough. "The one who abandoned you?"

Sam absolutely overheard.

Over his shoulder, Bentley shot her a look. I appreciated that.

"We were just talking about dinner," I said. Time for a subject change. "Are you still grilling tonight?"

"I am, yeah," Bentley said. "Are you gonna be around for dinner, Sam? We've got plenty."

"Oh. No, I couldn't ask you to do that. I don't want to step on any toes or—"

"You're not." Bentley turned my way. "You want him to stay, don't you?"

Bentley wasn't asking because he was unsure. If I hadn't wanted Sam here, I wouldn't have told Bentley that we were just discussing dinner plans. As always, he knew what I wanted. Also knew that I wouldn't say it on my own.

"It's the least I can do." I gestured to the weeded flower bed. "Or, I guess, the least Bentley can do. He cooks. I do not."

Sam swatted some sweat from his brow again. "Alright. Yeah, thank you."

"Don't worry about it. I could use some help getting the grill going though." On his way past, Bentley pecked my cheek. In a lower tone, at my ear, he said, "I talked to Grace. She's ready for your interview."

* * *

I followed Grace inside. Although I encouraged her to unpack and not throw all her dirty clothes on the floor that Bentley had cleaned tirelessly while she was away, her nose was glued to the glass, watching her father and mine. "You know he's drilling him, right? Because I know my dad. Today, *he's* playing detective."

"Yeah, I figured that was why he sent me in here with you."

"Well, your interview can wait." Ducking slightly, so only the top of her head was visible, she eyed them carefully. "Respectfully, your dad's kinda hot."

Good genes. Gross to think about on my end, but there was a reason the assholes I'd arrested had nicknamed me Barbie. "He's, like, five times your age," I said.

"Still hot." She shot me a smile over her shoulder. "He just showed up? Didn't call, didn't text?"

"Then showed in my mulch beds." Leaning back on the bed, I propped myself up on my elbows. "But I'm not complaining. Not about that part, at least."

She struggled around the piles of linen on the carpet and plopped down beside me on her bed—the only clean surface in this room since she'd arrived and tornadoed through it. "What part are you complaining about?"

"The fact that he won't tell me why he killed a man."

A few months ago, her jaw would've dropped at that. Her eyes would've bulged. Now, she only arched a brow. Supposed that was the typical reaction once you stabbed your kidnapper half a dozen times in the back. "You can't find any information about it?"

"A lot of the files I've found so far are redacted." Exhaling, I shook my head. "But that's not why I followed you in here. How was camp?"

"Camp." A careless shrug. Unzipping her duffel bag between us, she yawned. "I learned how to make a soufflé. Had my first crème brûlée. All of which were fantastic. And before you ask, yes, I will make you some later. Not the highest priority right now, Maddie. Tell me about your hot dad."

I grimaced. "Please don't call him that. And please stop finding old men hot. You don't need daddy issues. You've got a good one."

"What is he? Fifty? That's not an old man." She tore through her suitcase, raining more clothing to the floor. "But not the point. Didn't he leave you when you were, like, six years old? And then he just waltzes back in? Does he have a good reason? Do we hate him? Are we cool? I need to know how I'm supposed to handle this."

I was supposed to be the mature adult here, but damn it, she was funny. "He did, he did, he does, we don't, and we are."

"Um, I'm gonna need more detail than that."

So, I explained.

When I was finished, and the two of us were chomping on some beef jerky she had made at camp, she plopped backward and hung her head off the bed beside me. "Oh. So that's what you meant about the whole killing a man thing."

Didn't even want to know what else she thought I may have meant.

"And you think you can trust him?" Grace asked. "Even though he's a murderer? Or manslaughterer, I guess."

Shaking my head, I raised a shoulder. "I don't know."

"Do you believe him? About the whole trying-to-take-you-with-him thing?"

"I don't know. But he knows I'm a PI. It'd be a dumb thing to lie about. I'll find out if he is."

Still dangling her head backward off the bed, Grace flapped her lips together in a trill. "If anything changes, and we do hate him, just let me know."

"Got yourself a deal, kid." I repositioned myself on the bed so I could lie beside her, also with my head hanging off the edge. "But enough about me. Tell me about the trip."

It was hard to tell if her smile drooped or not, given the angle. Her tone gave it away. "I told you. It was fine. But that's not even what you came in here for. So let's do it. Ask me questions. Not about camp. About Daisy."

She was avoiding talking about camp. It wasn't my place to push. If Bentley wanted to, that was his responsibility as a parent. Mine was to be the parent's girlfriend, and the private investigator. I hoped, at least. "Your dad explained all of this to you, right?"

"That she's probably dead?" Contrary to the blunt annoyance in her voice a moment prior, there was grief there now. "Yeah. He had that talk with me a month or so after she went missing. And I'm not gonna blame you, or him, if you don't find anything. I get it. She was a tweaker. People like that go missing, and they don't get found. I'm not stupid, Maddie. So my expectations are on the ground. But my hopes are up. My hopes have *been* up."

I cocked my head to the side. "What do you mean?"

"I know the statistics. I understand the odds. But I don't think she's dead. I never have. Dad thinks I'm crazy, and I'm sure you're going to think I'm crazy too, but I just know she's out there somewhere. I can't tell you how or why, but I know. Have you ever just known something like that? Something that is totally illogical, but you just know it's true?"

Yes. My gut had good instincts. Maybe Grace's did too.

"Whatever. Not the point," Grace said. "Ask me the questions."

"Alright," I murmured. "To start, just tell me about her."

"Like, what she's like?"

"We can start there, sure."

With a harrumph, Grace nibbled her lower lip. "Funny. Really funny. Funnier than you." I chuckled at that, and Grace did too. "Never mean. Almost too nice. No, *definitely* too nice. Total people pleaser. Like, she just let people walk all over her. I know when people are on drugs like that, they can act kinda shitty, but she would just do dumb things. Like, dance around the kitchen when there was no music playing. Or stay up for days on her computer. Or go out into the yard at night and count the stars. We used to do that." She laughed again, softer this time. "I think the most we counted was somewhere around five thousand before I fell asleep."

When Bentley had talked about Daisy, he'd looked anxious and devastated. With Grace, the devastation was no different, but the anxiety was replaced with a certain joy. Something in the way her brown eyes twinkled, or maybe in the way she fingered the heart pendant around her neck.

"Is that new?" I asked, gesturing to it.

Giving a somber smile, she shook her head. "She gave it to me. I started wearing it after everything happened. I kept having dreams about her, and I usually just keep it locked up in my jewelry box, but... Anyway."

We all needed those little sources of comfort from some place. "She was never mean, you said?"

"Not really, no. Why?"

"Your dad just mentioned that he and her fought sometimes."

"She still wasn't *mean*." Straightening, Grace frowned. She waited until I sat forward to continue. "Dad didn't do anything wrong. Not really. He was worried about her. I was too. I think it was a guilt thing, you know? Like it was his fault she was on the path she was. So he pushed too hard. It's not that he was controlling but overbearing. A helicopter parent. Like he is with me. When she started dating that piece of shit, he always told her she was a pushover. That she needed to stand up for herself."

"Bentley did?"

"No, the asshole. Kevin." That was a nickname I could get behind for a drug dealing, sex trafficking, abusive son of a bitch. "And she did. But she should've stood up for herself to *him*. Not to dad." A deep breath. "I think they fought like most parents fight with their teenagers. They never went for low blows or anything. Dad wanted her to get clean, and I don't think she knew how. I don't think she had anything to get clean *for*. Dad would get pissed because he saw that, and then she would get angry, but there was never any meanness. It was just more intense than most teenage tantrums because the stakes were higher, I guess.

"But, aside from that, I don't know. Daisy was smart, but not in a book smart sort of way. Street smart. She was artistic. She loved telling stories."

And Bentley hadn't thought to mention this? "Like, she was a writer?"

"She always just said she was a storyteller. But yeah, she wrote them down sometimes. Usually, she just told me stories before bed. She wasn't big on reading, but Mom used to read to me. When she died, any time Daisy came over, if she was there at bedtime, she told me a story."

"What kind of stories?" If they were fictionalized versions of her life, they could tell me a lot about who she was. And who surrounded her. "Like, sci-fi? Fantasy?"

"A little of everything. Some fantasy. Romance, some horror, even. Mysteries. Really, she was all over the place."

If she was writing them on meth, that made sense. "Do you have any of Daisy's stories? Did she ever email you something she wrote?"

"I think she used my phone to login to the app she wrote on a few times when hers was broken," Grace said. "I deleted it when she was done, but I can probably find it. And I know all the passwords she used to use. You want to read them?"

"I want to read everything I can find on her," I said. "It would be great if she had a journal somewhere, even if it's just fiction. Reading it will tell me a lot more about her."

"Then, after I get a shower, I'll find it." Yawning, Grace stood. "Anything else you need to know?"

"Let's see what I can find in her writing." I stood as well, stretching my arms overhead. "Then we'll go from there."

Chapter 21

Dinner inside—with air conditioning and no bugs—was preferable to the patio chairs in the yard. Bentley had suggested the latter, but Grace and I'd convinced him of the former. So, that's where we were. Sitting around the kitchen table covered in steaming piles of fragrant barbecue, illuminated by bright sunlight that shined in from the window behind Sam's head. One big, happy, dysfunctional family.

It had gone well so far. Bentley and Sam seemed to really hit it off. Supposed two men and a pile of meat combined with a fancy grill had a way of connecting them. Even once inside, they talked about this, then about that, primarily the changes Bentley had made and was still making to his double-wide trailer.

"I really want to do new floors throughout." Bentley gestured to the linoleum in the kitchen and the dingy carpet in the living room. "Part of me says to do hardwoods, but I'm leaning toward LVP. They hold up better, you know?"

"Yeah," Grace said, nodding with wide eyes. "But we'll need to put some joists between them, and maybe a retaining wall."

I laughed. "What?"

"Just trying to join in on the conversation." Grabbing a soda from the fridge, she glanced at me over her shoulder. "Water or pop?"

"Pop, please," I said.

"Hardwood is exactly what it sounds like," Bentley explained. "Wood floors. LVP stands for luxury vinyl plank. They're basically plastic, so they're water resistant, but a lot of them are designed to look the same as wood floors, and they hold up better."

"Wood floors would help your resale value," Sam said. "But those luxury vinyl planks, they do look good. That's probably what I would do."

"See, that's what I'm thinking too." Lowering himself into his usual spot across the table, Bentley talked through a mouthful of hamburger. "Because realistically, the resale value on a trailer, even if I move it onto a piece of land, isn't gonna to be close to the equivalent of a house of the same size. And it's not like I'm planning on selling anyway. Having wood floors, even though they're less efficient, would just be for vanity's sake. And that's not me. I'm not into all the fancy shit."

"Oh, I am." I shot Bentley a smile. "Hey, if I were to buy you some wood floors, could you put them in over at my house?"

"Probably." Finally, he swallowed and wiped his mouth with a napkin. "Why would you want wood? Tempy's nails are going to scratch the hell out of them. And you're not good about keeping your floors dry. You'll come in with snow on your shoes, forget to dry them off, walk all over the place, and ruin them. You should do LVP."

"But wood floors are pretty." And I had always wanted them. It was a small thing, a silly thing, and I saw the point about the resale value. But my car was worth more than my trailer at this point. It's not like I ever expected to make a profit on selling it. That was, if I ever sold it. I liked everything I had done to my trailer. The only thing I would like to change was the land it was on, because paying lot rent when my trailer was paid off just felt redundant. "I don't know. I just think it'd be nice."

"You know," Sam said, "I think we're going to have some flooring left over from this house I'm working on. They're as easy to install as the LVP, but they're wood. I wouldn't mind doing it for you."

"I don't think you can just take the leftover materials," I said. "But I appreciate the offer."

"No, really, it wouldn't be a big deal. I'm friends with the owner of the company. He let me take a damaged cabinet home yesterday so I could put it in as a bathroom vanity. He wouldn't mind."

"How's that?" Grace asked.

Oof. I knew where she was going with this, the nosy little shit. Granted, I was thinking the same thing. I'd planned to ask him about it later. When he wasn't surrounded by people he didn't know, doing his best to make a good impression.

"How's what?" Sam asked.

"How are you friends with the owner of the construction company you work for?" Propping her elbows on the table, Grace leaned in. "Didn't you just get out of prison? How could you have made friends this quickly? And where are you living? Because usually, when you're renting, you don't get to just put in a new bathroom vanity. Right? Didn't we run into that problem when we moved here, Dad? When we were waiting for the deed to come through on this trailer?"

Bentley frowned at her. "Don't pry."

"I'm not prying. I'm just—"

"Curious," Sam finished. "I'd have questions too if I was where you all are." He gestured between us. "I met Tom in prison. He was my cell-mate for five years, so we were close. His wife ran his businesses while he was in. Promised me that when I got out, I had a job."

"And where are *you* living?"

Bentley gave her another look, the kind that said to mind your business, but she didn't seem to notice. Or care.

"It's a little cabin. Not far, bordering one of the state parks a bit north of here," Sam said. His last explanation, he was confident in announcing. This one? He avoided eye contact and picked at the label on his plastic water bottle. "It's kind of a long story too. But a friend of mine told me when I got out, I'd have it waiting on me. We're signing some paperwork next week that'll make it mine."

"You own it?" Furrowing my brows, I tilted my head slightly. "This friend of yours, he just gave you a cabin."

An uncomfortable throat clear. "Yeah, sort of. Like I said, it's a long story."

"I bet it is." Sipping the Coke Grace had set in front of me, I leaned back and eyed him carefully. There were only a handful of reasons I could think of to gift a friend a home. Few of them were legal. "I'd love to hear about it sometime."

He gave a short nod. "Sure."

"Is this friend, by chance, connected to the person that you murdered?" Grace asked.

"Grace." Bentley's head shot in her direction, voice firm.

I gave her a look, but I couldn't say I was all that mad. That story, I still needed to know.

"What?" Grace asked. "It's true. He's a murderer. Forgive me for wanting to know why. And for wondering if it's somehow connected to his sketchy living situation."

"Manslaughter," I said under my breath. "Manslaughter–er?"

Grace snickered. I tried not to, but there was a slight snicker.

"Children," Bentley said, shaking his head. "You're children."

"And I wasn't judging him," Grace said, reaching across the table for the salt-and-pepper. "I stabbed a guy too. Don't regret it. Do you regret it, Sam?"

Bentley rubbed his temples. I said nothing, only studying Sam's expression. Which was somewhere between awestruck and confused. Like there was just too much here to even begin responding to.

That was fair. It was a mess. We were all messes. Despite trying his hardest to turn his life around, to appear normal and healthy, he fit right in with our brand of chaos.

"Did you really stab someone?" Sam asked eventually.

"Yeah. Like, somewhere between five and fifteen times? We think, anyway." Grace shrugged and took another bite of her burger. "I never read the autopsy report. What do you think it was, Maddie? Five?"

"Probably more like ten," I said.

Blinking hard, Sam looked from her to me. "You're serious."

"The Country Killer," Grace said. "He kidnapped me. It's a long story though."

Still in awe, Sam said nothing for a moment.

"You didn't read that in the news?" Bentley asked.

Swallowing, Sam gestured to me and said, "I knew about your knee. But this story didn't make it to the news stations I was watching."

"She's a minor." I nodded Grace's way. "Protecting her anonymity and all."

"Very kind of them." Grace chomped into her burger and continued speaking with a full mouth. "Would've been great if my school did the same thing, but they didn't, so everyone knows."

"Geez," Sam murmured. "I'm sorry. I can't imagine, especially at your age. How old are you?"

"Almost fourteen. And I see what you're doing here, so let's get back on task." Finishing off her burger, Grace straightened in her seat. "Is your friend somehow connected to that killing?"

Sam glanced at me, then at Bentley, as if trying to gauge whether he should answer this. I wasn't sure if it was because he was looking for a way out or if it just wasn't a story appropriate for children. Grace had seen plenty, so I doubted this would make any massive impact on her psyche. Not knowing what he'd done, however, and eating dinner with a man who was just released from prison? Yeah, I could see that being hard for her.

Bentley must've felt the same way because he didn't say anything. Likely because he wanted to know as well.

"Yeah. It is connected," Sam said. "I knew him. The man I killed. I sort of worked for him and his family. When it all went down, when I went to jail, there was a lot of information they didn't want getting out to the world. So they helped me out. Got me a good lawyer. Made sure I had money on my books. And then, this. A final farewell. The cabin."

"They bribed you," Grace said. "So you wouldn't snitch on them, they bribed you."

Pressing his lips together, Sam shook his head. "You could call it that. But there's a lot more to it."

Now, it was all making sense. He refused to tell me what happened that night, not because he was ashamed, not because he wanted me to think he was a totally reformed ex-con on the right track all of a sudden, but because he couldn't.

Someone had paid his lawyer fees, given him a home, taken care of him in prison, so that he would keep his mouth shut. Maybe what had happened that night was something he would take to the grave. Maybe, while he wanted a relationship with me, he feared I was too much like my mother. That I would betray him, and he would end up chopped into a million little pieces and dissolved in acid.

That's what I had to imagine, at least. For someone to go to such lengths to keep him quiet, he'd been involved in something deep. Something powerful. Hence why he'd killed the mayor.

I had already assumed it was messy. Now, I knew for certain.

Maybe it was drugs. Illegal gun trade. Hell, maybe it was human trafficking. I didn't know. But I had a feeling that while Sam wouldn't admit it, the world was a better place without Benjamin Russel in it.

Did that change my opinion of him? Did that make me feel as though he was an evil person I didn't want in my life? No. Not one bit. I knew what it was like to get in over your head. I knew that if I ever opened my mouth about Jackson, Simeon would kill me.

No one liked secrets to be kept from them. Myself included. But sometimes, it was better for everyone this way. At least, for now. Maybe, eventually, I would press for more information.

Today, however, I wanted to make up for lost time. I wanted to believe he was a half decent man. Killer or not, he was my father. The only family I had left. I had to believe that he was the one I took after. That my line of morality, the blurry gray between black and white, didn't come from my violent, horrible mother, but from the man who'd come back that night to take me with him; the man who'd tried to pull me out of school so he could get me away from my abuser —from his abuser—the man who'd done something just as messy, just as gray, to pay for lawyers, get an apartment, and take care of his daughter. Even if he'd failed, a feeling I knew all too well, he had tried to be the father I needed. He couldn't be then, but maybe he could be now.

I just had to know if I was right. If the man he killed deserved to die.

"How so?" Grace asked. "What's more complicated about it?"

Scratching his head, the color drained from Sam's face. "Uh, you know, I'm not sure right now is a good time to get into it." He glanced from me to Bentley. Like some type of secret message. *She's a kid, I don't think that this is a conversation for her.* I agreed. But I wasn't Grace's mother, and it wasn't my place to discipline her. "Maybe another time?"

"In other words," Bentley said, "Stop harassing him, Grace."

"I'm not harassing anyone," she said. "He killed someone. I want to know why. I feel like that's something I deserve to know about the person I'm sitting across from at dinner. Don't you? You don't want to know why he did it?"

"I think that it's a sensitive topic and really not our business." Bentley's tone sharpened. "He's not forcing you to air out your dirty laundry—"

"*My dirty laundry?*" Grace snorted. "I was kidnapped. That's not exactly dirty laundry, Dad. What I did, I did to defend myself. Forgive me for wanting to know if he was doing the same thing."

"That's valid, but—"

"No *but.*" Grace's face screwed up in a combination of annoyance and fury. "There's no *but* about it. I have the right to know—"

They kept on arguing, and I kept my gaze on Sam. He opened his mouth a few times, as if to interject, to hose off the flames his fire had started, but no words came out. I didn't blame him. I wouldn't interrupt a disagreement between a father and his daughter either.

But the fight was over him. Which explained the gradual greenish look to his skin. The bottle of pop before his plate, clutched between his fingertips, began to tremble.

Damn, this was tough. It was never comforting when Bentley disciplined Grace in front of me, an occurrence that had gotten more frequent since everything had happened. Usually, I minded my business. Usually, however, I wasn't the source of the argument.

I wanted to help them both, but I didn't know how to help either of them.

"I'm sorry," Sam said, voice cracking as his eyes met mine. Grace and Bentley were still going back and forth. "Is there a restroom somewhere?"

"Yeah, right around that bend." I pointed down the hall off the living room. "First door on the left. You can't miss it."

He tried to muster a smile, but one didn't come. He only muttered a, "Thanks," and an, "I'm sorry," as he grabbed his bag and all but sprinted in that direction.

Only then, when he was out of sight, did the bickering stop. Shaking his head at her, Bentley traced his tongue along his teeth. Grace rolled her eyes and picked at the hot dog on her plate.

"I'm sorry," I said. "Maybe I shouldn't have suggested this."

"You didn't suggest anything," Grace said, looking at me and refusing to cast her gaze at her father across the table. "Dad did. And I don't mind that he's here, but—"

"You could have fooled me," Bentley said.

"Why do you care?" Grace said. "Why are you so concerned about his feelings? Because you're trying to impress Maddie? I don't think the way to her heart is through the father who abandoned her—"

"I care because he is another human being." Firming his voice again, Bentley held up his pointer finger, motioning for her to let him finish speaking. He wasn't being overly strict, nor mean and aggressive, but firm. Soft-spoken, but confident in the words used. "If you're uncomfortable with him being here, we can tell him to leave. I will respect that, Grace. But if that's not the issue. If it's just about you prying to get information because you feel you're entitled to it, that's a problem. Talking to people the way that you were just talking to him is not okay."

"I was just asking questions." Brows furrowed, she leaned toward him. "I want to know who he is. I want to know what he's done. And I don't think that makes me a bad guy."

"I'm not saying you're in the wrong for wanting information." Bentley didn't match her aggressive tone. He stayed steady, as usual. "But you and I both know the way you asked those questions was inappropriate. Even when you've been overbearing about wanting information out of Maddie, you would still back down when she got uncomfortable. You saw how uncomfortable that man was, and you kept pressing. There's no reason for—"

"Of course. I'm the problem. Right? I'm always the problem. It can never be anybody else, it's always me."

"Don't twist my words. I love you, and I'm trying to raise you to be a good person with compassion and care for other people's feelings."

"Oh, so I'm just a sociopath now? Is that it?"

Bentley grumbled some curse words, and I politely escorted myself from the table in silence.

I'd missed Grace this week. Bentley had too, undoubtedly. But I hadn't missed this. I almost forgot about these almost nonstop arguments over any and every small thing.

Fourteen-year-olds weren't known for their patience or tactfulness. Grace was no different in that regard, but the trauma had made it a thousand times worse. No matter how good a dad Bentley tried to be, this wasn't something that could be repaired overnight. With all the hormones of adolescence combined with the literal nightmare she had survived, there was a long road ahead.

I didn't know where I stood on it. Was I supposed to scoot off to the side so they could pass, like I just had when I stepped away from the table? Or was I supposed to use my body as a speed bump to slow the chaos down?

While I wasn't sure which road was mine in that relationship, I knew Sam was my intersection to cross. So that was where I went. The hall beside the bathroom.

Leaning against the wall, I exhaled deeply. So messy. Everything about my life had gotten so messy. Things were simple, easy, before the

Country Killer came back. Ever since, everything was a damn shit show.

How could I clean it up? How could I fix all the messes that surrounded me? Those two questions summed up my life perfectly. When a problem arose, I liked to tackle it head on. But there were too many boundaries here. Between Grace, Bentley, Sam, Teresa, and the $500,000 heading into my bank account, I didn't know where to begin.

The bathroom door creaked open. Sam jolted, hand flying over his heart. He looked better now. Less pale, eyes less sunken, relaxed. Laughing, he dried his hands on the thighs of his dirty jeans. "Didn't realize you were right there."

"Sorry." Forcing a smile, I hooked a thumb toward the racket in the dining area. "And sorry about that. She's a sweet kid. She's just been through a lot, and she's a little paranoid."

"Don't apologize." His smile may have been sad, but it was more genuine than mine. "I don't blame her. I'd be asking questions too if I were her. It's just—It's complicated."

"Everything is."

He pressed his lips together and gave a nod.

I responded with the same mannerism. Because what more was there to say? Sure, I could grill him like Grace had, but what was the point? He wasn't going to give. If he did, I was sure we would both regret it.

What if he'd killed people for that man? What if that had been his job? What if he'd trafficked drugs for him, or guns, or people? I should have wanted to know, but maybe I didn't. Maybe it was best to live without knowing everyone's dirty secrets. I sure as shit didn't want him to know mine.

Clearing my throat, I gestured to the bathroom. "I did need to use that."

"Oh. Right." Sam scooted out of the way for me to pass. "Sorry."

Just when I had crossed the threshold into the bathroom and Sam was walking out of the hallway, an indistinguishable yell, which I had to assume came from Grace—although, I wouldn't be surprised if it was

Bentley letting out a girlish shriek in response to his teenager's antics—sounded from the dining room.

Stopping, Sam turned my way and pressed his lips together. "Maybe I should stay put for now."

I chuckled. "Maybe."

Once inside, as I did what I needed to do, a droplet of red caught my eye from the trash can. I knew my cycle, which had synched with Grace's, and she hadn't come in this bathroom since she had been home. The only person who'd been in here was Sam.

Call me paranoid, but I needed to know why there was blood in the trash can. Sam was an IV heroin user at one point, even if he was clean now. There were a host of infections I could contract from him if I wasn't careful. So, careful as I could be, still sitting on the toilet, I used an additional piece of toilet paper as a makeshift glove and reached into the bin. An invasion of privacy, maybe. But maybe Grace wasn't wrong to be paranoid.

Carefully, I lifted the tissue. As I did, an orange cap clicked to the tile floor. And my heart sank.

An orange syringe cap.

Chapter 22

Trying to stay as quiet as possible, I shut the bathroom door behind me. "Let's go," I said.

Sam gestured to the living room we'd come from. "Back in there? Because it sounds like they're sorta going at it. I don't want to intrude. I don't mind waiting here if you want to go back and handle it."

I nodded to the back door. "Out there."

"Oh. Right. Probably best to let them do their thing."

He started that way, and I said, "You got your things?"

He gestured to his backpack over his shoulder. "Yeah, why?"

Because you won't be coming back.

I didn't say that aloud, of course. We didn't need two father daughter battles sounding from different parts of the house. Instead, I kept walking. Straight past Sam, right out the door.

It was a beautiful evening. The sound of children's laughter floated from somewhere in the distance. That pretty blue sky was turning orange and pink as the sun set behind Sam's head. Scents of fresh cut grass and burgers and hot dogs filled the air.

So pretty, so pleasant, and I was about to ruin it.

"I can't do this. I thought I could, but I can't. I can't have you in my life. I wish I could. I want to. I want a relationship with you, but I can't

184

have one, can I?" When I started, I didn't know how to stop. "Because some people don't change. You tried to convince me that you have, and you almost had me fooled, but I can't. I *won't*. I won't be lied to by the people I care about. I won't ruin my life and the lives of the people I care about the most just because I want a relationship with my daddy."

All that fell out in one breath. A chaotic, rambling tangent. I didn't want to be mean, I didn't want to hurt him, and I certainly didn't want to demonize him for being an addict. But I was one too. After so much time in law enforcement, if there was one thing I'd learned with absolute certainty, it was that addicts couldn't be friends with other addicts. In a family of addicts, if one of them chose to continue abusing or using, the one who needed to stay sober, who *wanted* to stay sober badly enough, had to cut the rest of them off. They had to go no contact, because if they didn't, they would fall right back into the life that had brought them to jail or rehab.

Those were the statistics, and I refused to be one of them. I was clean, and I wanted to stay that way.

As Sam had been with everything since we met again, he was calm. There was hurt in his eyes, so much hurt, but not anger. He wasn't trying to guilt me into changing my opinion.

It just sucked. Sucked for both of us.

"I understand," Sam said. "I'm sorry."

And for whatever reason, that lit a fire in me. Hurt, that was what I felt a moment prior. Now, my chest was burning. Flames caught there and all but burst out of my orifices.

No rambling tangent in response? No profession of his regret? No heartbreaking plea for me to understand that it was one time? No, I *only relapsed a few days ago. I'll get my shit together. I swear I will, kid. I wanna be in your life, and if I have to stay sober for that, I will. I swear I will. Just give me a chance.*

I knew that'd be bullshit. Nobody got clean for another person. But I wanted to hear that. I wanted to hear that I mattered enough. That he would at least try.

But he wouldn't. He just confirmed as much.

"That's it?" I asked. "You're not gonna beg me to understand?"

With tears welling in his eyes, he opened his mouth. But nothing came out. He only looked at me with those teary eyes.

All but stomping my feet against the damp grass, I shook my head. "Fine. Fine, I'll beg. This will be the only time. Because I want you here. I want a father. I want a god damn family, Sam. I never had one, and maybe that wasn't your fault then, but it is now. Because you can choose to get your shit together and be here for me, but you're choosing to walk away.

"After everything you said, all the promises, you won't even stay clean for me. I wouldn't even care that you were using, but I can't have my sobriety ruined because of you, so can't you at least lie? At least pretend that having me in your life matters more than the drugs? Gotta give her credit there, because at least Mom pretended she loved me. At least she was here, damn it. She was horrible, but she was here, and you weren't. Not when I needed you. And I don't need you anymore, but I want you. I want a relationship with you. I want a god damned father, Sam, but not if—"

"What?" Blinking hard, Sam cocked his head to the side. Throughout my rant, he'd kept his head down, shoulders hunched, doing his best to keep it together, to stay humble. The confusion only started in those last few sentences. "Maddie, I'm sober."

"Bullshit. I found the needle cap. I saw the blood. You have a lot of balls to do that in my boyfriend's house, by the way. After meeting his daughter for the first time, too. The audacity to—"

"I didn't get high in that bathroom." Confusion dissipating, he held his shoulders just a little higher. Not cocky, but less ashamed. "You're not crazy. I'm not trying to make you think you are. Because I would be thinking the same thing if I were in your position. But look." Pulling his backpack off his shoulder, he unzipped it, fished around inside, and held up a small glass bottle. His finger disguised the label until he passed it to me. "This is what the needle was for. And I probably shouldn't have left the pen cap in the bathroom. I just didn't think about it."

Passing me his bag, I read the label and a feeling of overwhelming stupidity washed over me. Insulin.

"Look through it. There are no drugs in here. Outside of my anti-depressants but they're not a controlled substance. I swear, Maddie, I'm not using. I don't ever want to again. I'm trying really hard not to." The tears in his eyes flooded over. "I want to be that, kid. I want to be your dad. I know I haven't gotten to be, but I really want to be. I thought you were upset about what went down in there, and if that's the case now, I understand. Really, I do. I get it completely." Another hard swallow. "I'm a killer. That's more than a justified reason to not want me in your life. But if it's about drugs, I'm clean. And I'll never bring them around. I'll never bring that life to you. But I... I'm sorry you found it anyway."

What a way to announce to my father that I was an addict.

How stupid I felt. I did this so often. Although my trust issues surely came from this man, my mouth would be the death of me. "I'm sorry. I shouldn't have jumped to conclusions. I just—"

"Don't apologize," Sam said. "It's gonna take time for you to trust me. For you to let me in. As it should. You were a kid, and what I put you through when I left, everything your mom put you through, you have every reason not to have faith in me. And keep doing that. It'll hold me accountable. But if you wanna test me, every few days, or once a week, or just when I walk in the house, you can. I won't be offended. I wanna make things as right as I can."

"I want that too." And I did. Sam had done virtually no wrong since we'd met again. But I did like the idea of testing him every few days. At least until I could find some trust for him. "Maybe that'll work."

Sam's smile got a little bit bigger. "So, we're okay?

Maybe. "I need you to answer that question."

"Which one?" Sam asked.

"If he deserved it."

Expression softening, shoulders sinking again, he stayed silent. I sat with it. This conversation wasn't over 'til he answered that question.

It must've been a solid minute before he finally said, "I wish I could tell you everything, kid, but I just *can't*. I'm not proud of the things I've done, but it's—"

"That's not what I asked. I don't need to know the whole story. I just want to know the son of a bitch deserved it, Sam. There's gotta be a reason you got manslaughter instead of murder, and I need to know if it's as deep as it looks."

A deep breath, followed by shutting his eyes and turning away.

"I'm no stranger to doing bad things out of necessity." My voice was as soft as the summer breeze. "I exist on a morally gray line. I just need to know if that's the case here, too."

Meeting my gaze again, his shoulders still drooping, Sam did his best to remain calm as I caught a slight clench of his jaw. "The bastard deserved it."

For now? That was all I needed to know.

* * *

THE REST OF DINNER WENT WELL. SHOCKINGLY WELL, IN FACT. There was some tension between Bentley and Grace, but Grace seemed to have made her amends with Sam. Or maybe she just realized that Bentley was right. Of course, she would never admit that. Not verbally. Teenagers defied their fathers for sport.

Regardless, as we were cleaning up dinner, Grace asked if Sam would like to help her cook dessert. And so, they did. Sam, with a bit more excitement than you would typically expect from a middle-aged man who was asked to bake cookies with a thirteen-year-old.

Once we were finished eating, it was after nine. Sam said he had to get ready for work in the morning. Grace said she "smelled like bus" and needed a shower. I smelled like outside, and definitely needed one as well. So, I ran to my house to shower. While I was at it, I cleaned up Tempest's paws. The hike had done a number on them. Most of our walks were on pavement, at least lately, and she needed a full bath in the tub. I was just finishing her up when Bentley knocked on the door. Apparently, I had left my jacket in his car.

In typical Bentley fashion, he had to rush to return it to me. But, as he stepped inside and petted Tempest and asked, "So what did you and Sam talk about outside?" I realized his intentions weren't all virtuous. They were nosy.

But I pried into people's lives for a living, so who was I to judge? I sat him down on the couch and explained. Finishing up with, "I need to stop jumping to conclusions. But it was kinda valid, right?"

"Dude killed a guy. Totally valid." Pausing, Bentley nibbled his lower lip. "That is something that you needed to know, though."

"That 'the bastard deserved it?'"

"No, the diabetes. Everybody should know what their parents' medical history is like. You should probably take steps now to avoid developing it. Maybe. What type was it? One or two?"

Typical question for a man in medicine. "I have no idea."

"Either way. That's the sort of thing that you should consider in life. Or, I guess, something that *I* should consider. I'm the one who cooks for you. I can start cooking more vegetables. Meats. Cheeses. Less carbs. We do eat a lot of carbs around here, don't we? They're just easier. Pastas, breads, cookies, and..."

Smiling, I shook my head at him.

He returned it. "What's that smile for?"

"I just love you."

"I love you too."

Just as he leaned in for a kiss, my front door swung open. No knock. Tempy only perked her head up from the floor at my feet, knowing who it was already. There were two people who walked into my house without knocking, and one of them was sitting beside me already.

"Oh." Grace rolled her eyes at the almost kiss she interrupted. Crossing her arms, she shot Bentley a look. "Sorry."

"Don't apologize," I said. "What's up, kid?"

Another glare at her father. "Can I talk to Maddie? Alone?"

Bentley's jaw tightened. "Yeah, probably best I get to bed anyway. Just make sure she gets home for me, alright?"

Grace rolled her eyes at that, despite me agreeing. As if to say, *Oh, I can't even walk a few dozen feet on my own? I'm that incompetent?*

Once Bentley pecked my cheek, gave Tempy a scratch behind the ears, and shut the door behind him, the air thinned out.

Grace's eyes were softer when she sat on the couch beside me, holding out a small yellow Post-it note. "Daisy's login. This is the app she used to write her stories. I just checked, and it did open to her account. So if you download it on your phone, and you log in, you have access to all her stories. She probably put some notes in there about everyday life and things like that too."

"Wow. Thanks."

Grace gave a short nod, eyes falling to the floor.

I bumped my elbow into hers. "Are you okay?"

"I am." She hooked a thumb toward the door. "I don't know about us."

"I think you're finally going through the, *I hate my dad*, phase."

"I don't." She frowned. "I hate the way he treats me. Like I'm stupid. Like I'm a kid. But I don't hate him." She paused again, then exhaled deeply. "I'm sorry. About the way I talked to your dad. I know I was being a little pushy, but you wanted to know. And I could tell you wanted to know, and so did I, but it's better that the annoying teenager drills him than the estranged daughter. Because if you're mean to him, that might end your relationship, but if it's me, what does it matter? And did it help? Did you learn anything?"

So that was why she'd acted like that. Not because she hated Sam. Not because she was afraid of him. Not because she was nervous about having a convict in her house. Because she knew I wanted to know more about him. "You didn't need to do that for me, Grace."

"Did it help?" she repeated.

"That's not the point—"

"That is the point." Grace's gaze hardened. "You help me whenever you can, and I'll do the same when I can. I don't think there's anything wrong with that. But I am sorry if I was mean. I didn't mean to hurt his feelings. I just wanted you to get the information you need. So, did you?"

Frowning, I tucked an arm around her shoulders. "I got what I needed. But I don't want you to do something like that again. Don't fight with your dad on my behalf, either. He's trying really hard to be the dad you need, and I'm sorry if you feel like he's failing in some ways, but he's doing everything he can."

A risky thing to say, a thing I questioned the moment it fell from my lips. Yet, she only cozied her head closer to mine. Didn't snap that he was failing, didn't rampage that he was awful. Only sighed, followed by murmuring, "I know."

Chapter 23

After some puppy cuddles, Grace headed home. I checked out the window to make sure she walked inside and texted Bentley to let him know. He thanked me, said he'd see me tomorrow, and to sleep well. Considering the last twenty-four hours, and the fact that I had been awake for a large part of them, sleeping would have been the most responsible thing to do. I did not, however. The top of my priority list? Getting to know Daisy Miller.

That wasn't to say reading through her stories was an easy task. Not because they were poorly written, but because they were poorly *organized*. Most of them were listed as *Document 1, Document 6.7, Document 42, Document 0.53.* Altogether, there were over five hundred documents. With no idea where to start, I just dove in to the first on the list.

The first story I happened upon was a horror. It was well-written and had my skin crawling. Although I wasn't much of a reader, it trapped me in the first few pages. It started like any typical horror story. A group of teenagers in the woods in the middle of the night. Had to laugh at the irony. But it followed the perspective of a sixteen-year-old girl who watched as each of her friends were killed by some mysterious creature. It lurked in the shadows, and she never saw its face. Had to wonder if that had something to do with the "shadow people" that meth users frequently saw in their hallucinations.

I didn't get to the end of it, though. Halfway through, the shadows on my walls were starting to freak me out.

The next story was a thriller. Or maybe a mystery. I could never tell with those sorts of things. The genres teetered too close to each other.

Again, we were in the point of view of a teenage girl. Guessed that whole "write what you know" philosophy was Daisy's cup of tea. This time, a friend of the main character had gone missing. They were just regular high school students. Probably the type of person Daisy wished she had been. Someone who wasn't burdened by addiction and foster families.

I knew that all too well. The essence of the story was an interesting plot that had popped into Daisy's head, paired with a fantasy she daydreamed about daily. When I was a kid, I would daydream about that too. Not solving the disappearance of my best friend but being a normal kid like the ones I saw on television.

Regardless, it started getting creepy about midway through, and I exited that file and moved onto the next. And boy oh boy, I had a blast. A paranormal romance titled *Moonlit Whispers*. It was dual point of view, in the perspectives of a young woman, twenty-four-year-old Selene, and Damian, a four-hundred-year-old vampire. Apparently, they were fated mates. As cheesy as it sounded, and as much as many would mock it, it was my favorite of the stories I'd read so far. They were all good, because the writing was good, but reading the inner struggles of the young woman and the old man in a young, hot man's body was beyond entertaining.

I read the entire novel in a night. It was only about forty thousand words, so I couldn't call myself a speed reader. But damn it, the thing ended on a cliffhanger. The last chapter was a fight scene with another super old vampire. The love interest was bleeding out, having sacrificed himself for the main character.

Where the hell was the next one? She couldn't just leave me hanging like that.

Spending the next half hour digging through Daisy's files, searching for it, or even an outline for it, I found diddly squat. Not so much as notes mentioning the main characters' names.

Frustrated and panting as I dropped my phone to the couch, half-tempted to hunt the author down on social media to offer up a kidney for at least an outline of the next chapter, I stopped at the obvious realization.

There might never be a sequel. The chances of Daisy still being alive were slim to none. I wish that weren't so. I wanted to stay blissfully ignorant and hope that all this investigating would lead to more than a body, but the fact was, Selene and Damian's story may never get finished.

And, on that sad note, I sighed deeply. A glance at the clock told me it was 6 AM. I had stayed up all night reading a vampire novel without getting an ounce of work done. Didn't regret a bit of it, but the fact remained.

Sleep wasn't a bad idea, but that ending had my heart racing. If I couldn't find out what happened next, maybe I could find out what happened to Liz.

So, that was where I went. I opened my laptop and began revisiting the information on hand. There wasn't much. But I kept coming back to that kid. Andy McAvoy.

There was something odd about him. Something just didn't make sense there. So I went back to the footage his father had sent Harper and me.

It all looked normal at first. Andy entered his home beside the car wash the family owned at 8:30 PM the night Liz disappeared, so he couldn't have been present in the woods an hour away. He didn't leave again until 7:12 the next morning with his father.

But I kept spinning the clip back and watching it again anyway. I couldn't say what didn't feel right, but maybe a few more time lapses of that night would do the trick. By the twentieth or so, I was ready to crack it up to paranoia.

Then, at 7:10 AM, something caught my eye in the corner of the image.

It was almost impossible to make out. I was amazed I caught it. But at that car wash next door, a red car pulled into the lot. Two minutes later, Andy and Andy Senior stepped outside.

And where'd they go? I couldn't be certain from the angle of the camera, but their driveway was on the right of the porch. They walked to the left, toward the carwash. Toward that red car.

Who in my research had I stumbled upon that drove a red car? Darren. The twenty-something-year-old guy who received a naked photo of Liz only days before her death.

Was I missing a thread here?

Hurriedly, I clicked back over to Liz's social media. After finding Darren's profile, I flipped over to his friend's list. Sure enough, he was friends on Facebook with both Andy and his father. Were they all related?

Couldn't say I was surprised when I clicked into Darren's tagged photos and found a big family picture. There were more than a dozen people in it, most of whom I didn't take much note of, but there they were. Andy McAvoy Senior with an arm around Darren before a Christmas tree.

They were family.

Was this the missing piece? Was this why Andy junior had run? Had he seen something in Darren's car that night? Liz's body, perhaps?

* * *

"Detective Ashley Harper," she answered on the fourth ring.

"Oh. Hey." I'd expected to get her voicemail, so her voice jarred me. So much so that I had to straighten and wipe the Cheeto dust off my shirt from my reading binge. As though she could see me huddled on the couch with orange fingertips, covered in dog hair, and bundled in throw blankets. "It's Maddie. I'm calling from my landline. Did I wake you?"

"No, haven't really slept." She stifled a yawn. "What's up? You find something?"

"Maybe, yeah." I clicked between the Facebook page and the video footage from the car wash. "Do you have Darren Murphy anywhere in your records? Has he come up in the investigation?"

"Vaguely. One of Liz's coworkers at the ice cream shop, right?"

"Right." Zooming in on the image of his car in the parking lot, I squinted into the windows. "You know if he has a record?"

"I haven't run it yet. There're only, like, ten million people I need to cross-reference here. Why? What do you got?"

"Not much. But he's Andy McAvoy's cousin."

"Where you going with this, Mads?"

"The carwash Andy works at. Darren was there that morning. His car was, at least. Can't make out the driver that well. But I'm wondering if there's a connection. Maybe Andy saw something, and that's why he ran? Maybe it had nothing to do with the drugs."

"Hmm," Harper murmured. "That would check out. Want to go interview him?"

"Thought you'd never ask."

Chapter 24

Quick Quarters Laundromat. A small, red brick building on the edge of town, roughly fifteen minutes from the carwash, with second story apartment. It was nothing special. One of the windows was busted, covered in plastic to keep the weather at bay. Little window boxes lined each of the four panes of glass on the second floor. The garbage on the second story walkup was overflowing, but the sidewalk was well-kept.

If I had to guess? Darren's chore was taking out the garbage, and he couldn't even do that for the mother of his child. Or rather, for himself and his child. Even from here, just stepping out of the car, I heard the baby crying from inside.

"Bet he's a real winner," Harper said, gesturing to his Dodge Charger in the parking lot. "Keeps that thing sparkling but can't even take the garbage out."

"Wonder how long she's been awake with him." Walking ahead, the baby's cries only got louder. "Screw that, man."

"Kids?" Harper asked. "Same."

"No." Laughing, I climbed the first stair with Harper at my tail. "Screw having kids with someone who considers working at an ice cream shop and selling weed a career yet won't even help around the house."

"Oh," Harper muttered. "I say screw them altogether."

Again, I laughed.

"You don't?"

"I don't what?"

"Say 'screw 'em?'" she asked, waiting for me to limp up the next few stairs. "You want kids now?"

"I don't know." I did know. Especially considering how much I loved spending time with Grace. "Maybe. But not if I end up with anyone like this little shit."

"Eh." Harper knocked on the door a few times. "Most of the time, moms end up doing all the work. It's screwed up, but that's how it goes. And then they wonder why women today don't want to have kids. We're making the money and still expected to do everything at home."

A fair argument. One I had thought about frequently, especially when I had been with Ox. But now that I was with Bentley? Now that I was trying to form a relationship with my dad? There were too many men like Harper described, but I was lucky to have found a few who weren't.

Judging by the mess Angela was when she answered the door, she had not been so lucky with Darren. Angela couldn't have been older than twenty-five judging by the fullness of her cheeks and lack of wrinkles on her skin. But stress was taking its toll. Her hair hadn't been washed in days, from what I could tell. Deep circles of purple lined her pale blue eyes. A splotch of dried-on white gunk, which I had to assume was baby barf, decorated the shoulder of her old band t-shirt all the way to the middle of her chest.

On her hip sat a sobbing infant, the same one she had complained about on Facebook. He didn't look like he was doing much better than his mom. His pale skin was blotchy from tears, chafing around his nose and eyes from the excessive liquid. He was well-fed, nice and plump, and his clothes were cleaner than his mom's, so I didn't suspect neglect.

Not on her behalf, at least. As for Darren? Definitely a neglectful father and partner.

But did I have enough to believe he was a murderer?

"I'm sorry, can I help you?" Angela said, voice coming out more of a snap. "A little busy here."

"We're sorry to bother you so early," Harper said. "I'm Detective Ashley Harper. Is Darren home? We were hoping to have a word with him."

Slowly, Angela's already pale face got whiter than snow. "What about?"

"Just a few questions," I said.

"I make sure he goes to all of his drug and alcohol classes." Voice taking a certain tone, she re-situated the fussy baby on her hip. "And he's always pissed clean for his P.O. So what'd he do this time?"

"It's not about past charges," Harper said. I was glad she had. Because now that I wasn't a cop, I treaded carefully when invited into an investigation that wasn't mine to begin with. "We were just hoping to chat with him. Is he here?"

"He's not. Do you want me to tell him to call you?"

"His car's out front." I nodded in that direction. "Really, it'll only take a few minutes."

"H-he left the car with me." She glanced inside, then re-situated the baby again. Otherwise informing me that her frustration was with the guy who was probably comfy on the couch while she had to deal with us. "He stayed at a friend's last night."

"I'm sorry to hear that," Harper said. "Are you two doing alright with the new baby and everything?"

"Assuming this little guy is his son," I said, reaching out my fingers for him. His crying had subsided a bit as we spoke, and he extended his chubby hand my way. Angela didn't pull him back, but her brows slowly furrowed. "Darren's come up in an investigation of ours. We just want to make sure everyone's safe."

A sickly green color floated to the surface of her skin. She swallowed hard, then she shook her head.

It was a small thing, especially considering the words that came out of her mouth next. That slight shake of her head told me more than she realized. No, everyone was not safe. But she didn't know how to say so. Or maybe, she was afraid to say so.

"We're fine. Just a little stressed. This one's teething, and Darren can't handle it. He got out of the house for a while to get his head on straight. Do you have a card? I'll have him call you."

After reaching into her coat pocket, Harper extended a business card. "Call anytime. Day or night. Either of you. If there's anything you need us to know, or even if you just need help. Hell, are you hungry? Could we treat you to breakfast?"

"He's got an appointment with his doctor in an hour." Angela gestured to the baby. "Thanks though."

As she reached out to tug the door shut, my eyes caught on her wrist. Specifically, the black and blue bruise that wrapped around the inside. As though someone with a much larger hand had grabbed her and squeezed with a lot of force.

Catching the door with my palm, I held it open. "One more thing. Was Darren home three nights ago?"

"I-I don't know off the top of my head. He's out with his friends a lot. I don't keep a roster of them all. But again. I'll have him call you."

"Thanks," I said. "We appreciate it."

Angela didn't give so much as a smile as she snapped the door shut in our faces.

Harper shut her eyes and eased out a deep breath.

Descending the stairs, I glanced her way. "Did you see the wrist?"

She let out another calming breath and said, "Wonder how many more bruises we can't see."

"Too many, I'm sure."

* * *

HARPER CHECKED HER WATCH AS SHE EXHALED A PUFF OF SMOKE from her cigarette. We were outside the Medical Examiner's Office now, waiting for Alex to come in and do the autopsy on Liz Turner. It was just after 8, and Alex's shift didn't start until 9, but I had called her on my way here. She said she'd be in by 8:30 to help us get this case moving.

"Did you get any information from his probation officer?" I asked Harper. Common practice in law enforcement. If somebody was suspected of a crime, and they were already on the record somewhere—especially if they were on probation or parole—we tried to get any information we could from one another.

"Yeah, I just got off the phone with her." Flicking some ashes to the pavement, Harper did her best to waft the smoke away from me. Never had been a fan of the smell. The sun shone high in the sky, however, wind too strong for any of it to get close. "She said she would come back to the house and make Angela let us inside."

"Not gonna do us much good if he ran. And he probably did if he knew what we were there for."

"Hence why he didn't come to the door. I'm sure they know there are two blonde girls asking around about Liz's disappearance," Harper said. "She's going to get me a list of names though. People he might be staying with. After this autopsy, I'm going to call Andy McAvoy down to the station, too. And his dad. I have the feeling they both knew about this. Not just the kid."

"That's what I'm thinking too," I said.

"But what if it wasn't him? We should look into Angela. Depending on what we find with the cause of death, she could've been the one to do it."

"Maybe." Biting my lip, I shook my head. "But I don't think so. I don't think Andy junior and senior would've covered for Darren's baby mama. For Darren, yeah, but not for her."

"True. But we might be able to pressure Angela to give us more information if we point out that she had motive and means. Worst case, we're looking at this all wrong, and it was neither of them. A lot of this case has been grasping at straws."

God, I hoped one of the straws had the answer. "True. It could all be a coincidence."

"Very seldom do I believe in coincidences. That's not how things go in this line of work."

"Also true," I murmured. Most of the time, if it looked like a duck and quacked like a duck, it was a duck. But sometimes it looked like a duck and quacked like a duck, but it was actually a goose. I didn't want to put the wrong guy away for this, especially since we hadn't talked to him yet. "I need to meet him. See if he's got the killer vibe."

Chuckling, Harper exhaled another puff of smoke. "You and your vibes."

"When has my vibe been wrong?"

"True. We both would've died that day if not for your vibes."

"See? You got to trust my vibes." I smirked. "But, uh. Which day?"

"Well, aren't you humble."

"Never claimed to be."

"The shooting. We would've died that day if not for your vibes."

Ah, the shooting. The only officer shooting I'd ever been involved in, and the first time I had killed someone.

I wasn't proud of it. Any cop who was proud of killing a civilian wasn't a good one. But I'd done what I had to that day.

I had only been a cop for six months or so. Harper and I were working together, I was still in the flirting phase with Ox, and I hadn't gotten my K-9 training certification yet. I had, however, a keen sense for crime. Harper hadn't. She'd gone to school for criminal justice, the whole nine yards of college and a degree, preceded by a nice little life in the suburbs.

We'd been patrolling together, pulled somebody over for failing to come to a complete stop at a red light. Harper approached the vehicle, and I stayed a few feet behind. I could tell she'd been about to let him off with a warning. He seemed like a nice guy at first glance. Attractive, around our age, if not a bit older. White. Well-dressed in nice button up and slacks. But driving an old, beat-up clunker.

I'd pulled her aside and said something fishy was going on. Harper hadn't agreed but ran his registration to ease my mind. But it hadn't been registered to his name. I'd told her to call for backup. Again, she hadn't agreed and began trekking back to the car. I'd stayed right behind. When she asked him whose car it was, why he was driving it, he hesitated. Then, he'd reached. I hadn't fired until I saw the gun. And it had, in fact, been a gun.

We learned later that the car was stolen. There'd been two bricks of heroin in the trunk. Why anyone carrying two bricks of heroin would steal a car was beyond me, but the fact remained. I'd killed that guy. Now, I had a lot of regret over that. But he'd planned to shoot us and drive off. I really hadn't had another choice. To this day, I couldn't put my finger on exactly what put me off about him, either.

"My vibes are never wrong," I said.

"Haven't been yet," she said.

It was quiet for a few heartbeats, and I thought about that. My *vibes*. I didn't remember the first time that I used that phrase. I remembered the first time Ox heard me say it, though. "There's no such thing as a *vibe*," he'd said. "We can't arrest somebody because they give you a *vibe*, Maddie. And we certainly can't convict them because of a *vibe*."

The memory made me smile. Talking about him with anyone else was all but impossible. Even though it was strange, even though it didn't make much sense, if there was anyone I wanted to talk to about Ox, it was Harper.

"Ox hated my vibes," I said.

"If there wasn't evidence, if it couldn't be proven, Ox didn't believe it."

"Worse than that, he said it was stupid." I chuckled. "Actually, he said *I* was stupid."

"Correction. He'd say you're *being* stupid, not that *you* were stupid."

"Like that was any better. God, I miss his mean ass."

Slowly, the lighthearted nostalgia faded, replaced by solemn silence for a few ticks. "Me too."

So easy. It was so hard to talk about him with anyone else, but not with Harper. Outside of myself, she was probably the best friend he ever had. I was the sugar that mixed with Ox's spice, and Harper was somewhere in the middle. Spicy and sweet. While I could be a bitch, more often than not, I was bubbly. Fun and easy going. Harper was a bit more serious than me. Solemn and contained.

Out of everyone, I shouldn't have been the slightest bit surprised that she'd been the one he'd had an affair with. Realistically, they would've been a better couple than Ox and me. It would've burned like a son of a bitch if they'd gotten together after we'd broken up, but if they had met first, maybe we would all be living entirely different lives right now.

Maybe he would still be alive.

"How have you been with all that?" I asked. "The grieving, I mean."

"Some days are better than others." A certain sadness, or maybe awkwardness crept over her face. "Nobody else really gets it. You, you get it. But everyone else down at the station? They didn't know him. They knew he was a prick, but that's all they know. And he was."

"He really was." Chewing my bottom lip, I swallowed the knot that wadded up in my throat. "Doesn't feel real. I just keep thinking that we're not talking right now. That's why I haven't heard from him in a while."

"We weren't really talking anyway," Harper murmured. "It'd been a long time since the two of us really talked."

Cocking my head to the side, I furrowed my brows. "Really?"

"Spring of twenty-twenty one. He felt guilty. I felt guilty. I think he kept hoping you'd take him back. He knew that wouldn't happen if we were still friends, so he just sort of stopped being mine."

"You guys were still close. For, God, how long? I mean, the three of us were together almost all day, every day, for going on a decade. And then, a year before he's gone forever, you guys..."

Awkwardly pressing her lips together, she avoided my gaze.

"I'm sorry," I said. "I didn't want that. The way it all happened, that wasn't what I wanted."

"You don't need to apologize. Ever. You did nothing wrong. Literally, nothing at all. It does suck though. All because the two of us were drunk and stupid one night."

"Drugs and alcohol," I said. "Nothing else ruins as many lives."

"Maybe war. War might ruin a few more."

I laughed. So did she. And for a moment, that was all we did. Laughed, looked at one another in the early morning sun, and then got teary-eyed. That was when the laughter ceased.

"So," Harper said, "What are you gonna do with the life insurance money?"

Again, my face scrunched up. "How do you know about that? Did he leave money for you, too?"

She snorted. "No. He left some money to Candace in HR. Monroe in narcotics. A few other guys he might have cussed out over coffee once." I was the one who snorted that time. "I figured if he was leaving money to all of them, he surely left you some. If not all of it."

Swallowing hard, I nodded. "I'm probably gonna donate it. I don't need it. Lots of other people do. And it feels weird. Like guilt money. I'm sure that's what it is. And I don't want that. I'm not the only one who got hurt. We all did."

"We hurt you the worst," she said, voice and eyes full of sincere regret. "We all got hurt, but we were the ones who hurt you. It's not fair that you took the fallout for our mistake."

"Either way. I don't want the money. There are a few causes he really cared about. Inner-city kids. Drug and alcohol rehabs who could use the cash. Maybe I'll donate it to them. They could use it more than me."

Her frown only deepened. "Don't do that, Mads."

"Why not? It's better it goes to people who need it than into a savings account that will never get used—"

"Then spend it. Don't put it in a savings account. Or rather, don't put it *just* in a savings account. Move somewhere. Build that dream house you guys were always talking about."

I huffed a laugh. "That was another lifetime. That house is hardly my dream anymore. It'd also be really weird to buy myself a place we wanted together when he's dead."

"Then find a new dream. Move to the suburbs. You always loved the suburbs."

I put my finger into my mouth to signify gagging.

"You hate the suburbs now?"

It wasn't that black and white. But sort of. "There's something I like about the culture in my little trailer park. I know it sounds stupid. Who wants to live in a trailer park? But I do. I like my trailer. I like my neighbors."

"Oh, I know you like your neighbor."

"Not just that. I mean, yeah. I love Bentley. I don't want to move away from him. But it's where I grew up, you know? And little by little, I'm replacing all those bad memories with good ones. The solution isn't to run from your problems. The solution is to overwrite the bad with good. I'm building a nice life for myself where I am. I don't need to move to the suburbs. I certainly don't need a half a million-dollar home only for it to be a cookie-cutter box drawn by some architect who uses the same blueprint for all the thousand houses in a development."

"Then put it in savings. Keep it for when you inevitably get arrested for doing something you shouldn't."

"I have no idea what you're talking about. I am a perfectly upstanding citizen."

"Right. And Ox was the one who killed The Country Killer."

Silence.

I figured she'd known. Harper wasn't stupid. But she'd covered it up. Because things would've gotten complicated for me if she hadn't.

It was unlikely that I would've gotten charged with murder. I may not have gotten manslaughter either. But my gun license likely would've gotten taken away, which would be very inconvenient for my line of work. I may have served time for something, either battery or interfering with an investigation.

Although, simply because everyone knew about my connection to Simeon Gunn, the DA might have charged me with murder just hoping I would become the informant she needed to take down the largest dealer in the state.

In TV and movies, self-defense was always displayed as this 'no big deal' situation. Hollywood was a damn liar. Killing someone was a big deal. The lengths I'd needed to go to get back in the field after my shooting early in my career were exponential. Cops, private investigators, even people in their own home who killed intruders, could face serious charges. In some states like my own, death penalty was still on the table. At any given moment, all around America, there were innocent people sitting in jail because they had defended themselves.

And, after all, Eric Oakley had fled. I'd chased him. I'd shot him when I hadn't had to.

But I'd had to. By my moral compass, I had to. That bastard had to die. If I hadn't killed him that day, he would've gotten away, and he would've killed again. The fact that Ox had died in the shootout said it all. What I'd done that day was for the best, but it could have ruined my life.

And I was grateful Harper hadn't let that happen. "Thanks."

"But, in all seriousness, use that money, Maddie. Go on a vacation. Take Bentley. Grace, maybe. Go somewhere you've always wanted to see or buy something you've always wanted. And besides, I'm sure he wrote you a letter or something, right? Something he left with his attorney? That's what my mom did when she died. What did he say in it? Did he tell you to spend it to get the hell out of that trailer park? He was so worried about you getting hurt there."

"He was so worried about me anywhere that he couldn't watch me," I said. "But I don't know."

"You don't know what he said in the letter?"

"Nope."

"But he did leave you one?"

"He did."

"And you haven't read it?"

"Nope."

"Why not?"

"Because if I don't read it, he still has more to say to me." Why? Why was opening up to Harper so damn easy? "The moment I read that, I'll never talk to him again. Never hear from him again. And I want that. I want to hear from him again."

When I looked up, there were tears in Harper's eyes. "I'm so sorry, Maddie."

Swallowing, I shook my head. I shook my head until the lump in my throat thinned out. And then, I had nothing else to say.

Luckily, a pleasant voice interrupted the awkwardness. "Oh, hey!" Alex called from the other end of the parking lot. "You beat me! Look, just like the old days! All three of us together again."

I had to rescind my previous statement. Harper and I both had a combination of sweet and spicy. Alex, though? She was all sweet.

Chapter 25

After almost ten years in law enforcement, I should've been used to this. I was not.

Pinching my nose together, I tried to disguise the scent of the rotting body on the table by breathing through my mouth. Problem was, then I could almost taste the remains instead. The place also stunk of formaldehyde and bleach, which was hardly pleasant either. The stink of that shit made it feel like I'd swallowed a hot poker.

And as far as the mental toll? This was never a part of the investigation I liked partaking in. Sure, sometimes it made sense to be present at an autopsy. It was often the quickest way to discover new evidence, especially in a case like this, where there wasn't much. But this made it too real.

Liz Turner wasn't a stranger anymore. She was real now. As annoyed with her as I had been while I'd investigated her personal life, as frustrating as I'd found her entire demeanor, everything she stood for, everything she didn't, a sight like this had a way of awakening anyone's humanity.

Liz Turner was just a young girl, naked and dead on a metal table, given only a thin sheet to conceal the shred of dignity she had left. But who was I kidding? There was no humanity, no dignity, in something like this. That pretty blonde hair in the pictures was bleak and dull now. Her once cherry-red lips were blue. Her golden white skin was just as cold and colorless as the metal she lay upon.

Prior to this moment, I had wanted to find her because it was the right thing. It was my job. But now that I smelled her rotting flesh, saw that colorless, lifeless corpse, she wasn't a bitch anymore. Maybe she had been one. That was more of an objective fact than an opinion, really.

But why did that matter? She was barely more than a baby. No matter how awful she was, no matter how many bad things she did, no little girl deserved to be on this table.

"Oh, calm down," Alex said. "It's not that bad. Don't be dramatic."

"Is that how it works?" I asked. "You slice open enough bodies, and then the smell of rotting flesh just doesn't bother you anymore?"

She pointed to her nose. "Vapor rub around the nostrils."

"Ah," Harper said sarcastically. "Genius."

Wiggling her brows, Alex gave me a teasing smile. Then she looked down at Liz, and it fell. Clicking a button on the recorder above Liz's head, Alex cleared her throat. "The victim is Elizabeth Turner, Liz Turner for short. Eighteen-year-old who went missing several days ago and whose body was discovered yesterday afternoon in a creek north of Pittsburgh. While there are several injuries to report, pinning down an exact cause of death will be difficult. Several of her wounds could explain her death. What is inarguable is whether they were self-inflicted, considering the body dump." Alex lifted Liz's palm to examine it. "Victim has no obvious defensive wounds, outside of a small abrasion on the knuckle of her left pointer finger."

"The friend she was with when she went missing claimed that that came from an altercation with her," Harper said. "No guarantee, obviously, but worth noting."

Returning to Liz's head, Alex lifted it carefully. "While examining her yesterday at the site, I noticed a large contusion to the back of her skull. That could also be the cause of death."

"Large contusion to the skull?" I asked. "No one mentioned this to me."

"Shit, I'm sorry," Harper said. "I'd just gotten off the phone with you when Alex noticed it."

At least I knew now. "You think somebody hit her?"

"Not with an instrument, no," Alex said. "There's usually web-like fracturing when someone is hit with something. Like a hammer or a baseball bat. That's not what this looks like to me."

"What does it look like?" Harper asked.

"I wasn't sure at first. But I couldn't stop thinking about where I've seen this before last night, and then it hit me." Alex lifted a glass petri dish. Inside, there were a few tiny gray rocks. "You see what I see?"

Harper said, "Maybe the fracture came from when she was dropped into the creek?"

"No," I murmured. "That's gravel."

Exhaling deeply, Alex nodded. "Suggesting to me, at least, that she either fell onto the pavement while whoever killed her was loading her into their car, or that was how she died."

"You think she was hit by a car," I said.

"That's my working theory."

"You have any other evidence to support that?" Harper asked. "You know I trust you, but I need a story to tell the judge for a warrant."

"I believe I do." Alex took a few steps down the table and lifted the sheet enough to expose Liz's thigh while giving her the modesty that the rest of the sheet provided. There, on her left thigh, was a massive bruise and a small cut. It was only a few inches wide, jagged and messy. Not like that of a knife. "I couldn't see this yesterday while I was examining her, but while you guys were filling out the intake information, I was having a look. I pulled a small piece of plastic out." Again, Alex gestured to a petri dish on the wheeled, metal table beside Liz's head. "It's reflective, so I'm thinking a head or taillight."

"Point of impact?" I asked.

"Maybe. I'm hoping to find some more particulates that you guys can use to connect to the person who hit her. My best guess, she got hit

211

by the car, fell backward, cracked her skull, assailant saw she was dead, loaded her up, and dropped her in the creek."

"God damn," I murmured, eyeing the bruise around that slice on her thigh. "And you're not sure if she was dead by then? When he dropped her in the creek?

"I'm hoping that was the case, but no, not yet." Alex nodded to the scalpel laid out on the table. "I'm gonna check her lungs in a bit. You can stay for that, if you'd like. But I'm gonna fish around that wound in her thigh first and see if I can find anything else. In case you want to turn around, Maddie."

Narrowing my gaze, I shot her a certain hand signal.

But I did, in fact, turn around.

"Is that normal?" I asked. "For a bruise to appear if it was the cause of death?"

"They can, yeah. Which is why I'm checking her lungs next. There's also bruising on her chest that suggests someone attempted to resuscitate her. But..." Alex trailed off.

"What is it?" I asked, resisting the urge to peer over my shoulder.

"More particulates," Alex murmured.

"From the head light?" Harper asked.

"No, those were clear and reflective." Alex's voice was still low, focused. "I think this is a paint chip. Any of your suspects drive a red car?"

Eyes finding Harper's, I arched a brow. "Think this'll be enough for a warrant?"

"Might be after an interview." Digging around in her pocket for her phone, Harper started for the door. "Send us whatever else you find, Alex."

But I think you may have just solved this case.

Chapter 26

WHAT WE HAD SO FAR WASN'T ENOUGH FOR A CONVICTION, barely enough for an arrest, but sure as shit enough to bring him down to the station. While Harper couldn't get an arrest warrant for the murder, I showed her the nude photos Liz had sent Darren. They were timestamped several months back. Before she turned eighteen. That timestamp made the image child pornography. Darren had it, evidence showed how much he appreciated that photo, so voila. Arrest warrant for possession of child pornography.

After a quick trip to the station, then to the judge, we headed back to Darren's house, this time with a warrant for his arrest in hand. We took my car. Harper was running low on gas and didn't want to waste time with stopping.

When we arrived, Darren's car was still in the drive. So was another. A shiny, black Toyota.

Andy McAvoy the first. He was just opening his door to get in. Harper opened her mouth to speak, but I was already doing what she was going to ask. Boxing him in. Tucking myself behind his bumper, only a few feet away, I got my first good glimpse at him. And his face said it all. He had been cool, calm, and collected the other day. Now, terror shined in his eyes.

Neither Harper nor I wasted any time. He stayed reserved as he stepped from his vehicle, but the slightest tremble of his hands told me everything I needed to know.

All but leaping from the car, Harper said, "Well, hello there, Mr. McAvoy. Fancy meeting you here."

Even from a distance, I saw the sweat beading his brow. "Hey, Detective Harper." He dipped his head in my direction. "Miss Castle."

"Visiting your nephew?" Harper asked. "That's who Darren is to you, correct? On your side or your wife's?"

"Darren's my brother's boy." Stowing his hands in his pockets, Mr. McAvoy cleared his throat. "He in some kind of trouble?"

"Usually is, isn't he?" Harper asked. "It's funny, you know. I thought you might've mentioned that. When we met the other day, you said you'd never really heard of Liz. But your nephew *and* your son work with her. *Worked*, I'm sorry. Worked. Past tense. Your son's barely old enough to drive, so I'm assuming you've taken him to work. So you probably met her at some point."

Another uncomfortable throat clear. "I meant that I didn't know her well."

"You sure about that?"

While I saw what Harper was doing, Andy Senior was a waste of my time. I doubted he had anything to do with Liz's death. Maybe he knew something. Maybe he hadn't told us the whole truth. Maybe he could come in handy later in the investigation, at least with a conviction, but at this moment, he wasn't worth it. The man had a business, a wife, and a family. He wasn't running anytime soon.

Around the edge of the building, near the rear door, a figure poked his head around the corner. I recognized the rock band hoodie from his Facebook photos and the blond hair wound into a loose ponytail.

Sure, his face was a blur, but I had no doubt. That was Darren. And he was doing exactly as I feared he would.

Footsteps padding around the corner, I opened the rear door for Tempy. "Runner," I said. Having known that word, her ears perked the moment it left my lips. Starting that direction, still holding Tempest's leash, I called out behind me, "Is he armed?"

Mr. McAvoy didn't answer.

"God damn it, is he armed?" Harper repeated, her voice a lethal weapon all its own.

"No. No, I don't think so."

The voices became only chatter as I stomped after Darren. Behind the laundromat was a cluster of trees. I was unfamiliar with this area, but I knew Pennsylvania better than anyone. A cluster of trees usually led to a small forest. A patch of woods miles and miles long.

Unfamiliar wildlife was questionable territory for any officer. But I had Tempest. She was trained in arrests and narcotics. As long as he wasn't armed, he stood no chance against my massive German Shepherd.

"Careful," I told Tempest.

She glanced up at me, tongue flapping in the warm wind, smiling. As if to say, *I know, Mom. But I'm good at my job. Trust me. I know what I'm doing here.*

Panting, winded, I said, "Take him down," and dropped the lead.

And off she went.

The sound of the wind in my ears was like that of a hurricane, despite the blue sky and the swaying trees. My heart pounded like it never had. The gun at my hip smacked my thigh, and I closed my hand around it. Lifting it from the holster, an overwhelming sense of dread fell over me in a way it never had. The birds were chirping, and the forest was singing, and the sky was blue, and my feet were slamming the soil, and Tempest was out of my sight. I knew she was there, nearby, but I couldn't see her, and I never should've dropped the lead.

My vision flickered.

It was all so similar. These woods were different, but they weren't. They were the same. One second I was here, and the next I was six weeks in the past, chasing The Country Killer through the whistling wind, hearing the chirping birds, all beneath a blue sky.

I was holding the gun, and it was lighter, but it felt just as heavy as the hunting rifle. It was so god damned heavy that by the time I caught up to the sound of growls, my hand was shaking.

That was why my hand was shaking, I told myself. Because it was heavy, not because it felt so similar to how it felt six weeks ago.

Thirty feet ahead or so, in a clearing just before a cliff side, a precipice that dropped I didn't know how far, was Tempest. Tempest, and Darren.

Jaw clenched around his forearm, she shook her head back and forth. As if to say, *Stop squirming. I'm not letting you go. I don't want to make this hard for you, but I will.*

Shouting a profanity, Darren whipped her across the face with something. Something black. Something roughly the size of my hand.

Boom!

A gun. He just fired a gun.

"Don't you dare!" I screamed. I wasn't sure if that was even what escaped my lips, but that was what I meant to say. It came out as more of a pathetic, girlish shriek.

Sobbing, screaming in agony, he managed out, "Tell her to let go! Tell her to let go!"

I took a step closer. "Drop the gun—"

"I'll shoot!" He pushed the barrel into her forehead when she whipped her head back and forth again. "If you don't tell her to let me go, I'll kill her. I'll do it! I'll kill her, damn it! I'll blow her brains out!"

"You know what happened to the last guy who hit my dog?" Again, I meant to speak, but a girlish shriek left me instead. "I put a bullet in his head, and I'm not afraid to do it again. If you don't—"

"We just want to talk," Harper cut me off. I probably should've been nervous about what she'd just heard me say, but the only thing I was afraid of now was how close that bullet was to hitting my baby. "Put the gun down, and we can talk."

"Get this god damn dog off me!"

I said, "Tempest, re—"

"Can't do that, kid," Harper said. "You put the gun down, and then we'll tell her to release."

There were no words for how furious that made me. It was protocol, sure. And yes, it was better by police standards to let a canine die than a cop or civilian.

But by my standards? I would take a bullet for that dog. I'd lose a limb for her. I would do *anything* for her. And to hear Harper say that arresting this kid mattered more than Tempest's life? Hell, I was half tempted to shoot her instead.

But I was frozen. I couldn't think. I could barely breathe. Never in my life had I felt this way on a case.

"We're not gonna hurt you," Harper said. "We just want to talk. That's all. Why'd you run, Darren?"

"You know why I ran!" he screamed. "Just—just let me go. Please just let me go."

"What happened, Darren?" Harper repeated. "What happened to make you think you need a gun? Why are you running?"

"Make her let go!"

"Tempest, rele—"

"Not 'til you put that down." Harper took a few small steps closer, voice calmer than I could've dreamed of being. She kept her gun aimed in his direction, but she couldn't line up a clear shot around Tempy. Neither could I, but that was the fault of my quivering hands. "You don't want to hurt that dog. You don't want to hurt anyone, do you? I bet you didn't want to hurt Liz either."

Darren let out a long, shaking sob.

"Just tell us what happened, Darren," Harper said, inching closer. "Put the gun down and tell us what happened. We can help you."

His sobs turned into more of a snorting laugh. "Cops always say that, and you're always lying. You make it worse. I tell you, and you make it so much worse."

"Yeah, well, that's not the case here," Harper said. "See my friend here, we've been going through some shit for a while. She loves that dog more than she loves anyone. Especially me. If I let anything happen to her, because I told her not to give the command to release you, she's gonna kill me. So I am dead ass serious when I tell you that I'm gonna help you if you tell me the truth. I know the DA. This doesn't have to be bad."

Darren snorted for half a second, then cried again when Tempest wrenched her head back and forth. "How can you make murder 'not bad?!'"

"Because it wasn't murder. Liz was hit by a car. We know that car was yours. And we know you tried to save her," Harper continued, tone level, compassionate. "We know you didn't mean to hurt her, Darren. We know it was an accident. So just put the gun down, and let's talk."

Sobbing still, shaking hand trembling against Tempest's face, I watched his finger on the trigger.

No matter how hard I tried, I couldn't line up a shot. Not without hitting Tempest.

"Please don't shoot her," I whispered.

"It was," he sobbed out. "It was an accident." Another cry. "I didn't mean to hit her. I didn't mean to kill her."

"What happened?" Harper repeated.

"She called me. Sh-she needed a ride. So I went to pick her up, and she was really messed up. Super drunk, and really high. And Liz wasn't easy to get along with when she was sober," he whispered that last part through trembling lips. "We made it a couple miles down the road, and she was crying, and then she was running her mouth. She said her boyfriend broke up with her. That he was the best thing that ever happened to her, and he broke up with her because he found out she was cheating.

"And I said something. I don't remember what. She didn't like it. It pissed her off. And she just—" Another shaking sob. "She just exploded. She said that I was a worthless piece of shit. She was only screwing me for drugs. That I didn't deserve Angela, that she was going to leave me, that I'd kill myself like my dad did.

"And that the world will be better for it. That I didn't deserve to live. That I was a lowlife, and my son was going to be a lowlife just like his daddy." Still holding it, he lowered the gun. A deep breath of relief fell from my lips. He could raise it again, but for the moment, it wasn't aimed at my baby's head. "She said he'd be better if I left. If I left him now, before he's old enough to remember me. Because nobody should have to know me.

"I told her to get out. I told her to walk her ass home. I didn't care, just get the hell out of my car. She did. She yelled something at me, I don't know what, but it pissed me off. And the second she closed the door, I shifted the car back into drive, and I gassed it. But I didn't see that she had gone in front of the car. She was trying to walk around me. To the other side of the road, I think. And I hit her." He sobbed harder now. "I didn't mean to."

Moving carefully, Harper took another small step forward. "And that's when you got out to give her CPR?"

Speaking through trembling lips, he nodded. "But she wouldn't wake up. I tried, and I tried, but she wouldn't wake up. I had some drugs in the car. I knew if I got caught with those, I was going back to jail. I just panicked. I didn't want her to be right. I don't want to be a piece of shit. I don't want to end up in jail again."

"This wasn't murder, Darren," Harper said. "Your life isn't over. We can probably get this charge down to aggravated assault. If you just let me talk to the DA, we can get this figured out. Trust me, okay? Just let me get this figured out for you. This doesn't have to be the end."

"I killed someone," he said, looking back at us with tears in his bloodshot eyes. "Liz is dead because of me. It's too late."

"No, it's not," Harper said, still approaching slowly with her gun raised. "If you put that gun down—"

Darren looked at me. "Tell my son I loved him. And that I'm sorry."

In as long as it took to exhale, he lifted the gun to his head and pulled the trigger.

Collapsing to my knees, I didn't even feel the pain.

Tempest finally released.

I wasn't sure if it was because she knew he was dead or if it was because she knew that I needed her.

Jumping on top of me, Tempest licked me all over. As if I was the one who needed to be checked for injuries. A gash on her cheek was dripping blood onto my pants. It was at least an inch wide, maybe half an inch deep. She didn't seem to notice, or care.

It was all I could think about. All I could see. The blood. All that blood. The blood draining from her face, the blood all over the rock Darren lay on, the blood all over the forest floor. That blood wasn't Tempest's, wasn't mine, wasn't Darren's. That was Ox's.

After everything I'd lived through, one might think that I already had PTSD. It wasn't until this moment that it registered. I was here, and I wasn't here. Ox was here, and he wasn't. Darren was, and he wasn't.

It was such a difficult thing to describe. I saw Harper rush to Darren. Collapse by his side. Saw her checking for a pulse. Saw her speaking into her radio. Saw her rushing back to me. Felt her hand on my shoulder.

But I wasn't here. I was, and I wasn't. Everything I saw was almost pixelated, everything I heard was muffled, and everything I felt was more of a tingle than the way it typically resonated.

Was there a word for this? This wasn't a flashback. Or maybe it was. It was, but it wasn't. Harper's hand felt as real as the sight of Darren's body on that rock, but that didn't feel real either.

None of this felt real. The world around me didn't feel real.

Not until Harper took my face in her hands and said, "It's okay. It's okay."

Only then did I realize I was crying. No, not crying. Sobbing. Weeping. I was weeping for a man I didn't know.

Maybe it wasn't for him at all. Maybe it was for me. Maybe it was for Ox. Maybe it was for Tempest. Maybe it was for that little boy who would grow up without a father.

I had no idea. I had no idea what I was experiencing. But I knew what I was feeling. Grief and pain and terror. They grabbed hold of my heart and held it hostage.

No matter how many times Harper told me it was okay, even as she wrapped her arms around me, even as Tempest licked me all over, nothing felt okay.

This was the worst thing I'd ever felt in my life. This was just as bad as watching Ox die.

Maybe because, for the first time, I was feeling the weight of his death. I was feeling grief. I was mourning. I told myself that I'd been doing that for the last six weeks, but it wasn't until I watched Darren blow his own brains out that I truly grieved.

Chapter 27

THE NEXT FEW HOURS WERE A BLUR.

I hated that Harper spent the following thirty minutes calming me down. She kept telling me everything was fine. Tempest was fine, I was fine. Made no comment about Darren. But there was nothing to say about him. He was dead. That was a fact.

I just didn't know why it'd hit me this way. Maybe it was the setting, maybe it was the grief finally settling in. Maybe it was because this man thought it would be better to kill himself than to face living a life without his son. My dad probably felt the same way a time or two.

I didn't know. What did matter was that the case was solved. Liz Turner was dead, and so was her killer. Hopefully, her parents could find some respite in that.

While we waited for EMS to arrive, Harper informed Mr. McAvoy. He screamed, he cried, and I tried my best to not do the same. But it was like the dam had broken now. Exactly as Bentley had said it would, everything I had been pushing down bubbled up, and at the worst time. I managed to keep it together until Mr. McAvoy pulled away. But while Harper informed the other officers, while she spoke with EMS, I sat in my car, nuzzled up with Tempest, and cried.

By the time Harper finished up all the paperwork she needed

attended to, all the discussions that needed to be had, I had mostly pulled myself together. She asked if I could take her back to her car. I agreed, of course.

While we were driving, she asked if I wanted her to come with me to the vet for Tempest. I wasn't sure what I needed in that moment, but I didn't particularly want to be alone. That wasn't my usual situation. And I had my best friend again. Things may not have been the way they used to be, but she and Tempest were the only things that felt real, that tethered me to reality. I clung to that.

From there, we went to the vet. They gave Tempest a few stitches, some antibiotics, and we went on our merry way. It was only a little after three by then. Harper asked if I wanted to get lunch. I did. And so, through a drive-through we went.

I still didn't have the words to describe how I felt. Down in the dumps, that was one way. A state of disassociation, derealization, that was another. I was somewhere in the middle of it all. Confused, sad, and out of touch.

It was finally settling in as we drove back to Harper's car. She explained that she was going to bring in Andy Junior and Senior to get more information, to make sure they weren't aware of what Darren had done. I asked what her plan was if they had been. What if they knew exactly what Darren had done and did nothing? What if they'd helped him cover it up?

She said, "Guess it would be hypocritical of me to charge them, wouldn't it?"

"Darren killed an innocent girl," I said, shifting the car into park beside hers. "I killed a killer."

Biting her lower lip, she nodded. "But I'm not protecting you because you killed a killer. I'm protecting you because I care about you. That's the same thing, isn't it?"

The kindness in her eyes, that compassion, warmed my heart. "Guess that would make you a hypocrite."

She gave me a dry smile. "Guess we all are, in our own ways."

I huffed a laugh at that. She did, too. It was probably time that we parted ways, but she looked at me, and I looked at her, and our shared gaze alone was worth a million words. She spoke up anyway. "Can I say something?"

"Unless you forgot how to."

"An opinion. Can I give you my opinion?"

"You rarely hold it back."

She inhaled and said, "I think you need to get some help, Maddie."

Breathing out a deep sigh, I grabbed a fistful of my hair close to the root. The idea had been to swing it away from my face, but I just held it there for a moment. "I think I do, too."

"I'm here for you. I don't know if you want me to be, but I am. If you need anything at all, you call me. I don't care what's going on. I don't care how mad you think I'll be. You call me, Madison Castle. And I'll be there."

Tears welled in my eyes, but I was able to blink them away this time. "I want you to be."

"If you need a therapist, I know a good one. One who won't tell anyone the things you're most ashamed of."

"I guess I can afford health insurance now, huh?"

"I think Ox would approve of that."

"The health insurance. Never had much faith in psychology."

"The people who need it the most tend to feel that way."

I laughed, and so did she. Eventually, she sighed deeply. "I got a lot of paperwork to do. But keep in touch, alright?"

I was looking forward to doing just that. She started for the door handle, but I stopped her. "Harper?"

Holding the handle, she looked my way.

"Will you sit with me?" The look on her face told me she didn't know what that meant, and admittedly, neither did I. It sort of just fell out. "While I read the letter. From Ox. I didn't want to read it with Teresa. Feels weird to read it when I'm sitting beside Bentley, and I'm usually sitting beside Bentley. But I-I think I want to read it. I think I need to say goodbye. If I don't, I'm gonna bawl my eyes out every time I see somebody blow their brains out."

"Honestly, I think it's a perfectly rational response to bawl your eyes out when you see somebody blow their brains out."

"Not for me."

She laughed. I smiled. I tried to, at least. It wasn't as prominent as I'd intended it to be. But it was the best I could do.

"You sure you want to read it right now?" she asked. "Right here? Just a parking lot in the middle of nowhere?"

"I'm afraid I'm never gonna read it if I don't do it now." I hated how tight my chest was. "I have to face it, Harper. I have to deal with the fact that he's gone. That I'm never going to see him again. That nothing will ever be the same again. Not with him. He's not coming back, but we're here. Reading it with you, that makes the most sense to me."

Releasing the door handle, eyes full of sympathy and grief of her own, she nodded. "Sure, sweetie. I'll sit with you. You just want me here for moral support? Or do you want me to read it with you?"

"With me, I think."

"Alright."

After finding it in the glove box, I tore the envelope open. And then, I stared at the words.

For a few seconds, I just stared at them. I didn't read them. Not like his handwriting was ever the easiest to read to begin with, but I reminded myself that it was time. Before I gave the money away, before I put it in savings, before I bought a house, before I figured out what the hell to do with it, I needed his insight. So much of my life was based on his insight.

In the last year, I'd stepped away from that. That was for the best. I'd needed to become my own person outside of him, a life separate from him. I had that now, but the money was his, and I needed his advice on what to do with it. I needed to read this letter.

So, I read it.

MADDIE,

If you're reading this, I guess I'm dead. That sucks. Guess my ex-

fiancé is still the person who means the most to me, even at my death. Either that means I'm a pathetic old man who never remarried, or something went down at work.

I bet you were there, weren't you? If I died on the job, you were there to witness it. Not because you're to blame. To clarify, considering you blame yourself for everything that is not your fault. But because if it was bad enough, a big enough case to kill me, I would've wanted you there. And you would've been there.

That's the funny thing about the two of us. We never really liked each other, but we were always there for each other. And I guess that's why I gave you this. Because you've never had enough, Maddie. And I know it'll piss you off to hear me say that, but you deserve so much better than life has given you. No one's ever taken care of you. That's why I always tried so hard to. That's why I pissed you off all the time. Because I wanted to be what you didn't have. Someone you could count on.

I hope I was that. Even though you couldn't stand me lately. And don't feel guilty for me saying that either. You can't stand me, and I can't stand you. That's just us. It's why we loved each other, even though we hated each other.

But anyway. I got this life insurance policy when you said yes. Because I didn't want you to be screwed if I died. I already had the one from work, but I wanted you to have enough. I wanted you to have a life without me if you lost me. I didn't want you to be stuck. I wanted you to be able to go anywhere you wanted to. Do whatever you wanted to. Work cases for free if you cared enough about a family and still have money sitting in the bank.

And then I got shot. You were still the beneficiary then. My lawyer came to see me in the hospital. He suggested I remove you. And that's when I thought about all of this. I almost died, and when he said I should've taken my ex-fiancé off my life insurance policy, all I could think was, "Why?"

Why shouldn't she get it? She's everything to me. You're everything to me, Maddie. I didn't show it enough. And I didn't show it how you needed me to. When we were together, and then now that we're... what-

ever we are. Friends, I guess. But I mean that. I love you. This is the best thing I can do to prove it.

If I haven't said it before this letter, I want you to know how sorry I am. Not just for what I did, but because it was Harper. Because I took your best friend.

Writing this, I just paused to think of what to say after that. I don't think there's much I can follow that up with.

Just know that I'm sorry. I'm sorry I'm dead. I'm sorry you're hurting right now. (I hope you're hurting at least a little bit over my death. Is it mean to hope that you are? It's not that I want you to hurt. I just want you to be a little bit sad that you will never see me again. I hope that you don't feel nothing about my death. Because that would suck more than dying. But whatever. Not the point.) I'm sorry that through this, you don't have your best friend to hold onto because of me.

It's messed up, isn't it? That everything between us ruined so many lives. Mine, yours, hers. And if I'm dead, and I'm not an old man yet, you guys are probably the only ones who care. The people who hate me the most are the people I cared about the most.

Let's hope it's at least a year or two later. Maybe we'll hate each other a little bit less by then. Maybe I died when we were on good terms. I hope, at least. I really hope.

This is stupid. Just some morphine -induced ramblings from a guy in a hospital bed who got pissed off at his lawyer and is really damn tired of this stupid catheter.

Anyway. Do something good for yourself with this money, Maddie. Please, please, don't relapse with this money. Stay clean. Right now, to me, as I'm writing this, you are. I'm stoned out of my mind on morphine, but you're sober. And I want you to stay that way. I want you to get everything you ever wanted out of life. I want you to be happy.

So do whatever you have to do with this money to feel that. (Outside of drugs.) Fix up your trailer. Put it on a piece of land. Put it in savings. Buy a house. Invest in the stock market. I know you hated gambling, but that's what people with this much money do. They invest in the stock market. Or index funds. No idea what those are, but it sounds like the sorta thing someone with half a million dollars should know about.

Above all else, please do that. Be happy. Get what you want out of this life. It's never long enough, not for anyone.

And I don't care what you do with the condo. If you want to sell it, if you want to rent it out, if you want to live in it, it doesn't matter to me. I hate the idea of Bear staying out there with a new family, though. Would it be crazy for me to ask you to bring him to me? Bury him in my casket? God, that's gross. Ugh. Maybe that's the morphine talking.

But maybe you could pay somebody to do it? I'm sure with 500 grand, somebody would be willing to dig up a dead dog for you.

Again. No idea what the hell to follow that up with. I'm out of shit to say. All that's left is I love you. And I do. I love you.

-Ox

TEARS WERE STREAMING DOWN MY FACE BY THE TIME I GOT TO the end. Harper was in a similar state, judging by the tears that fell onto my arm.

Sniffling, swatting my tears away, I broke the snotty silence with, "Know anyone who'd dig up a dead dog for me?"

Chapter 28

IT WAS ALMOST 6 BY THE TIME I MADE IT HOME. BENTLEY HAD
texted me a few times throughout the day, once to send his usual good
morning and again to ask how my day was going. I responded to both,
then partook in the usual small talk. Rarely did I tell him exactly what
was going on throughout my day on a case like this. That, I saved for
dinner. But I had plenty to tell him about now.

And yet, when I pulled into the drive, and saw him cutting our
grass, giving me that usual sweet smile of his, everything about my day
left my mind. All the details, everything I'd learned about Daisy, the
investigation, even Darren's death.

He must've seen it on my face because his smile dropped when I
got out. After shutting off the lawnmower, he walked my way. Only
scratching Tempest's ear, he cocked his head to the side. "You okay?"

I just said, "You were right."

"Usually how it goes. What was I right about?"

"The dam. It broke."

Softening his gaze, realizing what I meant, he reached out for my
hand. "You wanna talk about it?"

"I—" I was about to say no. That I was fine. But that was a lie.

"Yeah, maybe. I guess. If you're not busy, and if you're not dealing with your own shit. I don't want to—"

"I'm not busy." He gestured to the lawn chairs. "I need a break anyway."

* * *

So, I told him. About my day, about what Darren had done after. More because I felt the context was necessary than anything. I told him that Harper had been there for me through it all. That maybe we were on the way to working through our shit. That she was right about one thing: that I needed to go to therapy. That I was a god damn shit storm, and I needed to get better. I didn't realize how broken I was until today. And now, there was no denying it.

I hated that, feeling weak. Vulnerable. That's what today was, wasn't it? A sign of my weakness. A sign that I couldn't handle my issues. I'd broken down because I was too much of a coward to just accept things as they were and move on.

I said that, how much I hated showing the disaster I was. Bentley cut me off, saying, "You're human, Maddie. Only a sociopath would have been through the things that you've gone through and felt nothing about it. It's okay. It's okay to admit that you're not okay."

Maybe he was right. It made it easier to keep going, though. To keep talking.

Throughout the evening, that was all we did. We talked. Talked about everything and about nothing.

Soon enough, Grace came out of her bedroom to ask what the plans were for dinner. Bentley started cooking, and she retreated to her room. When she was gone, I asked him how the two of them were. He said they had been talking, but that they probably had a long road ahead of them. I was sure of it.

The evening stretched on in our usual, boring way. Dinner, TV, followed by passing out on the couch by 7 PM. Boring, it may have been, but it was safe and comfortable, and I was grateful for every second of it.

At 2:30 AM, when Bentley was going into work for some overtime, I awoke to the sound of his keys jingling on his hip. He told me to go back to sleep. I considered it, but I'd gotten a full night's rest. So I kissed him goodbye and stared at the wall for a while. When that got old, and after I let Tempest out, I spent some time scrolling online for health insurance. No idea what the hell I was looking at—figured I should ask Bentley's advice when he got home.

From there, now that my case was resolved, I didn't have much else to do. Except look for Daisy. Or at least a trace of her. The only place I could do that was within the cavern of her own mind. So, to that writing application I went.

After digging a while for the next part of that paranormal romance I'd read the day before and finding nothing, I made my way to a new story altogether. The timestamp in the corner suggested it was written only a few months before she disappeared. Last edited only days before.

And, oh man, this one was different.

It was a journal. It was titled *Sins and Silk Ties*. But there was no way to call it a story because I knew every character in it. Bobby, the main character's very protective, overbearing big brother. Gabby, the big brother's young daughter. And the main character, with an eerily familiar, heartbreaking back story. A dead sister. A mother with a meth problem. An absent father.

There was no denying that this was Daisy's story. The main character was even named Lily. A little word play on the flower name.

What stuck out about it wasn't the fact that it was a self-insert. It was a love story. The love story between a young, broken girl, and a much, *much* older man. Mr. Deluca.

She'd met him at her place of employment. A strip club named Club Cabaret. Which wasn't all that different than Club Xstasy, was it?

He'd started out as a regular. A nice man with an astute nature. Attractive. Smart. Spoke like he graduated from Harvard. Brilliant, kind, and dominant. A quality that Daisy liked in a man. Or at least, one that was attractive in her nineteen-year-old innocent mind.

He swept her off her feet. Gave her massive tips. She didn't even make him pay for more. She gave it away because he was just oh-so-charming.

Regularly, he asked if she would quit her job. Said that he wanted her to live a better life. One quote read, "You're too perfect to be a whore forever, little bird." He'd given her that nickname because of a hummingbird tattooed on her hip.

Lily was young. Or rather, Daisy was. She found that quote endearing.

I found it manipulative and insulting. That isn't to say I advocated for young girls becoming sex workers. Daisy had gotten in over her head and used the only thing she knew that could make her money. She survived however she had to, and I respected her for that.

Degrading her for that survival, shaming her for doing what she needed to, while simultaneously complimenting her left Daisy, or Lily, thinking she needed him. Mr. Deluca could save her. Sweep her off her feet and fly her away from all her problems.

Only to create more.

That much, I knew, because I knew men like him. Mr. Deluca didn't want to save her. She was a vulnerable, naive girl, barely more than a child. He loved the power that came with that dynamic. If he got what he wanted, he wouldn't have her as a partner. He would *own* her. Throughout the narrative, he said so a few times. That she was *his*. As if she was a sports car he could show off, as though she was an item for him to possess.

And the sad part was, in Daisy's young, twisted mind, that was romance. I couldn't blame her. I'd been young and dumb once too. The possessive, controlling, jealous, handsome guy had swept me off my feet as well. As much as I loved him, Ox was not a good partner. But he didn't even come close to how bad Deluca was. In his mind, whether the young girl realized it or not, she was nothing more than something for him to play with on his command.

The fact of the matter was, he was a typical hero in a romance book. For whatever reason, maybe purely cathartic release, so many women—like myself once upon a time—found this appealing. As if being controlled, being owned, by another person was a good thing in any reality.

It was a sad thing. A sad thing too many women fell victim to. And how so many women ended up losing their lives at the hands of a man who was supposed to love them more than anything.

If not for the fact that all the other characters were so clearly based on those closest to Daisy, I may have chalked the character up to be only that. A character. But Bobby was Bentley. Gabby was Grace. Mr. Deluca was someone too. He had to be. And if I was right, I had a damn good feeling I knew what happened to her. Or rather, *who* happened to her.

The more that I read the story, the more I hated the guy. I understood why Daisy liked him. She'd been young and dumb. She'd read all his red flags as green, like the fact that he would call her twenty times in a row if she didn't answer the first.

As someone a bit older, slightly wiser, I desperately wanted to reach through the screen, straight to the girl telling the story, grab her by the shoulders, shake her, and say, "He's not in love with you. He's obsessed with you. Run. Run as fast as your damn legs will take you."

By the time I was at the end of the story, at the place where Lily quit her job the night after Deluca beat up her abusive boyfriend, only for the two of them to run away together, my stomach was in knots.

I felt as sick as I had when the Country Killer had still been at it. While Eric Oakley had been evil in his own way, Deluca was terrifying in another. Terrifying because he was real. He was the villain we all didn't want to acknowledge lived around the corner. The nice guy. The handsome, wealthy one, who seemed perfect. At least, perfect to a young, vulnerable girl. He was the dark side of every woman's fantasy. The one they liked to read about in books only because they'd been burned by one just like him in the real world.

Just like him, minus the part where he made you disappear. Or at least, didn't make you disappear in the way you wanted to.

What scared me the most was that I knew the story. Anyone working in law enforcement knew it. Young girl with a lot of damage plus dominant, good looking, rich man didn't equal *Pretty Woman*. Not usually. Usually, it equaled tragedy.

In a case like this, I might have suspected he was married, and the wife found out. Maybe she'd killed Lily. But average people weren't great at covering up murders. Then again, it wasn't like anyone was really looking for Daisy.

The other possibility was that he never cared about her at all and only wanted her for sex trafficking. Because, contrary to what the Internet might tell you, most sex-trafficked people got into that position from a partner.

But that was what didn't make sense. Kevin, her abusive boyfriend, had already trafficked Daisy. By definition, that's what human trafficking was. Forcing or coercing someone into sexual acts. It wasn't all kidnapping women in Walmart parking lots.

So I had to wonder, how could it get much worse? Was he simply that good at covering up a murder? Was his wife?

I didn't know, so I kept reading. It was almost 6 AM by then, so bundled up on the sofa with a cup of coffee in hand—my fourth—I continued down the rabbit hole. The next story I read was shorter, twenty-thousand words or so, about a sci-fi world where men didn't exist. Had to laugh about that one. In fairness, it wasn't like Daisy had seen many great men.

It wasn't her best work, but it kept me entertained. More than that, it piqued my interest. Not because it was all that entertaining, but because at the bottom, right after the final the end, was a phrase I knew all too well. *AO3*

D.M. Followed by a bunch of numbers, then *@AO3*

AO 3, short for Archive of Our Own. A website where amateur writers shared their stories. One I'd spent too much time on in my younger years when I'd been broke and had no other form of entertainment.

No wonder Daisy was a good writer. She'd been writing for a brutal audience for years since this story was dated 2016. Also explained the quality difference between this one and the former.

Being the experienced woman I was, I headed for Archive of Our Own. With Daisy's user tag—God, I hope it was Daisy's user tag—I searched. And without much effort, I found her. And holy shit, if I thought this girl had written a lot, I had no idea. Clearly, this was all she did. Because there were hundreds—maybe thousands—of stories published under this user tag.

When I clicked on to a few of them, not only did I recognize the writing style, but the stories themselves. The rich boyfriend one, the paranormal romance, the horror, the mystery. Unless Daisy had just been stealing somebody else's work to copy and paste onto here—which was senseless on a free site like this—these were hers.

She was the creator of this profile, and she had a hell of a lot more work for me to uncover. Given the racy scenes in the last one, I figured it probably wasn't best for me to recruit Bentley and Grace to help me get through her backlist faster. But, much to my joy, I didn't think I would need them. Not yet, anyway. Because the most recent story I clicked on was written in May of this year. Published at least.

It was called, *Bird in a Cage*.

EVERYTHING'S SO BEAUTIFUL HERE
    Nothing to complain about
    There's a pretty swing to my left
    Ornaments overhead to wonder at, to play with
    My cage is gold, with platforms and perches of the same everywhere i look
    Bells hung with ropes, swings swaying between them
    Even a tree to climb and watch the sun rise and set between the bars, behind the

Door. locked.

BIRD IN A CAGE.
Yes, where the hummingbird belongs.

MY, OH MY, WHAT I'D GIVE TO FLUTTER THROUGH THE TREES LIKE the ones beyond the chains and bars do.
Yes, no, yes. no, no, no. not where a bird belongs.

HOW DID THE WIND CARRY ME HERE?
Easy. so easy to cage me.
Roped up in chains of gold
Ornaments of twine, cheap yarn, were a thousand times more beautiful than all this gold

"DAISY WROTE THIS?"
I jumped.
Coffee splashed over my shirt, dousing Tempest on my right. With a chuff, she hopped off the couch and settled onto the floor at my feet.
Behind me, Grace peered over my shoulder at the words on the screen. "Sorry. I came out for a drink."
Normally, I'd tell her it was fine. But after what I had just read, what I believed I just learned, I couldn't form the words.
Bentley told me not to give her false hope. Even if the hope was true now, if I had just reason for believing Daisy was still alive, it was information he deserved to hear first.
"It's alright." Reaching forward to snap the laptop shut, I cleared my throat. "And yeah, I think she did."
Grace caught the corner of the screen. Holding it open, she

squinted at the words on the page. "Are you sure? She was never big into poetry."

Shit, what was I supposed to say? What was I supposed to *do*?

Still squinting at the page, she cocked her head to the side. "Wait, when did she write this?"

Shit, shit, shit. "I'm not sure. Let me do some more digging and talk to your—"

"Hang on. Wait a second." With more force than the girl typically possessed, she snatched the laptop from my thighs. Scrolling with one hand, Grace walked around the back to join me on the sofa. "May 15th? She just uploaded this two months ago?"

"I'm not sure." Like she had, I snatched the laptop and gave her a look. One that said, *That was rude.*

She paid no attention to my annoyance. "Someone did. Someone uploaded this poem two months ago." A short pause, as though she needed to collect her thoughts. "Wait, Daisy published?"

Didn't know if I could describe Archive of Our Own as publishing. "I don't know yet, Grace. Can you give me a minute to collect my—"

"This is weird." Leaning closer over the laptop, she shook her head. "This style, I mean. For any writer, this style's weird. What makes you think it's Daisy's?"

"I don't know if it is."

"But you said you *think* it is." The sunrise peeking in through the windows illuminated the concern in her brown eyes. "What makes you think that?"

Damn it. "I should talk to your dad about the stuff I find before—"

"You didn't tell me. I saw what you found." She gestured to the laptop screen. "And I'm telling you that this doesn't look like Daisy's style. Which Dad doesn't know, but I do. If you tell me why you think it's hers, maybe we can make sense of this together."

Bentley was gonna be pissed. But she made a good point.

So, with a sigh, I showed her the web of connections that brought me here. By the time we were back to *Bird in a Cage*, Grace was biting her lip and studying the poem. Rather than the frantic excitement, she scrutinized it as closely as I did.

"Well, yeah, I guess I see why you think its hers, but does this look like anything else you've read of hers?" she asked.

"No. She does long narratives, not poetry." Scratching my head, I studied the words closely. "And her grammar is pretty damn good usually. But look." I pointed to the fifth line of the first stanza, then the first and second lines of the third. "She doesn't capitalize the word 'I,' or the first word of each sentence here. That's not the norm in poetry, is it?"

"Not unless there's a stylistic reason for it." This girl loved literature, so even if it'd piss Bentley off, it *was* best to consult an expert here. "It's strange too. There's no rhyming, so it's not following a typical poem format. I'd say it's free verse, but there's no artistic reason to style like this."

"What do you mean? With the grammar?"

"More syntax than grammar." She pointed to that third stanza again. "She could structure this entire stanza differently for a better rhythm. Here, let me show you."

After copying and pasting the stanza into my notes, she did just that. Restructured the stanza. Rather than the original,

My, oh my, what i'd give to flutter through the trees like the ones beyond the chains and bars do.

Yes, no, yes. no, no, no. not where a bird belongs.

Grace rewrote it so it read,

My, oh my,
What I'd give to flutter
Through the trees
Like the ones beyond the chains and bars do.
Yes, no, yes.
No, no, no.
Not where a bird belongs.

"See how differently that sounds when you say it in your head?" Grace asked, pointing to the page. "By separating the sentences into different lines, you're putting pauses between clusters of words. Varying sentence structure was important to Daisy. She always said that good writing will have a rhythm to it. It'll read like a song in your head. So there has to be a reason she wrote it like this."

Huh. That added up. "Do you think it could have something to do with the capitalization?"

"Mayb—" She gasped. Eyes bulging, she murmured the poem aloud to herself again.

"What?" I asked. "What do you see?"

Slowly, a greenish hue filled her cheeks. She swallowed hard. "Acrostic poetry. That's what this is."

I may have enjoyed a fair deal of fanfiction once upon a time, but I was no English expert. "And what is acrostic poetry?"

"Spelling out a word with the first letter of each line. It makes the poem awkward, most of the time. You get what the author's telling you, but it's not gonna be their prettiest writing, because that's not the point. It's supposed to send a message." Again, she pointed to the poem, but this time, she stroked her finger vertically down the page. "All the capital letters. Read them."

I did. And my stomach sank.

Entombed by my hero.

"Holy shit," I murmured.

"She's alive." Grace's voice wasn't full of hope. It was low, slow. Scared. "She's in a cage."

Chapter 29

Rubbing a hand down his beard, Bentley's eyes shone with a look I had only seen a handful of times. Eyes wide, almost empty. The vein in his forehead pumping. Fingers trembling. Scared and excited at once. "That doesn't mean she's alive."

I wasn't sure if there was a word for this emotion in the English dictionary. The fear of hope. Not the fear of good. There was nothing he wanted more than to learn Daisy was still alive. What he didn't want was to have hope again, only for it to come crashing down. That was the worst thing he could imagine. I could tell just from looking at him.

"It doesn't." Reaching across the table, I twined my fingers between his. "But it does mean somebody logged into her account and posted a story under her name."

"What if she shared it with someone?" he asked. "What if that's why there are so many stories? It's possible, isn't it? Maybe she had a friend that got on the account sometimes."

"That's possible—"

"It's not, Dad." Grace came out of the hallway with her arms tucked against her chest. Her expression wasn't much different from Bentley's. There was just a hair more hope than fear. "I've been reading Daisy's writing since I was a kid, Dad. My whole life, I've been hearing her stories. I know Daisy's style. I know how she talks, and all of this is hers. Some of the stories, she only told me. I looked through the account, and these are *her* stories. Please don't tell Maddie to stop looking. Please."

Forehead crunching down into his eyes, Bentley turned my way. "You told her this. You told Grace before you told me."

Damn it. "I did. I'm sorry. It wasn't—"

"Your decision to make, but you made it anyway?" Bentley asked. "We talked about this, Maddie. You said you wouldn't—"

"Dad—"

"This isn't about you, Grace. Go to your—"

"I'm not going to my room!" She may not have stomped her feet, but she may as well have. Also immediately regretted it. "I'm sorry." She lowered her voice before he could yell at her in response. "I didn't mean to yell, and I'm not trying to fight with you. And I get why you didn't want Maddie to tell me. But she really didn't. I was reading her laptop over her shoulder when she figured it all out. Then she explained, but she didn't just *tell* me.

"And I know I've been a pain in the ass lately, and I'm sorry for that too, but I don't think she's dead, Dad. I never have. I told you that. And does this make me happy? No, not at all. I read the story." Tears welled in her eyes. "Somebody has her. Somebody's holding her captive. I don't know why she even has access to the Internet or why he is letting her publish her stuff online. But this is Daisy."

Silence.

Aside from Tempest panting in the corner of the room, not a huge fan of arguments or yelling or the tones the three of us were using, the room was eerily silent. So silent that I didn't know how to fill the space.

One way or the other, I was in trouble. Bentley wasn't happy with me, and I couldn't blame him. I never would've told Grace first if she hadn't seen it.

Also I knew he would get over it.

What he wouldn't get over was his regret if I was right.

That fear of hope was still in his eyes. Now, tears accompanied that wordless emotion. I wasn't sure if they were that of joy that he and Grace were finally not hating each other again, or the awakening of the possibility that Daisy was still alive.

When he met my gaze, he exhaled slowly. "We need to talk about this later."

"All of it?" It may have been a question, but it left Grace as an annoyed chirp. "Because that's not fair. I get how you feel right now, but—"

"I wasn't talking to you, Grace Rycroft." The glare he shot his daughter was worth a thousand words. "You can stay out here. But I cannot fight with you right now. Please stop with the attitude."

Ah, so I was the one he'd scold later. Which was fair enough. He had the right to be upset with me. And better that he was annoyed with me than her.

Grace still had her arms crossed, but her tone was understanding. "I'm sorry."

Sighing again, Bentley brought his attention back to me. "What can you do with this information? What comes next?"

"I can talk to Harper about getting in contact with the Columbus PD. They might be willing to dig into this deeper. Or they might tell us what they already told you. That she's an addict, and she'll be home when she comes home. Harper is our best bet, but it's gonna take some string pulling. I do have some connections with the FBI. They might be able to trace this. Wherever Daisy was when she uploaded this story, I mean. If we can track down the IP address, we might be able to find a roundabout location of where she is. If it's in PA, that gives me a lot more leverage. I can't make any promises, but the states are close. Mr. Deluca in the book said he lived close to the border. And if that's the case, it gives us a lot more legal power."

Bentley ran his hand through his hair and grabbed a fistful at the back. "Do you really think she's alive?"

"I really think she was at the time this was published. And I think it was her cry for help," I said, despite the cringe he tried to disguise. "I don't know if he's reading her stories, or if he was keeping her alive for one specific thing, or if it's way bigger than I can wrap my head around. But this was Daisy. And this was only a few months ago. If he's kept her alive for that long, it stands to reason he's still doing so."

If Daisy believed that Mr. Deluca was going to kill her, she would've said so in a manner of words. That wasn't what the story said.

The story suggested he wanted to keep her as his pet. That she was his pretty bird in a cage.

The tears in Bentley's eyes budded over. He tried to disguise them by clenching his jaw and looking away. Grace and I met one another's gazes, each waiting for the other to break the silence. Attempting to speak without words.

Was he mad? Sad? Scared? All the above. Was this the right way to handle this? Neither of us knew, but we looked at each other for what Bentley was most afraid of.

Hope.

"Do you have any idea where to start?" he asked eventually. "Outside of talking to the FBI and Harper, I mean."

"I do," I said. "But I'm not sure if you're gonna like it."

Chapter 30

Fanning the pages beneath her nose, she pulled in a deep breath. That smell was unlike anything in the world. Her favorite smell. They were simply her only joy. And so was this place.

The library.

She'd been to so many now, she'd lost count. Some were dingy, with linoleum floors and yellowing white walls. Others were practically churches with domed ceilings, stained glass windows, and intricate art above mahogany bookshelves that stretched as high as a tree in the forest.

This one was of the latter. It had the domed ceiling, the stained-glass windows, and those beautiful bookshelves.

As a girl, she loved libraries as well. Bella never understood it. Could she read a book? Sure. But reading a book was only reading a book to her. Often felt more like a job than a thing of pleasure.

For Daisy, however, it was safety. An imaginary world that came to life when her eyes flicked over the black ink peppered across cream pages. Like a movie in her head, and a myriad of emotions. Emotions that weren't hers. Emotions she felt, but ones that didn't hurt.

Of course, she loved a book that made her cry as much as the next person, but it was momentary pain she could walk away from. She knew that by the time she got to the end of the story, at least if it was a romance, the ending would be happy. Or, if it wasn't a happy ending, it would at least be resolved.

Daisy didn't know what that felt like. Resolution. An ending that didn't feel like nonsense. Those nonsense endings, Daisy knew all too well. They were *all* she knew. Conflicts without resolutions. Like the one she was in now.

At least here, she got to do her favorite thing. Escape into an imaginary world. The pain she'd walk away from between the pages was a relief because, even if only for a while, she got to hurt over pain that wasn't her own.

Setting her stack of books on the table, Daisy lowered herself to the old wooden chair. No matter how much the ones she sat on usually cost, no matter how high-end they may have been, this was the most comfortable spot she'd sat in since the last library. Because here, for now, she was safe.

The first one she flicked open was worn, tattered. She couldn't make out the title. Gold Russian? Gold Hush? Gold Rush made more sense. It came from the free stack in the back of the library, tucked against the wall. The books people had donated, the ones the library took out of rotation. The pages were a bit yellower than she may have liked, but that was okay. At least these, she could take home.

Home. What was that?

The irony was, these books were the world's trash. Between the faded words, the dog-eared pages, the water stains, no one else wanted them. No one cared enough about the world that lived between those pages to care for them.

But Daisy did. The irony of that wasn't lost on her either. She'd wanted that once. To be taken care of. To be loved and cherished despite the yellowing of her pages, and the dog ears, and the water stains.

Now? Now, all she wanted were these books. Her books, and to be free of her damn cage.

Gold Rush was a mystery, Daisy discovered within the first few pages. The first chapter depicted a murderer slashing a young man's throat in a park. The next chapter began with a detective being called to the scene. Daisy hoped she wasn't stepping into the middle of the series, because the best part was watching the characters before their arc reached its peak, but from what she could tell, this was gonna be a good one.

Derivative? Maybe. But there was something magnificent about a good mystery. Even if it wasn't the best she'd ever read, they all kept her entertained, and that was all she was looking for. A break from reality.

Within the first chapter, she realized it was exactly her kind of story. The main character, the female detective, was a trope all on her own. Smart, determined, witty, but kind. Compassionate for the victim.

If Daisy ever made it home, maybe she'd do something like that. Become a detective. Then again, she was sure there were laws prohibiting such a thing. With her record, she doubted she'd even be able to own a gun.

But that's what she wanted to do. She wanted to solve crimes, help people. And do it respectfully. That much was important to her, because she knew what it was like to be the victim the cops didn't care about.

After reading a few chapters, Daisy went to the computer in the corner. It was a good book, after all. She wanted to save it for later, when she was lonely and had nothing else to do.

And, as she often did, she logged into her various writing accounts. She didn't write, though. That, she saved for when she was home. Being out in the world was a rare occurrence, of course.

No, she went to her comments.

The fanfiction world was a bizarre one. There was always an argument of some kind ongoing, and Daisy didn't spend too much of her time with that. But as a writer, she was vain.

She would never admit it, of course, but writers were sensitive creatures. They had to be able to connect a reader to another world. And there was nothing a writer loved more than hearing that somebody else enjoyed their story. After realizing there were a few comments, some asking when Daisy would release the next *Moonlit Whispers* novel, the paranormal romance she had been working on for years, skimming over the few negative reviews who didn't appreciate her excess dialogue and lack of description, she found a comment from a user that made her heart drop.

Gabby_Reynolds_365.

Gabby Reynolds was one of the main characters in the last story she'd written. The last story before everything changed, at least.

365 was the street address that had always felt like home. Grace and Bentley's.

The comment read,

Gotta admit, Mr. Deluca is a total ass face. I see the allure, I guess, but I'm dying to know what happens next. Because there's no way in hell that guy's Prince Charming. Will the next chapter be up soon? What about Bird in a Cage?

Me and my dad's girlfriend have been reading them like crazy. She used to be a cop, actually, and she's convinced that this story ends with Mr. Deluca behind bars. Please tell me there's another coming soon! Contact me when you do!

Stomach bubbling, hands sweating, Daisy stared at that sentence structure, those words, until it felt as though her heart would explode. That was Grace. Daisy knew that was Grace. It had to be. She read the story, she put together who she was in it, who Bobby was, who Lily was, and then she read Bird in a Cage.

They were looking for her.

As much as she wanted to congratulate Bentley for finally moving the hell on, this wasn't good. It was a fantasy, but it wasn't good. There was nothing she wanted more than to respond to that comment, to give her the exact location, but if Daisy did that, she would never make it home.

God damn it, what was she supposed to do? What came next? How would she—

"Any good reviews?" A husky, all-too-familiar voice spoke over Daisy's shoulder. He touched it too. Massaged it slowly, working his hand down to her bicep where he squeezed ever so slightly.

Stomach still full of knots, Daisy forced a smile. "Yeah, and some people bashing me for my lack of purple prose."

Giving that famous, or maybe infamous, laugh of his, he leaned down for a kiss. "Can't please them all."

No, she sure the hell couldn't. Rock and a hard place was a familiar state for Daisy, however. Especially lately.

"There're some really lovely ones too." Forcing the smile higher, as she had learned was her best defense mechanism, Daisy found his hand and held it tight. "Can we stay a little while longer? There are a few more books I was hoping to find, and maybe check out—"

"You know we don't check them out." His tone hardened, but his face stayed soft. After all, there were people nearby. "And I think she's hungry. You need to feed her."

Looking over her shoulder at the baby in the stroller, Daisy's heart pumped faster.

She couldn't respond to that comment. Not when she looked at those big blue eyes, that silky brown hair, and those outstretched hands, waiting for Daisy to hold her in her arms and rock her to sleep with a full belly...

Daisy couldn't let this little girl grow up in this horror novel either.

* * *

Maddie's story continues in **Smoldering Lies**, coming soon!
https://www.amazon.com/dp/B0CSQHVT1V

Want a free copy of the Maddie Castle prequel novella? Sign up for my newsletter and download a copy today:
https://liquidmind.media/maddie-castle-newsletter-signup-1/

Join the L.T. Ryan private reader's group on Facebook here:
https://www.facebook.com/groups/1727449564174357

LOVE MADDIE? NOBLE? CASSIE? HATCH? GET YOUR VERY OWN L.T. Ryan merchandise today! Click the link below to find coffee mugs, t-shirts, and even signed copies of your favorite thrillers! https://ltryan. ink/EvG_

The Maddie Castle Series

The Handler

Tracking Justice

Hunting Grounds

Vanished Trails

Smoldering Lies (Coming Soon)

Want a free copy of the Maddie Castle prequel novella? Sign up for my newsletter and download a copy today:

https://liquidmind.media/maddie-castle-newsletter-signup-1/

Love Maddie? Noble? Cassie? Hatch? Get your very own L.T. Ryan merchandise today! Click the link below to find coffee mugs, t-shirts, and even signed copies of your favorite thrillers! https://ltryan.ink/EvG_

Also by L.T. Ryan

Find All of L.T. Ryan's Books on Amazon Today!

The Jack Noble Series

The Recruit (free)

The First Deception (Prequel 1)

Noble Beginnings

A Deadly Distance

Ripple Effect (Bear Logan)

Thin Line

Noble Intentions

When Dead in Greece

Noble Retribution

Noble Betrayal

Never Go Home

Beyond Betrayal (Clarissa Abbot)

Noble Judgment

Never Cry Mercy

Deadline

End Game

Noble Ultimatum

Noble Legend

Noble Revenge

Never Look Back (Coming Soon)

Bear Logan Series

Ripple Effect

Blowback

Take Down

Deep State

Bear & Mandy Logan Series

Close to Home

Under the Surface

The Last Stop

Over the Edge

Between the Lies (Coming Soon)

Rachel Hatch Series

Drift

Downburst

Fever Burn

Smoke Signal

Firewalk

Whitewater

Aftershock

Whirlwind

Tsunami

Fastrope

Sidewinder (Coming Soon)

Mitch Tanner Series

The Depth of Darkness

Into The Darkness

Deliver Us From Darkness

Cassie Quinn Series

Path of Bones

Whisper of Bones

Symphony of Bones

Etched in Shadow

Concealed in Shadow

Betrayed in Shadow

Born from Ashes

Blake Brier Series

Unmasked

Unleashed

Uncharted

Drawpoint

Contrail

Detachment

Clear

Quarry (Coming Soon)

Dalton Savage Series

Savage Grounds

Scorched Earth

Cold Sky

The Frost Killer (Coming Soon)

Maddie Castle Series

The Handler

Tracking Justice

Hunting Grounds

Vanished Trails (Coming Soon)

Affliction Z Series

Affliction Z: Patient Zero

Affliction Z: Abandoned Hope

Affliction Z: Descended in Blood

Affliction Z : Fractured Part 1

Affliction Z: Fractured Part 2 (Fall 2021)

Love Maddie? Noble? Cassie? Hatch? Get your very own L.T. Ryan merchandise today! Click the link below to find coffee mugs, t-shirts, and even signed copies of your favorite thrillers! https://ltryan.ink/EvG_

Receive a free copy of The Recruit. Visit:

https://ltryan.com/jack-noble-newsletter-signup-1

About the Author

L.T. RYAN is a *Wall Street Journal, USA Today,* and Amazon best-selling author of several mysteries and thrillers, including the *Wall Street Journal* bestselling Jack Noble and Rachel Hatch series. With over eight million books sold, when he's not penning his next adventure, L.T. enjoys traveling, hiking, riding his Peloton,, and spending time with his wife, daughter and four dogs at their home in central Virginia.

* Sign up for his newsletter to hear the latest goings on and receive some free content ➜ https://ltryan.com/jack-noble-newsletter-signup-1
* Join LT's private readers' group ➜ https://www.facebook.com/groups/1727449564174357
* Follow on Instagram ➜ @ltryanauthor
* Visit the website ➜ https://ltryan.com
* Get merch ➜ https://ltryan.shop
* Send an email ➜ contact@ltryan.com
* Find on Goodreads ➜ http://www.goodreads.com/author/show/6151659.L_T_Ryan

***

C.R. GRAY goes by a lot of names, but the most know her as Charlie, a fantasy romance author who's finally diving into the genre she's always wanted to write in - mystery and thriller. She's from a small town outside of Pittsburgh and hopes she does her city justice in the books she works on!

If she isn't writing, she's chasing after her three adorable, but incredibly stubborn, puppers - who may or may not have some of the same bad behaviors as Tempest in the Maddie Castle series. When she isn't writing, she's watching Criminal Minds or binge reading a Kathy Reichs or Kelley Armstrong novel for the millionth time. (They never get old!)

Made in United States
Orlando, FL
30 December 2024

56719227R00147